I take a deep breath and sink into the backseat of the cab as it careens through the streets of Manhattan.

It occurs to me now, that sometimes the big things in life happen quietly. All this time I was waiting for a crash, a big *something* to hit me and change the course of my life. But life-changing moments aren't all smashing into icebergs and getting mowed down by buses. Sometimes it's as simple as opening your eyes.

In midtown, the cab lurches and takes off up Third Avenue. I look through the windshield and take in the vastness and the beauty of the city up ahead. There has to be something for me out there in that boundless assemblage of stone and brick and glittering brilliance. Doesn't there? Maybe one of the lights I'm seeing has its source at the bedside of a boy I'm destined to marry. Maybe this very cab has gone to and from the business I'll someday run. Maybe tonight I can finally put my life in motion.

Happiness Sold Separately

is also available as an eBook.

Happiness SOLD SEPARATELY

LIBBY STREET

New York London Toronto Sydney

An *Original* Publication of POCKET BOOKS

DOWNTOWN PRESS, published by Pocket Books
1230 Avenue of the Americas
New York, NY 10020

This book is a work of fiction. Names, characters, places and incidents are products of the author's imagination or are used fictitiously. Any resemblance to actual events or locales or persons, living or dead, is entirely coincidental.

Copyright © 2005 by Sarah Castellano and Emily S. Morris

All rights reserved, including the right to reproduce this book or portions thereof in any form whatsoever. For information address Pocket Books, 1230 Avenue of the Americas, New York, NY 10020

Library of Congress Cataloging-in-Publication data is available.

ISBN-13: 978-0-7434-9923-1
ISBN-10: 0-7434-9923-9

First Downtown Press trade paperback edition July 2005

10 9 8 7 6 5 4 3 2 1

DOWNTOWN PRESS and colophon are registered trademarks of Simon & Schuster, Inc.

Manufactured in the United States of America

For information regarding special discounts for bulk purchases, please contact Simon & Schuster Special Sales at 1-800-456-6798 or business@simonandschuster.com.

For our parents

Acknowledgments

Many thanks go to our amazing agent Wendy Sherman for giving us the chance of a lifetime, and for believing in us and our writing. Thanks also to Elan Drucker for loving Ryan almost as much as we do; and to Shari Smiley at CAA for taking us on. *Dank* and *danke* to Jenny Meyer and Emily Russo. Amy Pierpont, you are the best editor two very green writers could ask for. We appreciate all you've done for us, and for Ryan. Megan McKeever, thank you for the reading and shipping and all the things you do for us behind the scenes. Last but not least, on the business front—Steve Sarfatti, a.k.a. Uncle Steve, Esq., you are not only an outstanding interpreter of legal mumbo-jumbo but also a tireless advocate of our work, and we love you for it.

On the personal front . . . we have come to the conclusion that our families are the most supportive and selfless in the world. Brian and Rocky Bushweller, Randy and Shawn Morris—thank you for the backing, financial and emotional, which has made this all possible. Giuseppe Castellano, you are a prince among men—an incredible husband and a wonderful friend. Jennifer Bittle, the friendship the three of us have is indescribable and special beyond all measure; we love you.

Our gratitude to: Katie Morris, Mary Morris, Stephany Bushweller, and Alyssa Feldman for your early readings and advice. Sam Bennett, Joshua and Jeremy Bushweller, and their families for sharing in our joy. Richard Stern for your encouragement. Nate Trier, copy editor extraordinaire and resident expert on struggling musicians. And, finally, to the rest of the Delgonquin (including honoraries), who make us laugh and get us hammered when necessary, Jay and Laura Cooper, Jimmy P. Hoover, Julie Tripi, and Jay Bittle—thank you.

Happiness SOLD SEPARATELY

CHAPTER One

Have you ever had the perfect day? A day when the world smiles on you with sunny skies and fills each hour with such bright and lovely things that, as you snuggle down to sleep, you say to yourself, "Now, that was a wonderful day"?

Me either.

I've been wondering lately, how many people actually have days like that? Are people having them all around me and I just don't know it? For instance, could the guy standing in front of me be smiling so enthusiastically because he just met the love of his life? Or the woman behind me, will she glide into bed tonight and say, "This was *the* day—I'll remember this day always"?

Okay, probably not.

I don't imagine you have to wait in an interminable ATM line on a truly perfect day. Surely, on a truly perfect day, cash materializes in your pocket on command. Sadly, in my world, the closest thing to perfect is when the ATM actually spits out money instead of that admonishing beep and *Sorry, cannot process your request at this time* message.

You see, my life is fine. It is neither outstanding, nor bad enough to require medication. I've never been privy to a perfect day, but I haven't had a lot of especially bad days either. I guess you could say I live in that vast cushiony-soft gap between superb and suicidal. In other words, I am your typical twenty-five-year-old modern American female.

I am a well-educated, reasonably intelligent, fairly productive member of society. Like every other modern American girl I'm slightly heavier, shorter, and more impoverished than I want to be. I'm pretty sure I'll never find Mr. Right, but on that point I am more than willing to be proven wrong. In my world, managing to get fifty bucks out of the ATM is one of life's greater pleasures, right up there with Hershey's chocolate and outlet shopping.

I step up to the ATM machine with the standard mixture of trepidation and hope. Every ATM encounter is a gamble, and, as is usually the case, the odds tip in favor of the house—Chase Manhattan. I swipe my card and say a little novena to Saint Jude, patron saint of lost causes. "Please, let there be enough money in there." I'm not Catholic, but it can't hurt. I hate it when I'm the one sad girl who has to keep swiping and frantically punching in dollar amounts in decreasing increments till finally leaving the place red-faced with ten bucks.

The machine coughs out the sweet *whir, swish, click-click-*

click and bills sputter out to freedom. I grab the money swiftly, before it can get sucked back in.

The piercing whine of a cell phone rings out. The three people in my vicinity not already on the phone riffle through their pockets and purses.

The ringing continues. They all look at me. I lift my giant black tote to my ear. Yep, it's me.

I shuffle through the crowd and out onto the street, digging through the gum wrappers and convenience-store receipts that have gone forth and multiplied in the dark recesses of my bag. I flip the phone open. "Ryan Hadley." Damnit!

"Aw, you did the work phone answer." It's Audrey. She screams out to Veronica, who is no doubt right next to her, "She did the work phone answer!" Back to me. "That's a round on you, baby!"

"Yeah, yeah" is the only reply I can muster.

"Where are you?"

"Sixty-eighth Street. Two stops," I say.

She screams, "Well, hurry up!"

I get an earsplitting *crash-thump,* followed by a muffled "Oops."

Veronica picks up, "Listen to this."

In chorus they belt, *"All the women who independent . . . we all love the overdraft / All the honeys makin' money . . . we love living check to check . . ."* The tune almost sounds like "Independent Women" by Destiny's Child, but not quite. (Sadly, Audrey has only three CDs in morning workout rotation: Beyoncé's *Dangerously in Love*, the Destiny's Child remix album, and the *Charlie's Angels* soundtrack, circa the year 2000.)

As Audrey continues to belt out lyrics in the background, Veronica says, "We call it 'Ode to My Overdraft,' subtitled 'Credit-Dependent Women.'"

"You are so Destiny's Bastard Child," I say.

"Girl, you're gonna be Destiny's Bitch if you don't get here soon."

Then comes the oh-too-familiar snap, crackle, pop of signal loss.

I blurt, "I'm losing you. I'll be there in fifteen minutes!" as I follow the throng of people disappearing underground and race onto the Uptown 6.

Audrey and Veronica are my best friends. Together we're the ultimate triple threat—a blonde, a brunette, and a redhead. Audrey is fair and petite, occasionally fragile and slightly pristine, but we love her anyway. Veronica is tall, slender, and as fiery as her hair, though not nearly as ruthless as she'd like you to believe. And I'm, well, somewhere in between. Given enough Lycra and Lancôme, any man is putty in our hands. At least, that's the theory.

When we met, sophomore year in college, the Triple Threat was more than just theory. Our alma mater is the kind of university with stately brick buildings, stone spires, and tree-lined greens. On the surface it looks like a very distinguished bastion of higher learning. It woos unsuspecting parents into believing their child will receive a top-notch Ivy-ish education at a bargain price. It is actually a members-only gathering place for barely postpubescent borderline alcoholics. Oh, yes, we did very well there.

Lately, however, the Triple Threat has become a little more

dour than dangerous. We are free from romantic attachments (can't get a date to save our lives), tired of stupid men (angry about aforementioned dating problem), and most importantly we are all in the midst of "financial crisis."

Now, to the modern American female a "financial crisis" is defined as the condition in which too much rent and/or food money has been spent on too many beers and/or clothes, resulting in a maxed-out overdraft and/or credit card. The only recourse available to a modern American female in the throes of "financial crisis" is excessive beer and cigarette consumption at local dive bar with best friends.

The Gaf, our dive bar of choice, is just around the corner from my apartment and the perfect place for chronic financial crisis recovery. Actually, The Gaf isn't a great bar for anything except financial crisis recovery. There are never more than three other people there, the bartender is older than Rome, and it's dark—good for hiding.

The old mahogany paneling and Irish pub paraphernalia give The Gaf that added je ne sais quoi—the kind of je ne sais quoi only overcome by good beer at low, low prices. But when you add in the great jukebox and the owner's take on the New York smoking ban, you have what we like to call paradise. At least once a night, Bill, the owner and chief bartender of The Gaf, tells whoever will listen that he left Ireland to "escape tyranny" and that he won't let "the fascist imperialists" tell him what he can and cannot do in his bar. Thus, to Bill, every cigarette smoked in The Gaf is an act of civil disobedience; we are more than happy to support him in his efforts.

As I amble into the bar and see Audrey and Veronica at our

favorite window booth, I finally feel the great weight of work lift off my shoulders. I hang my purse on a nearby hook and flop in next to Audrey.

I'm about two bottles behind in the conversation, so the girls give me an encore of "Ode to My Overdraft" in a sad attempt to catch me up. And I thought Audrey's predilection for vintage Beyoncé was a *harmless* fascination.

At the conclusion of the fifth and final verse, Bill erupts in applause and gives us a round on the house. God bless Bill.

"Ryan!" bellows the usually composed Audrey as she slams her beer down on the table. "How was your day?"

"Fine," I reply.

"And Veronica?"

"The usual," she replies, lighting a cigarette. "And you, my dear?"

Audrey shrugs. "Same."

Ah, the depressing side of financial crisis and romantic drought—same old, same old.

"So, we all got nothing?" I say, disappointed.

Audrey wiggles in her seat. "Oh, wait! I almost forgot! I saw the Fonz today!"

"Heeey," I imitate, giving her his trademark thumbs up.

"Where?" asks Veronica.

"Coming out of Starbucks at Forty-ninth and Seventh," replies Audrey.

"What did he have?"

"A grande, I think."

"What was he like?" I ask.

"Shorter than I thought; kind of older too."

"Well, he's got to be my dad's age," says Veronica.

"Or older," I add.

"Yeah," says Audrey, deflating rapidly from her momentary high.

"Wow," I groan, "the highlight of the week is a Henry Winkler sighting?"

What happened to all the excitement, the thrill of being a modern American girl in the big cruel city? We used to have actual stories or, at the very least, daydreams. These days a real whopper of a night on the town involves two pitchers at The Gaf and dinner for three at a burger joint on the corner.

"Are we losers?" I ask the girls.

"No," chirps Audrey.

"Absolutely not. We're young and vibrant," says Veronica weakly.

"We don't have it that bad. Besides, Ryan, things will pick up," declares Audrey.

Okay, things aren't *that* bad. I mean, in the four years since college we've managed the basics—crappy jobs, tiny apartments, great friends. Not bad, especially considering we decided to begin responsible adulthood in New York City. But there's no zing anymore, no thrill. What happened to waking up in a city that doesn't sleep and finding we're king of the hill, top of the heap? All right, I admit it: I was lured into the greater New York metropolitan area by Frank Sinatra. I guess it sounds pretty ridiculous now, but at the time it seemed perfectly reasonable.

I was an "ambitious, headstrong young woman driven to achieve the American Dream. Where better to do it than New York City?" Well, that's how my father explained it to my mother when I left home. Pretty great of him, right? The thing you have to understand is that his idea of life in New York came mostly from Doris Day movies. To live the kind of big-city life he envisions requires a closet full of brightly colored shift dresses (with matching shoes and handbags) and several years of finishing school. My New York dream, on the other hand, was much more realistic. It involved only two things—Central Park in fall and a man named Harry. In other words, it came mostly from Nora Ephron movies. The sad reality is, after about six months in New York all the modern American girl dreams about is surviving her twenties without a substance abuse problem or sexually transmitted disease.

When I first got here, though, New York seemed so full of possibilities, so ripe for my conquering. To my wide and untrained eye, the people, the pace, the scale of it, was only a detailed backdrop for my storybook triumph. I got off the train and glided through Grand Central Terminal feeling weightless, buoyed by the knowledge that college had prepared me for *something*. The specifics of that something were hazy at best, but I was confident it would be big, special, or at the very least highly lucrative. I was sure I would find an exciting and fulfilling life of wealth, success, and handsome men waiting for me right around the corner.

In a way, I was right—people live very well on Park Avenue.

"Do you think we've done everything right so far?" I ask the girls.

"What do you mean?" asks Veronica.

"Do you think we've done it all right? That we are where we should be?"

"I think we're doing just fine," replies Audrey sweetly.

I nod to Audrey in agreement. Yeah, *fine*. But shouldn't there be more? Lately, I can't seem to shake the feeling that I'm missing something—that there's more out there. I feel like spectacular, extraordinary things are always happening to other people—but never to me. It seems like the longer I live in New York, the further away I get from my New York dream.

For example, my big personal success for the day will be making it to my apartment without falling down.

"I think I'm going to go home and pass out," I say to the girls.

"Me too," replies Audrey.

"Your place tomorrow?" asks Veronica.

I nod as I wrestle the hook for control of my bag.

A few air kisses later and I'm on my way home, already dreaming about the one *perfect* thing I know I'll have today—six and a half to seven hours of wonderful, comalike sleep.

CHAPTER Two

Saturday. No date tonight and a bit of a hangover—classic. I wake up and briefly consider getting dressed, then realize that my bed is warm and comfy and that the remote control is within arm's reach. Thus, I begin what has become my Saturday ritual:

1. Tell myself, "Must clean the apartment."
2. Sit on sofa/bed and vegetate in front of *E! True Hollywood Story* or *Lifetime Original Movie*.
3. Get out cleaning supplies.
4. Lay on sofa/bed and vegetate in front of another *E! True Hollywood Story* or *Lifetime Original Movie*. (These programs always come in convenient double block or marathon format.)
5. Dust coffee table.

6. Snack.
7. Nap.

This is the carefully choreographed exercise I'm doomed to repeat until a staggeringly large wad of cash drops in my lap, making it possible for me to hire a maid.

Given the size of my apartment, the chronic procrastination is really pretty pathetic. My apartment is small—very small. Not cute or petite, mind you, just teeny tiny. It is so small, in fact, that I've been known to distribute microscopes to first-time visitors.

I can fake a cozy sort of feeling, but it requires the careful placement of mirrors. Mirrors, you see, give the illusion of space. In its mirrorless state my apartment has the kind of special snug feeling usually reserved for persons having committed one or more violent felonies.

My building, however, is a beautiful "UES Pre-war." In non-broker speak that means it is located on the Upper East Side and was built before 1942. It has a distinguished brick facade with scary little gargoyles over the entryway. You enter the building by way of a big blue door—rather *Notting Hill*, or so I thought when I first walked through it. That, unfortunately, is where the similarities end.

After trudging up five narrow flights you come to apartment 5C, my extremely humble abode. It's obvious that my so-called studio was once the maid's bedroom in a much nicer apartment. Years ago (probably the eighties) some sick developer looked at this extra bedroom and said to himself, *We'll drop a bathroom down here by the door, a kitchenette here on the south wall, and* boom—*two hundred square feet of luxury.* And I, Ryan Lorraine Hadley, am the beneficiary of that exhaustive planning.

I have room for a sofa that pulls out to a bed, a dresser that doubles as a linen closet, an armoire/TV cabinet, a nightstand/end table, and a bookshelf/pantry. The revolution in multipurpose furniture has made my entire lifestyle possible. Thanks to my parents and IKEA, I have the infomercial equivalent of a home—"It slices! It dices!"

All that being said, believe it or not, my tiny studio is a rare gem in Manhattan. It's only nine hundred bucks a month, rent-controlled, with utilities included. Amazing! Then again, I do have to pay my rent (in cash) to a man who insists I call him Blade. But it's worth it, because it's all mine. Not a single roommate or crusty old lady who offsets her rent-controlled $250 monthly output by charging five hundred bucks for a drafty bedroom and a hotplate.

I suppose I could have gotten more space and cheaper rent if Audrey, Veronica, and I had decided to live together. We did deliberate on it, but in the last two years of college we found cohabitation to be a severe strain on our relationship. Audrey grew up in a family of seven kids and is, therefore, unbelievably territorial. This led to several violent arguments that began with "Do you *ever* knock?" Veronica, on the other hand, has a volume problem. She is loud—music, TV, snoring—and her stubbornness prevents any compromise. I am all sunshine and roses to live with, of course, but do require quiet time, alone time, and dance-around-in-my-underwear-at-all-hours time. Which, to be honest, is probably what I'd be doing right now if I weren't expecting company.

• • •

Almost ready for the girls to get here—I've managed to scrape some dust off the TV screen and spray a little citrus room mist. At least it can smell like I mopped the floor.

Audrey is first to arrive, at precisely 7:30—no big surprise there. Audrey had a strict Catholic upbringing and, until college, was taught exclusively by nuns. This has resulted in an unnaturally precise internal clock that doesn't allow for tardiness. That's what she calls it: "tardiness." I, on the other hand, require advanced planning if I want to get anywhere on time. This means employing strategies akin to those the Allied forces used in liberating France.

Audrey floats into the apartment looking adorable as ever; at five foot four and a size four she has this remarkable way of looking dainty and curvy simultaneously. This God-given optical illusion gives Audrey the enviable ability to look pretty even in grungy old sweatpants.

"You cleaned?" asks Audrey, handing me a giant bag of popcorn.

"Ha!"

"Bath & Body Works?" she asks.

I nod yes.

She takes a healthy sniff. "Convincing."

"Thanks."

"When's Veronica getting here?"

"Her mom sprang another bohemian dreamboat on her this morning. Probably not till nine or so," I reply.

"Oh, Lordy," says Audrey, rolling her eyes.

"My sentiments exactly."

The bohemian dreamboats are a parade of eligible artists, poets, and musicians thrust on Veronica by her well-meaning but clueless parents, Mr. and Mrs. Franklin Wheatley. The Wheatleys are a very wealthy Park Avenue couple whose biggest collective regret is that neither of them became an artist or poet.

Mr. Wheatley, a corporate attorney, rose to fame and fortune by representing chemical companies for $700 an hour. Mrs. Wheatley started her own headhunting firm in the booming eighties and soon made a name and big-time loot for herself. But each would much rather have been a folk singer. Unfortunately, neither had any talent in artistic pursuits, but bohemian dreams don't go down without a fight.

When the Wheatleys had children, they did everything humanly possible to raise two Park Avenue avant-gardists. Veronica and her brother, Jonah, were carted kicking and screaming to pottery class and mime lessons (among others) and were sent each summer to theater camp. The fruit of all this extracurricular labor is a daughter—a lover of all things Wall Street who plays a mean tambourine—and a twenty-two-year-old son who is just beginning his life as a perpetual student and stay-at-home stoner. Mrs. Wheatley, though, is a trouper. Since her retirement from headhunting a few years ago she has taken up two habits: wearing loud tribal caftans and matchmaking for Veronica.

The bohemian dreamboats usually last all of two hours with Veronica. She schedules the "dates" right after work, the better to startle them with her corporate attire and scary Wall Street attitude. Truthfully, though, only a state of extreme relaxation allows Veronica to appear anything less than formidable. That being said, she does have one thing to overcome in discouraging the bohemian dreamboats—her uncommon beauty. No matter how off-putting she tries to be, she's still just an all-American babe. So the guys, no matter how punk, or beatnik, or whatever they're trying to be, see nothing but long red hair, a slender body à la Cindy Crawford in her glory days, and miles of creamy white skin. To Veronica, being irresistible to artsy boys carries the same annoyance factor as, say, being attacked by a swarm of bloodthirsty wasps. I, on the other hand, would be more than willing to endure her mother's charity. I find even the hint of the artistic infinitely desirable.

I met this guy in a bar once. He was tall, had a killer smile, but what really got me were his paint-spattered jeans. When I asked, "What do you do?" he responded flatly, "I paint." And that was it. Come to find out later—his hand midway up my blouse—he was a painter of apartments, not canvas. Oops.

Audrey and I settle into my queen-sized foldout bed. We each get a down blanket, a beer, and a bowl of popcorn. I hit the PLAY button on *Bridget Jones's Diary*.

"How many times have we seen this?" she asks.

"I don't know. Ten, maybe twelve times?" I reply matter-of-factly.

"I never get tired of Mark Darcy," she sighs.

"Tell me about it. I wish I could just jump in there and steal him away from Bridget and live happily ever after in his great big London pad."

"Question," says Audrey, snuggling into her blanket. "Would you rather live in Mark Darcy's house in London, or Mr. Darcy's Pemberly?"

"Oh, tough one." I ponder a moment. "I need clarification. Can I have Mr. Darcy in modern-day London?"

"You cannot separate the man from his castle," Audrey replies gravely.

"In that case, it's a toss-up," I say. "Impossible to decide. And anyway, Audrey . . . beggars, like myself, cannot be choosers."

As Darcy's gorgeous mug flashes on screen, I get that feeling, the one I really wanted. . . .

Deep within every modern American female, whether she will admit it or not, lingers the image of an ideal man. It isn't necessarily photo quality, it rarely involves specific physical characteristics. No, this image is more like the promise of a feeling, a swept-off-your-feet, powerless-to-control-it, how-awesome-is-this-guy sentiment that she hopes someone special will someday inspire. Left to its own devices, the brain will keep this feeling dormant until truly warranted by a real-life flesh-and-blood person. However, there is one thing that can thwart the natural safeguards—the romantic movie hero.

A well-crafted fictional man can trigger this peculiar feeling, and, once entered into waking life, he and his emotional effect become the cinematic equivalent of crack. For the single girl in the twenty-first century, one man is the quickest, most satisfying high: Darcy.

Audrey and I stare into the screen, transfixed, lapping up all we can while secretly hoping it'll be enough to get us through the week.

Just as the Darcy-Bridget interview scene begins, the doorbell rings. I hit the door latch button, hope it's Veronica.

Several minutes later Veronica bounds into the apartment, haggard and a little out of breath. "One of these days I'm going to give you the money to get a place with an elevator," she says while slipping off her ridiculously high heels.

"Think of it as cardio . . . on stilts," I retort.

"I will not be one of those women who wear tennis shoes to and from work," she replies, massaging her painfully swollen feet.

"Fine, but don't come crying to me when you've got bunions the size of artichokes and can't wear anything but white orthopedic granny shoes."

She catches her breath and rolls her eyes at me. "Thank you, Dr. Scholls."

I change the subject. "So, what was he?"

"A magician," Veronica replies with disdain.

Audrey lets out a deep belly laugh.

Veronica nods her head in agreement with Audrey and continues, "My Mom says to me, 'Veronica, he's an amazing performance artist. Positively inspired.' It turns out his 'art' centers largely on pulling live animals out of a television set."

Audrey suddenly slaps me on the arm. "Ryan! The PAUSE button! It's the kitchen scene!"

We dig through the covers frantically, pillows and popcorn tumbling to the floor. Like a slow-motion scene in a cheesy war movie, we mouth "No!" and look at each other in panic while scrambling for survival. It's no use; the clicker has disappeared in the downy abyss.

I fling myself off the bed and smack my hand against the PAUSE button just in time, nearly breaking my leg in the process.

Mark Darcy's gorgeous mug is frozen on screen, so vulnerable and yet so manly. We all stare at the TV, tipping our heads slightly as we do, like three dogs whimpering for table scraps.

Audrey breaks the swoonfest. "Why can't I find a Mark Darcy?"

"Because he's a fictional character, and no one who looks that good in a suit and has eyes that soulful actually exists," replies Veronica.

"Colin Firth actually exists," I say.

"It can't be that hard to find a guy like him. Can it?" Audrey implores.

"You're right, Audrey," says Veronica, picking up her purse. She heads for the door. "I'll just run to the Boyfriend Store and pick up three Darcys. Would you like him in business attire or casual?"

"I'll take a Nineteenth-Century Darcy with a side of Ewan McGregor, please," I say. If you're going to order one up, you might as well aim high.

"Come on, there are nice guys out there."

Veronica gives Audrey her standard "Prove it!" look—head down and eyes up, like a viper daring you to come closer—and says, "Where? Is there some secret stash of Darcys out there? Maybe they're being held hostage by the weirdos we've gone out with?"

Wow, the magician must have been a humdinger.

"The guys we've dated haven't been that bad," responds Audrey meekly.

Veronica and I give an all-too-exuberant chuckle.

Audrey goes on the defensive. "All right, who?"

We comb the memory banks, sorting and compiling the dusty remnants of relationships past.

Results, top three best of the worst:

In third place, The Soccer Player. TSP was Audrey's first boyfriend after moving to the city. If I remember correctly, his given name was Dave, but his friends called him Crutch. I have no idea why and never had the chance to find out. He was so all-American, a big brawny Wonderboy. Unfortunately he was also 90 percent frat boy and 10 percent phallus. I mean that both literally and figuratively. He was hung like a horse, and behaved like a horse's ass.

"He could be very sweet at times," Audrey says.

"Why did you break up with him, again?" asks Veronica, a glimmer in her eye.

"Okay," Audrey says, throwing her hands up in defeat, "so he peed on my sofa."

"Oh, yeah, he was a winner," giggles Veronica.

"In his defense," Audrey continues, "he was extremely drunk and asleep at the time."

In second place, Herman, a CPA who cooked the books for the Yankees. Or should I say, "Hair-mon, emphasis on *-mon.*" No joke, that's how he used to introduce himself to people. "My name's Hair-mon. Emphasis on *-mon*. It's German." He was a trust-fund brat who had never seen a picture of Germany, let alone been to the "Fatherland." But, aside from the strange name business, he was quite normal—handsome, polite, halitosis-free. But Veronica quickly tired of listening to stories about how much a Yankee road trip costs, i.e., "Do you know they eat

$13,456 worth of food every day?" Yeah, nobody knows, and Veronica really didn't care.

"Go, Mets!" says Veronica, cracking open a beer and sitting down on the bed.

And number one goes to . . . Ryan, with Robbie the Maniacal Runner! Robbie and I dated for two months. The guy ran absolutely everywhere, to and from dates, to the grocery store. He would get up at 5:30 in the morning so that he could jog to work. In addition, he ate only raw or steamed foods. I, on the other hand, buy only frozen foods and cook things until they're only marginally identifiable. Not exactly meant to be, he and I. He also had a problem that can only be described as "the tofu breath." There are only so many ways you can offer a guy an Altoid, you know?

Our breakup was painless, though, as neither of us could really see the point of being together. Oh, but that wasn't the end. About three months later, I ran into him at a bar on the Upper West Side. He shouted to me from across a crowded room filled with yuppie types and their skinny arm candy.

I barely recognized him, as he'd gained about fifteen pounds and put blond tips on his cropped hair. He also talked a lot faster than I'd remembered.

"Ryan! Honey, I am so glad to see you!" he said. "How have you been? It feels like forever."

"I'm fine, Robbie."

"Look," he said, putting his hands on my shoulders, "I am so sorry about what happened with us. It was a nightmare, wasn't it?"

"I don't know that I'd say *nightmare*," I replied timidly.

"Well, I would."

Uh, thanks.

He went on, "It was just such a stressful time for me." At this point he glanced over my shoulder and grinned brightly. "Oh, Ryan. There's someone I'd like you to meet."

I turned around, expecting to see a skinny blond tart in running shoes.

"This is my boyfriend, Andy."

Say *what*?

Robbie pulled Andy beside him, sliding his arm around Andy's waist. "Andy, this is Ryan Hadley. Remember, I told you about her?"

Excuse me . . . *boyfriend*?

I smiled as best I could and said, "Nice to meet you, Andy," and tried not to let the "Oh. My. God." face out of its cage.

I'm sorry, but what do you say when an ex-boyfriend tells you he's gay? What is the appropriate response to that? In the end, I took the pretend-you're-waiting-for-someone-who-didn't-show-and-sneak-out-of-the-bar approach. I recommend it—worked like a charm.

"Okay, not Darcy. But not horrible, either," says Audrey.

Veronica rolls her eyes. "Well, we haven't dated any serial killers, if that's what you're getting at."

"That we know of," I add.

Veronica responds with a sly wink.

A frustrated sigh escapes my lips before I can check it.

Veronica nods in agreement and whispers, almost to herself, "Yeah."

The really sad thing is, they *weren't* all weirdos. Most of the guys I've dated have been okay, but that's just the problem—they weren't anything more. They were perfectly normal, even interesting on occasion, but there haven't been any sparks. I haven't felt anything like the real-life swept-off-your-feet, powerless-to-control-it, how-awesome-is-this-guy sentiment since college. Now, that guy . . . that guy was most definitely more than just okay. . . .

Veronica yanks me out of my memories with a boisterous, "Hey." She holds out a lit cig for me.

As I reach to receive a smoke, I notice a hard object under my bum . . . the remote. Typical, lost under my massive arse.

CHAPTER Three

The work week sucks. But then, it always begins with the relentless *buzz, buzz, buzz* of the alarm clock. Cacophonous buzzing is not a good way to start anything.

I once tried using the radio wake-up function, but it backfired. I integrated the music into my dreams and slept an extra forty-five minutes. So then I tried using a Britney Spears CD. It did wake me up, but it turns out that Britney is actually *more* annoying than that buzzing sound.

I slam off the alarm clock and open my eyes—in that order—and get ready for work.

The work week:

1. Wake up.
2. Bagel.
3. Shower.

4. Get dressed (black skirt or black pants combine with button down shirt or sweater, shoes. Done.)
5. Get on subway.
6. Get off subway.
7. Work.
8. Get on subway.
9. Get off subway.
10. Unsatisfying frozen dinner.
11. TV.
12. Sleep.

(Repeat)

Five days of robotlike repetition—the Twelve Step Program of work-born boredom.

As usual, when I step out of the train at the Fifty-first Street station I get caught up in a great wave of humanity. Like toothpaste being forced out of its tube, hurried commuters surge through the terminal, bottleneck at the turnstiles, and then squeeze up the stairs before finally squirting out onto Lexington Avenue. This is how I am daily released onto the sidewalks of Midtown—I am forced out by the people around me. My right foot hits the pavement and I brace myself for the rest of my commute. One of the many marvels of my urban life is this daily trek through heavy human traffic.

As a pedestrian in Manhattan, especially during morning rush, you are supposed to fold yourself into the crowd and allow the bustling professionals around you to set the pace—somewhere between a power walk and an all-out sprint. Unfortunately, I've never been able to master this particular "folding" maneuver. My walk to work is always a fight. I have never been able to move the way everyone else does.

Every morning the people around me make great purposeful strides toward their places of work. They march at a blistering pace up and down the streets and avenues, cradling their briefcases and messenger bags while chatting on cell phones. But these speed walkers aren't just harried and desperately trying to get to work on time, they're actually *eager* to get there. You can see it in their faces. These people speed along past me, often swerving to avoid running me over while I get jostled and bumped, poked and pushed. Try as I might, though, I can't seem to make myself go any faster or walk with any more purpose.

Lately it's gotten even worse. This morning, for instance, feels like the slowest yet. I am surrounded by a gaggle of freshly showered young professionals, all zooming vivaciously toward their daily grind. I'm moving in slow motion and everyone around me is in fast-forward. It disturbs me that I don't know how they do it.

Even more disturbing—I can see my office up ahead.

Now, to the modern American female, *work* is defined in one of two ways, it can be one or the other—never both.

Definition one: "work" is the place where you mingle with college-educated, suit-and-tie-wearing men. The mingling leads to dating, the dating to marrying. Hence, work = bar with fluorescent lighting, which one frequents in the day.

Definition two: "work" is the place where you slave day in

and day out in the hopes that you may eventually be promoted to a higher-paying job in which you will slave away day in and day out.

Thus, by *any* definition, work = sick, culturally encouraged masochism.

Don't get me wrong, there are modern American females out there who don't find their jobs tedious and unsatisfying, but those girls don't "work," they have careers. Career girls are something entirely different.

Career girls have plans. They know what they want to do and take steps to rise in the ranks and become whatever it is they want to be—usually something to do with fashion or finance, as far as I can tell. Veronica, for example, is a career girl. She graduated with a degree in economics and now works in one of those swanky downtown investment firms, the kind with too many names to remember. They have an entire building to themselves, complete with a lobby dripping in marble and, from what I understand, a very generous dental plan. Veronica therefore gets things like 401(k) statements and yearly bonuses. The bonuses aren't huge, but at least they are calculated in dollar amounts. Last year, my bonus was calculated in french-fry units—a gift certificate to T.G.I. Friday's.

Anyway, the important thing to note is that Veronica has a plan. She, and the other career girls, see the ladder to success and get on while plotting their way to the top. They know how long it should take between steps, have a clear vision of how far they have to go, and don't give a damn who's looking up their skirt as they rise. Veronica, the bitch, is actually ahead of her own schedule.

The rest of us, like Audrey and me—those of us who graduated from college with little more than a collection of embarrassing anecdotes and ex-boyfriends—we "work." We're the ones who populate your cities, muttering "Help me!" over and over again in our drab little cubicles. This, my friends, is the dirty little secret of the modern American female. We are not all driven, Steinem-fed liberated women. Mostly, we just have rent to pay.

Some of the women who "work," like me, *intended* to be career girls. College turned my fascination with computers and the Internet into an actual skill, so I thought I'd become a computer career girl. I had a modest little plan to rule NYC by beginning my own web-design outfit. It would be fashionable and brilliant. We'd go public after a year and the IPO would bust all previous records. Sadly, this was the full extent of my plan—not quite the solid beginning a business needs. Not to mention, the dot-com market bottomed out practically the day I graduated from college. So, instead, I got a job.

The job is horrible.

I work at Geiger Data Systems ("The Finest in Data Outsourcing"), where I am an overqualified "data-entry bitch," as my cubemate Will likes to call us. We are the indentured servants of corporate America, and yes, all we actually do here is enter other people's data. To someone, apparently, it is very important data because they always harp on us about getting it right.

Both Will and I have been at Geiger since graduating from college, and if it weren't for him I would surely have become cyber-sex–addicted and hygienically challenged. "Work" in a gray, fluorescent-lit cube farm can do that to you.

I enter my cube and heave the usual sigh, the sigh of impending torture.

I should get to work—big pile of crap to get through.

So, naturally, I peek my head into Will's cube.

"What do you feel like for lunch today?"

Will looks up from his *Rolling Stone*. "Ryan, it's 9:30 A.M."

"And?"

He ponders a moment, rubs his belly, and asks, "Mexican?"

"Perfect."

Good, I'm glad that's settled.

Will is completely gorgeous in a shaggy George Stephanopoulos kind of way. He has a quiet sophistication and deep-green eyes, which are shown off nicely by his wavy black hair. Not to mention that he grew up in Louisiana, so he's got that smooth southern drawl going for him, the kind that's a killer with the ladies—slow, subtle, and so sexy. All he has to do, in any bar in the nation, is walk over to a group of bimbettes and utter four little words—"How are y'all tonight?" Even the most jaded city girl turns to jelly in spite of herself.

To top it all off, Will is the singer in an amazing band called Delicate Blunder. Some of their songs are goofy, but onstage those guys are *so* utterly swoon-worthy. Amazingly, despite all he has going for him, I have never really felt anything for him aside from friendship. Why shouldn't I be madly in love with Will? Well, Audrey, Veronica, and I have our suspicions about his sexual preference—he's been eliminated from the dating pool on a hetero-technicality.

For women these days—especially those living in the city—discerning a man's sexual preference has become something of a recreation sport. It's the kind of thing you do on a park bench on a lazy Sunday afternoon, or while waiting in line at the grocery store. And believe me, it's getting harder. (Uh, see Robbie the Maniacal Runner.)

GQ, Maxim, and the staggering influence of *Queer Eye for the Straight Guy* have put many a gaydar on the fritz. Add to that the exponential increase in neuroses in this country and you've got a real challenge. Here in New York we have the out, the closeted, the semicloseted, the ambiguously gay, the ambiguously straight, the straight but cross-dressing, and—the most dangerous for the modern American female—those with an acute lack of self-awareness. This is what Audrey, Veronica, and I believe Will to be. We keep a running tally of his habits, things that point definitively to either gay or straight. We hope someday to know for sure so that we may inform Will himself.

"Am I getting a beer belly?" Will asks me.

I peer over the cube walls. "Are you asking me if you look fat in those pants?" Chalk one up for gay. "Come around, let me see."

Will does a turn and a mini-curtsey for me. Chalk up another one.

"No, Will. They do not make you look fat."

"Are you sure? Because . . ."

"Oh, shut up, you know you're a rock-hard rock-and-roll God."

Everyone within earshot groundhogs over the cube walls, no doubt expecting to see an interoffice snogfest to follow. There is a very low threshold for excitement in this office, as data entry is the most boring job in the history of jobs the world over.

And, because Geiger Data Systems' employee retention rate is slightly *lower* than that of your average McDonald's, the nameless cube-dwelling masses don't know how routinely Will and I play this little game.

Will gives me a conspiratorial wink.

He sits on top of my desk and licks his lips. "Hey, baby, let's give 'em something to talk about."

"How about . . . looove?" I say, and then pucker my lips.

"You're so nasty! I love it!" He leans in for a smooch.

I hold my hand up between us. "Wait, are you referencing the film or the song?"

"What song?"

"And you call yourself a rock star! Remove your ass from my desk at once!"

"Your loss."

Will hops off the desk and scurries around to his cube just as our boss walks into the farm. Typical—ruining a perfectly happy moment with nagging, um . . . I mean work.

Our boss is Dirk Anderson, Middle Manager, or The Dirk, as Will and I prefer to call him. His first name is so incongruous to the rest of him, I wonder what his parents are like. I think you have to be a particular kind of person to carry off the name Dirk. Dirk is either someone with a criminal record and biker tattoos, or the district chairman for GLAAD.

This Dirk, however, is a puzzle. His suits are cheap—really cheap—and come in an odd array of colors, like orangey brown and blue brown. The strange thing is, the suits are impeccably tailored. After many hours of deep thought on the subject, I have concluded that lurking somewhere in the cheap suit factory is an exact scale replica of Dirk Anderson from which they pattern all the cheap, oddly colored suits of the world. It's the only logical explanation.

"Ryan Hadley," says The Dirk with a sneer on his face. I think he might actually be attempting a smile. Tough to tell for sure.

"Good morning, Mr. Anderson," I say, trying out my best Cheery Office Person impersonation.

I expect him to give me some command, or a little jab about fraternizing in the office, but that's it. He passes me by, a clump of long hair, dislodged from his comb-over, flapping ever so slightly in his wake. He continues down the aisle of cubes, greeting Will and everyone else in his path. Bizarre. I mean, The Dirk peers out of his nest every once in a while, but saying hello to us?

I instant-message Will. *What was that?* I type.

Drunk? Will replies.

Too early. Lost it?

Through the cube walls, I hear Will typing furiously. *Whatever it is, it's creeping me out,* comes the response.

Finally, Anderson is out of earshot.

I whisper to the gray wall behind me. "Me too."

The electronic chitchat slowly winds down, and I stare blankly at the pile of data I'm expected to enter today.

Oh, well, only seven hours and twenty-three minutes till I can go home.

CHAPTER Four

"Coming up next: one woman's tale of heartbreak and triumph . . ." a breathy voice says from the TV.

I have just discovered that I have Lifetime Movie Network. I now have access to a never-ending stream of mindless made-for-TV movies, without those pesky reruns of *The Nanny* and *The Golden Girls* to sit through. I am at once excited and frightened. How many tales of heartbreak and triumph does it take to induce spontaneous combustion? Must not get sucked in.

I speed-dial Audrey at home.

No answer.

I speed-dial Audrey's cell.

No answer.

Veronica at home?

No answer.

Surely she has her cell phone?

No answer.

Okay, let's try this again. What I need is Mr. Darcy. Mr. Darcy covered in chocolate would be particularly nice right now. As there is no Darcy currently in residence, I guess I'll have to settle for the chocolate. Need chocolate. Chocolate and magazines. Chocolate, magazines, and cigarettes.

Turn off the TV.

Must get off my ass, even if only to stock up on brainless reading material and empty calories.

I slip on a pair of sneakers and a hat, a most important accessory since I didn't bother to shower today. I look in the mirror. Just as I suspected: disgusting. My hair is flat and stringy, and the freckles on my nose are all too pronounced without aid of foundation. Completing the picture is a crusty chunk of something plastered to my shirt. Yep, sexy as ever.

Down the stairs and, typical—it's raining. I never notice these things until its too late. The question is, how much do I care? Do I sacrifice myself to the rain gods or trudge up the five flights? This is, of course, a rhetorical question.

I hit the pavement, already in a sprint, and head around the corner to the bodega where Brock lives. I hop through the open doorway looking something like a wet ferret, and no doubt smelling like one as well. The previously crusty spot on my shirt has now gone semigelatinous.

Brock winks at me and says, in his thick Indian accent, "Rye-on! How are ya, beautiful?"

Brock. I love that man. He's an Indian émigré so full of the

American dream that his mood sways calmly between unrestrained joy and imperturbable optimism. His last name is impossibly long, but the Brock part he adopted when he became an American citizen. He will tell you, without much prodding, that he got it from the cover of a porn video. But the most noticeable aspect of Brock is his skin. It is positively the smoothest skin I have ever seen on another human being. I want to ask him how he manages it, but I can't get up the nerve to ask a man what brand of lotion he uses.

I give him a huge grin and say, "I'm just fine, Brock. How are you?"

His face lights up. "I got an interior designer. For the deli." He waves a plastic report folder. Brock is saving up to open The Delhi Deli, takeout curry.

I take a look at the plans. "Fabulous!" I exclaim.

"The usual?" Brock asks, reaching for the cigarette case.

"Yeah. Give me two."

I weave my way through the aisle of miniature feminine hygiene products and miniature shampoo bottles. I reluctantly pass the ice cream fridge, trying not to look jealous as a skinny, terminally-hip-schoolgirl type with thighs like toothpicks grabs two tubs of Cherry Garcia. I pick up *Cosmo*, *Glamour*, and *Lucky*—the triad of antiboredom.

When I get to the counter, Brock says, "Still raining."

I look outside, and beyond the rain-streaked window, walking casually down the street, is a total babe. He's looking down. Dark blond waves sweep playfully over his forehead. He holds his umbrella with the poise of a Calvin Klein model. Any minute now, a chiffon-clad stick figure will glide out of the shadows to meet him. Sinatra should be playing. Why can't I—

"Twenty-four dollars, twenty-three cents," Brock says, shattering my little fantasy.

"Huh?" I say in a daze.

Brock points to the bag of goods. "Twenty-four and twenty-three."

I quickly hand him two twenties and turn back to the window. The model-boy is just passing the door to the bodega.

Shock. Joy. Horror. Amazement. The wavy hair, those eyes . . .

I shriek, *"Charlie?"*

I said that really loud. Way too loud!

The Calvin model turns. Ohmygod!

I hit the deck, taking an entire stand of Hostess Cupcakes and pink Sno Balls with me.

There are only three instances in my life where I can remember not being able to breathe:

1. I was eight years old and Jennifer Dorré slapped me on the face, full force, in front of my little sister. I was struck with the raging fury of an eight-year-old scorned. I couldn't catch my breath—that is, until I heard my little sister laughing. I recovered soon enough and took my revenge out on a six-year-old while Jennifer ran home.
2. I fell off my neighbor's jungle gym and broke my collarbone. Couldn't breathe then.
3. Sixth grade. My first slow dance with a boy. I felt tingly and short of breath. I actually thought some-

thing was wrong with me and, in the middle of the song, excused myself to go to the bathroom.

This horrifying moment beats them all. I inhale deeply as I realize I'm lying on the floor of a convenience store, hiding from my ex-boyfriend.

In case you were wondering, this is the much-pontificated-upon "rock bottom."

Brock leans over the counter. "Are you okay?" he asks, alarmed.

The schoolgirl approaches with her armload of ice cream and looks down at me, confused. She then begins laughing—a big, guttural, "I-can't-wait-to-tell-all-my-friends-about-this" kind of laugh.

I whisper, "I'm fine. Where's the guy? Is he gone?"

"The guy?"

"The guy who just passed by. On the sidewalk. With the umbrella." I think I may be hyperventilating. "Is. He. Gone?"

Brock scoots back behind the counter as I huddle with one million puffy, individually wrapped calories.

"No one is there," Brock replies.

"No one?"

"No one," he repeats definitively.

I slowly raise myself up from the ground, daring to peer over the counter and out the window. He's right. The street is empty, except for the deluge of sad little raindrops.

Stand up, Ryan. Stand up!

I take a deep breath and try to compose myself.

"Oh, no, Brock, I've made a total mess!" Frantically, I try

and right the snack stand. I scramble to get the cupcakes back in their neat little rows.

"Rye-on, it is fine. You are fine?"

"I'm sorry. I'm so sorry!" I cry.

My face hot and red, filled with embarrassment to a degree I have never felt before, I snatch my bag from the counter and race out into the rain.

Synonyms for *humiliated:*

1. *mortified*
2. *embarrassed*
3. *shamed*
4. *disgraced*
5. *made-complete-ass-of-self-in-public*

But it was Charlie. Wasn't it? How could it be? He's in L.A. Oh God, what if it *was* Charlie?

The first time I ever saw Charlie was one of those perfect fall days in college, the kind when campus looked like something out of *Love Story* or *The Paper Chase*—sans the Harvard part, of course. The leaves had all turned, and the wind was crisp and held the musk of countless wood-burning fireplaces. I stopped at a coffeehouse for a hot cocoa on the way to class. It turned out to be the one time chocolate got me something besides chunky thighs.

The first thing I noticed about Charlie was how hot he was. Now, when I say *hot,* I don't mean that in my opinion he was attractive. I mean absolutely, drop-dead gorgeous, but there was more to it than that. Even on an ordinary day in a dingy coffee shop there was a spark about him. He had an air, something quietly unattainable yet calm and caring. It was written all over his face—and mine, because I couldn't stop staring.

He was sitting at a little table talking to a girl. He had on a big gray sweater and dark jeans with a scarf around his neck. So deliciously collegiate, straight out of an Abercrombie ad, with his sandy blond hair all perfectly imperfect and those amazing golden-brown eyes. The girl across from him was beautiful, zealously batting her eyelashes and flicking her hair. But I could tell he wasn't going to bite. She was trying so hard, and he didn't want her. He laughed at her jokes and listened intently when she talked, but he didn't want her. I could tell, and she couldn't.

I sat down across the room, sipped my cocoa, and pretended to read the paper, all the while measuring and quantifying what it was that made him seem more than just a good-looking guy. Was it the way he looked her in the eye? The way he leaned in when she said something? His laugh?

Then he caught me inspecting him and I did something so completely out of character that even to this day I can't tell you why I did it—I didn't look away. He stared, and I stared back. Then he flashed me the most amazingly tender smile—and, with our eyes firmly locked, I smiled back.

A real smile, a good smile, is in the eyes and the feeling behind them. Charlie's was so true, so incredibly honest, it was startling, exhilarating. When he broke the gaze I could still feel it, like the reverberating stun of a punch. My stomach flipped, flipped, and flipped—danced, really, I guess, the momentum of which carried me all the way to the computer lab.

It was that same kind of feeling that I got this afternoon, but this time the punch leveled me and decimated a completely innocent assemblage of junk food.

How can he *still* have this effect on me?

But it couldn't have been him.

Could it?

CHAPTER Five

I'm okay. I'm really okay. So what if I did watch both *Say Anything* and *Sixteen Candles* when I got home? So what if I have ruthlessly tried to quench that peculiar little thirst usually reserved for quiet nights on the sofa with Darcy—inexplicably caused by a possible Charlie sighting? And so what if I did walk five blocks out of my way to avoid passing the bodega this morning? It's just another ordinary day. I'm fine.

Anyway, I don't think I saw Charlie. It couldn't have been Charlie. There are eight and a half million people in this city; surely some of them bear a slight resemblance to other people, right? There's probably someone out there who looks just like me—poor thing. Besides, even if I did see Charlie, what does it matter? It's not like I even care. I don't care. I don't.

But I should ring Audrey just to be sure.

"Fletcher and Roth Advertising, Audrey speaking."

"Hey, it's me. I think . . . okay, yesterday I may have . . . it probably wasn't, but . . ."

"Ryan, just get it out, okay?"

"I think I saw Charlie yesterday."

Silence.

Then, in the infamous Audrey whisper, "Whoa!"

"Really? But it's nothing. Right? No big deal."

"Did you talk to him?"

"No . . . I actually, well, I kind of freaked out a little and—"

"Hold on, we have to get Veronica."

"Come on, it's really not that—" I hear a click and infectious Muzak is pumped into my ear.

If you want my body and you think I'm sexy . . .

"Okay. How did he look?" Veronica's in power voice mode. She's been doing some sort of high-powered wheeling and dealing this morning, no doubt.

"Are you kidding?" I say, a little too forcefully.

"That good?" Audrey replies.

"Well, it might not have been him. I only saw his face for a second before I . . ." Oh, best not to remember that.

Veronica prods immediately, "Before what?"

I read once that recounting a tale of horror is supposed to free you from the event—catharsis or something. Not the case. Really, not the case. I have just succeeded in magnifying my humiliation, despite all attempts to downplay my ridiculous behavior.

"Oh, Ryan," Audrey says warmly.

"Yeah," I reply flatly.

"I've got to go, guys. Seven-thirty at The Gaf?" Veronica says sternly.

"Sure."

"Seven-thirty sharp," says Audrey.

All righty, now I guess I have to get to work. Get to work and not think about Charlie. Then again, maybe I should go online for a little bit. I could Google Charlie's name and see what comes up. That isn't *technically* stalking, is it? Yeah! No, it would be wrong. He's in the past. No more thinking about Charlie.

Maybe I should just lean back and stare at the ceiling for a little while. . . .

"Ryan Hadley."

Oh, shit. The Dirk. I sit up too fast and the spring-loaded chair pops me out of my seat. Ceiling . . . desk . . . carpet. I have now planted my face on the floor for the second time in two days.

Desperately trying to pull myself together, I notice not a cheap Armani knockoff but a very nice pair of gabardine pants. Will!

He offers me a hand and lifts me up like I'm a feather. How do guys do that?

"You're late."

"Aw, you missed me that much?" he says with a wink.

"I can't decide between McDonald's and Wendy's. Happy Meal . . . Frosty . . . Happy Meal . . . Frosty. I've been going back and forth all morning."

"Funny, Ryan. How did The Dirk take my absence?"

"Steam from the ears, smashing of office equipment, cursing, the whole bit."

"Seriously?"

"I don't think he even noticed."

Will takes my hands in his and guides me back into my chair. "I have some news." His tone is an odd mixture of excitement and panic.

"Okay," I say, slightly disturbed by this sudden switch in mood. "What is it?"

"Don't get too excited, okay? Nothing's set in stone. . . ." He pauses, thus making me want to beat him to a bloody pulp.

Instead I say, "But?"

"But . . ."

"Will!"

"Remember how the guys and I sent out those demos a couple of months back? To the record companies?"

"Yeah," I squeal, about ready to jump out of my seat.

"It was a total shot in the dark. It almost never—"

I make the international gesture for *Move it along*: rolling my eyes while making giant circles with my hand.

"Yeah, well . . . one of them liked it and wants to take a closer look at us!"

"A record company?" I shout.

"Yeah!" he shouts back.

"Holy shit! Congratulations, I am so happy for you!" And more than just a little bit jealous, I don't add. "Do you have to send them more, or what?"

"We're setting up a gig this week. A guy is going to come and check us out."

"Amazing!"

"I know." He goes wistful, stares blankly at the stapler on my desk.

"You freaking out a little?" I ask.

He lets out a deep sigh. "Just a little."

"How about the guys?"

The guys—a seemingly random collection of musicians cast off by other bands, forming Delicate Blunder as a last resort. Dane plays guitar, Sammy the bass, and Ben is the drummer. Each has his own odd mix of cuteness and awkwardness. When you get right down to it, they're nerds with musical talent. I mean, Dane almost always wears a tie. Of course, it's usually paired with a Boy Scout uniform shirt, but it is a tie nonetheless. Sammy hasn't cut his hair in a decade and still plays Dungeons & Dragons. Ben's in graduate school, and though he's twenty-seven he doesn't look a day over nineteen. This could be a defining moment for all of them.

"We're all a bit in shock. 'Cause it's really happening. This could be *the* big break. Can you believe it? I could finally get out of this hellhole!"

Oh my God. I never thought about that.

I try to sound upbeat and supportive. "You will. I know you will."

Will gives me a big bear hug and practically skips to his cube.

I wish I had some kind of talent, something that could spin me out of here and into a whole new life. What kind of life, I don't know. Yes I do. A life of excitement, accomplishment, and money. Lots and lots of money. To be honest, I'd settle for anything that isn't this.

I wonder what Charlie's life is like now.

No more thinking about Charlie! I am going to think only non-Charlie thoughts. Maybe I'll surf Monster. . . . Oh no, the simultaneous hanging up of every phone in the office. That can only mean one thing—The Dirk.

Pretend to work, or actually work. Actually working would probably be best.

"Ryan Hadley."

"Mr. Anderson."

He smiles at me and pretends to look at my computer screen, but is actually looking at my feet. Possible foot fetish? I smile back, teeth clenched, so as not to gag. He smoothes his comb-over and proceeds with "the rounds."

When The Dirk has returned to his lair, I scuttle over to Will and drop a notebook on his desk. I flip it open to the "Dirk Observations" section.

"Three times a week. Always occurring between the hours of nine and eleven, or three and four," I say triumphantly.

"Nice work, Mrs. Fletcher, but what does it mean?"

"I still don't know," I reply glumly.

Will looks at me and then glances across the office toward a tiny desk near the front door.

"No!" I say, knowing exactly what he has in mind.

"She's really not that bad."

"Yes she is!"

I implore Will with a look that I think conveys the sentiment *Please, God, no.* The look he replies with is *Get your ass over there.* This is not going to be pretty.

Behind the tiny desk, and outweighing it by about fifty pounds, is Betsy. She is an institution here at Geiger, having worked in this office since the company's birth—amazingly, even longer than Will and me. Betsy is a secretary; the nameplate on her desk says Administrative Liaison. Behind her computer she has a poster of two kittens fighting over a ball of yarn. You see?

She is in her early sixties, with long, jet-black Clairol color hair parted down the middle. Her great girth provides her with a youthful plump that stretches out the wrinkles that are no doubt in there somewhere. I'm sure deep down Betsy is a very kind and considerate woman, but she is extremely talkative and a little bit morbid behind all that plump and circumstance. Worst of all, Betsy is a distress-seeking missile. She can smell fear, sense panic like a swarm of bees. She is always willing to come to the rescue, which would be great except her usual tactic is the it-could-be-worse method of cheering up, which isn't actually cheering up at all; it's inspiring guilt.

I once spilled a cup of tea on my favorite skirt (riveted to the computer screen by a trailer for *Pirates of the Caribbean* and dropped mug in lap). Fuming at myself, I raced to the bathroom. Powerless against her distress-seeking impulse, Betsy followed.

As I smudged the tea around, she told me that as a girl she dropped an entire kettle of boiling water on her thigh, giving her third-degree burns and a massive scar. That is the don't-cry-over-spilled-milk-because-my-cow-just-died approach to encouragement.

As I approach Betsy's desk, I see her head lift from her ergonomically correct keyboard. She adjusts her carpal tunnel preventative wristbands and gives me a great big Betsy smile.

"What can I do for you, Miss Ryan?"

"Not much, Betsy. I was just wondering about Mr. Anderson. Well, he's . . ."

"It *is* sad, isn't it? And to think, he still lives with his dear sainted mother. In Queens. Nice little place, from what I hear. Though, I must say, I have never been there. When I was a girl, everyone took their mothers in. It wasn't like today, with all those fancy places for people to . . ."

Something's got to give.

"Betsy, actually I wanted to know why he's been walking around here lately. You know, saying hello to all of us. I mean, I was thinking you might—"

"He is a nice young man."

"Yes," I reply quite convincingly, if I do say so myself, "but he's been . . . nice a lot more lately."

I would rather be getting a root canal.

I think Betsy's catching on. She gives me an eyebrow raise and a wink, then says, "It might have something to do with the evaluations."

Now we're getting somewhere.

"We're going to be evaluating him?"

"Yes, we are." She shakes her head coyly and gives me a look like *Isn't it silly?*

Evaluate The Dirk? What will I say? I have no idea what his job is. I mean, he tells me what to do occasionally, but that takes about sixty seconds via email.

"Well," I say cheerfully, "that explains it. Thank you, Betsy!"

I try to bolt away from the desk as fast as I can, but she catches me turning. "I can't wait to see what he thinks of my performance this year. I finally learned to work the word-processing thingy. . . ."

I try to scrub the shock from my voice. "*We're* being evaluated?"

"Of course!" she says brightly.

Of course, typical. Just great. Perfect.

I practically run to my cube. I must spread the word. Is there time to start a revolution? Unionize? Should I stand on top of my desk and shout in the manner of Norma Rae? Or . . . maybe I should do some actual work.

I draft up a little email and spread it. I sit and listen as the *ding* of new mail cascades across the office. It is followed shortly by whispering and impassioned instant messaging. The cube farm is abuzz. I have a feeling this could get ugly.

CHAPTER Six

"Why don't we go back to my place and watch *Bring It On*?" I say hopefully.

Veronica looks at me grimly. "You are not going to drown your sorrows in sap. You are going to drown them in beer." She signals our need for three beers to Bill the bartender. "Now, we have to figure out what you'll say when you see Charlie again."

"You say that like I *intended* to see him in the first place. It was a totally random street sighting. There is zero chance I'll see him again." I hope. "Also, you seem to be forgetting that my first instinct was to stop, drop, and roll. God only knows what would happen if I tried to *talk* to him."

Veronica raises her eyes to the ceiling, mulling it over.

Let me just take this opportunity to change the subject. "Hey, guess what? Delicate Blunder is getting a closer look by a record company! Isn't that great?"

Audrey exclaims, "I know! Isn't it fabulous?"

She knows?

"Can you two please stay on topic here for a minute?" Veronica gripes.

Audrey and I sit up straight and give Veronica the kind of rapt attention usually reserved for school principals and arresting officers. Veronica nods her approval.

"Ryan, Charlie isn't just an ex-boyfriend—he's *the* ex-boyfriend . . . the one that got away."

That's what I was afraid of: the truth. I suppose my uneasiness has reached my face, because the girls go silent. I secretly pined over him for months after our breakup. Even now, I guess, when things get really tough or life in the city gets too lonely, I think about him and what might have been.

Audrey crashes my pity party. "Why did you guys break up?" She and Veronica stare me down, trying to look very casual about having posed this question.

I have never told Audrey and Veronica all that happened when Charlie and I split, and I'm not going to. Ever. They know there's more to it than I've always let on, but I don't mind playing this little game nearly as much as I'd mind telling all the humiliating details. So, on the rare occasions that Charlie's name comes up, they gently try to garner little bits of information while I deftly bob and weave.

I reply, "He left. Picked up and went to L.A."

"Wasn't there something else?" asks Veronica, doing a very bad imitation of someone racking her brain.

"I don't really remember. It's been so long." That lie is so big and fat, I should probably open a window before we all suffocate under the weight of it. Must deflect. "I remember how we met."

After that first time in the coffee shop, I saw him everywhere. We would pass each other on the street, in hallways. He always smiled at me—that is, on those few occasions when I was brave enough to make eye contact.

Months this went on, and I began to see a pattern. I could predict, with almost 80 percent accuracy, when and where we might pass each other. Therefore, for an entire quarter, I was the best-dressed student in Marketing 342 (Tuesdays and Thursdays two to four P.M.—Tuesday being the day I saw him most often when I passed the library, Thursday most often at the music building). But, for all this time and no small amount of grinning, we never spoke.

During these months of silent flirtation, I considered no less than fifty different scenarios for approaching Charlie. Unfortunately, roughly forty-nine of them had an unreasonably high probability of failure—failure in this case meaning rejection, humiliation, embarrassment, or any combination thereof. I desperately wanted to be one of those ballsy girls who can stride up to any guy and make the first move, someone who puts herself out there, damn the consequences. But I'm just not one of those girls. I'm one of those girls born with keen foresight.

Even as a kid, I had the ability not only to see the possible outcomes of an action but also to understand their gravity. Some examples:

- Jumping off something tall, just for the hell of it
  Consequence: broken arm, leg, neck

- Crossing the road without looking both ways
  Consequence: truck, *splat*
- Putting straws up one's nose
  Consequence: bloody nose, brain damage, snot on an eating utensil

This very handy ability also kept me from making an ass of myself singing on the high school stage, falling into the spandex craze of the early nineties, and being summarily dismissed by Charlie in a crowded lecture hall. So I simply spent a minimum of four hours per week (not much marketing learned in Marketing 342) dreaming about who he was but never daring to stick my neck out. There is no shame in erring on the side of caution.

Thus, it wasn't until spring quarter of my junior year that I actually heard his voice.

It was ten o'clock on a Friday night, and I was coming out of the computer lab with Jessica, a friend of mine from html programming class. We'd just finished a month-long project, so naturally we made a beeline for the nearest bar. The night was warm and breezy and beautiful, the first really mild weekend after a frigid winter. The whole campus was out that night, everyone shedding their wool and testing out the short skirts and short sleeves they'd purchased for the upcoming spring break.

Jessica, a loud but very sweet rugby player, ushered me to her favorite pub on the strip of about twenty pubs just off campus. The place was called B-52's as the bouncer's T-shirt proclaimed, along with his name (Tim) and their slogan ("Get

Bombed"). The massive Tim gave Jessica a hug and waved us in without cover. The night had, by this point, already surpassed my greatest hopes. In college, getting in without paying a cover is something akin to achieving nirvana.

B-52's was like every other bar in town, extremely small and in total violation of every fire code known to man. The place was about ten feet wide. On one side was a slender bar with stools. On the other side, tables and booths covered every available inch of floor space. Add two hundred or so people and *boom;* it's Friday night at the fights, albeit with a lot more "Excuse me"s and no ref to give penalties for elbowing.

Jessica and I managed to weasel two good stools at the bar—that is, with a little help from Tim. It's astonishing how fast men will give up their seats to a lady when the suggestion comes from a three-hundred-pound halfback.

We got a couple of beers and talked about how ridiculous our professor was and how much we hated spending ten hours a day in the lab—all of the usual small talk for two people who really only see each other in class and know very little about each other's private life. And then, after precisely one and a half beers, Jessica spotted a group of her rugby friends playing pool in the back room. She asked me to join her, but for some unknown reason I said no. I decided to stay at the bar.

The second Jessica stood up, there was movement in the surrounding area. Every person within eyesight—in other words, every person in the bar—had designs on that stool. The person who snagged it was a bulky jock who smelled of Old Spice and Jägermeister. He gave me a perfunctory once-over, then resumed his conversation with a friend standing nearby.

I nursed my beer and people-watched in reverse. That is, in order not to look sad and desperate, I watched the crowd by looking in the mirrored wall behind the bar. As I drained the last drop from my bottle, I saw a ripple in the throng, someone stopping every three steps to shake hands and get patted on the back. As the ripple moved closer to me, I realized that at its epicenter was a mop of blond hair. My stomach went to knots.

The guy next to me turned and faced the aisle. Part of me wanted to turn, too, to cross my legs, toss my hair, and do the things that college girls are supposed to do in bars on a Friday night. But before I had time to carefully weigh my options, he was there—Charlie in all his glory.

Only a couple of weeks into spring, and he was already golden. A warm glow seemed to radiate from his faded-out Ramones T-shirt and illuminate his face and anyone in its presence. His beauty, his confidence, shown from him like a light. I guess it sounds silly, but I swear it's true.

Jäger guy slapped Charlie on the shoulder and whispered something to him. Charlie laughed, looked up to the mirror behind the bar, and caught me staring at him. I wanted to look away, but his proximity was so magnetic, I simply could not stop staring back. Charlie had an entire conversation with the guy sitting next to me, never once shifting his eyes from the mirror—and my eyes reflected in it.

When I heard him say, "Do you mind if I take this seat?" to the guy, my heart leapt.

I went to sip my beer but remembered I didn't have any left. How to look cool while waiting for someone to make the first move—one of life's great mysteries. Luckily, I didn't have to wait long. Charlie saw my empty bottle and, after casually reestablishing eye contact (this time face-to-face), said to me, "Can I get you another?"

"Sure," I said.

He signaled to the bartender, lifted my empty bottle, and got a nod of recognition.

Then he said the five sweetest words I've ever heard. "I thought we'd never meet."

I tried not to blush. If I could've taken my eyes off him for even a moment, I would have looked in the mirror to make sure I wasn't going pink all over.

I smiled and said, "We still haven't, really. I don't know your name."

"Charlie."

"Ryan," I said. He shook my hand, holding it just a little longer than necessary, and a little shorter than I would have liked.

Then, skipping all semblance of small talk, he asked, "What class is it you go to on Tuesday and Thursday?"

Conversation with Charlie was easy and effortless from the start. He listened, and I listened, and we laughed—big, hearty, open laughs—until the bartender announced last call.

Charlie was smart and funny in all the right places, his steady yet genial voice accompanied by a look so intense that at times it literally made my hands shake. Pretty amazing, since the law of male averages usually provides that the world be balanced by making all short men handsome and all tall men dull. Charlie, by being both tall and intelligent, was a very rare find indeed.

Topping it all off . . . he touched me a total of three more times that night:

1. He took my hand and led me through the crowd to a quiet booth in the back.
2. He felt the scar on my ankle when we were talking about scary animal attacks.
3. He gave me the most amazing, tender good-night kiss ever.

By the time he walked me home, I had a pretty good grasp on what made him irresistible. He was utterly without cockiness, self-confident yet self-effacing. Witty and charismatic, but without facade. He communicated without reservation or timidity. But most of all, Charlie Cavanaugh, this creature one part god, one part salt-of-the-earth everyman, had the eyes of a visionary.

"Audrey? Are you crying?" I say as I finish traipsing through my past.

"No," she says, dabbing a soggy napkin to her eye.

"Have I never told you guys how Charlie and I met?"

Veronica slowly lets out a deep breath. "I think at the time your recounting of it went something like: 'I met this guy. He's hot. I think I'm in love with him.' And after you broke up, you didn't want to talk about him."

Well, I still don't. Not really. I don't think.

"Have we covered the subject sufficiently now, Veronica?" I say, a bit exasperated. "Are we gonna go back to my place and watch *Bring It On*, or what?"

They both nod reluctantly. It's the tooth-brushing scene—lures 'em in every time.

CHAPTER Seven

I got an invitation from Will, in the usual way his invitations come—last-minute and very exciting. They typically involve the phrase "I got this thing. You wanna come?" (Chalk one up for straight.)

He once invited Audrey, Veronica, and me to a party. His exact words were "It's a party at this place. I'll meet you and we'll go." Okay. So we get there, and it's not just any party, it's a velvet-rope-postmovie-premiere-party/charity event, complete with celebrities and free martinis. It was fantastic—except that Audrey, Veronica, and I were dressed for a house party, not a premiere. I was wearing a worn-out T-shirt from college that featured the classic idiom *Death to Monkey.*

Needless to say, I did not end up going home with any of the roughly two dozen incredibly hot and gainfully employed actors in attendance. What I got instead was a pat on the head from

Regis Philbin, who thought that I was a mentally challenged young person from the "charity" portion of the guest list. I have since instructed Will to give a little more detail in his invitations. Thus, tonight's invite was "Remember that gig I was telling you about? It's tonight." My powers of persuasion are limitless.

I did manage to gather from Will that Delicate Blunder's show is at a new place in the Meatpacking District called O'Rourke's. From the nouveau-chic location and the hip one-word name we've decided it must be a bit posh. Therefore, the three of us are wearing no less than 90 percent black, all in sheer or semi-sheer fabrics. For me that means semi-sheer wrap top, big gold hoops (à la J.Lo), and dark indigo jeans, as tight as I dare. (I dare just enough for my size ten thighs to pass for size eight thighs in dim lighting.)

Of course, this outfit did not come to fruition without some effort. Audrey, Veronica, and I dug out all our most rock-and-roll–chick garb and trekked around the city helping each other with wardrobe selection. It took two hours and three apartments. For the modern American female, preparing to go out at night is more than just putting on makeup and clothing.

"Getting ready" is an art, a skill perfected by years of training—junior high dances, keggers, extensive teenage mall loitering. The modern American female must be sexy yet comfortable, alluring to the kind of man who opens doors, yet off-putting to the kind of man who thinks of groping as a first move. It's more than just looks, it's an attitude. That is the real reason it takes women hours to get ready.

To the uninitiated male, this intricate female process may seem tedious, protracted, even ridiculous. But for the modern

American female, the endless hair curling, eyebrow tweezing, and lotion applying are actually a carefully choreographed sequence of transformational activities. The woman begins her preparation a hapless work drone, and by the end is a sultry vixen. In order to be truly ready for action, the modern American female must feel emotionally, with every fiber of her being, like irresistible man-bait.

That's exactly how Audrey, Veronica, and I feel on the short subway ride to the bar. Clinging to those steel poles, we are fantastic. We are living art. We're like three babes in a music video, doing a slow-motion seduction routine in our best uptown-punk gear. We're like three sirens in a postmodern Diet Coke commercial. Okay, so we're actually doing a balancing act worthy of Cirque de Soleil. Do you know how hard it is to look relaxed and glamorous while teetering on four-inch turquoise stilettos in a moving vehicle?

Audrey slaps her hand on my leather-clad shoulder like she has something very important to say to me.

"What?" I ask.

"Nothing. I just thought I was going to fall," she whispers.

"And you thought you'd take me with you?"

Veronica hears us and we giggle seductively, tossing our hair back. Well, Audrey tosses her hair back—blond curls dangling willy-nilly can do that. My hair doesn't toss. Shaggy brown bobs (January *Glamour*, page 67) just sort of flop and swing. The men coming on and off the car don't seem to mind, though. They flirt and stare. We tease them with little backward glances before finally ascending the greasy station stairs and releasing ourselves on Manhattan.

We arrive at the alleged address of the allegedly hip club an hour before the show's to start.

"It's a hole in the wall," says Veronica.

Literally. It is a great gaping hole in a brick wall. The hole is lined with a curtain of heavy chains, but it's still a hole.

"Maybe Will gave me directions to Mickey Rourke's apartment by accident?" I ask.

"Where's your sense of adventure? Move!" Audrey says while pushing us through the chains.

We find ourselves in a semi-elaborate maze of brick walls and low ceilings. This gets better and better.

"I feel like I'm headed for the slaughter," I gripe.

"Well, it *is* the Meatpacking District," quips Veronica.

"Will you both stop complaining. I'm sure it's going to be very nice once we get past . . ."

The maze ends and opens to a large black space. I can kind of make out a bar and a stage, but it could be a mirage. *Nice* is not what I'd call it. I'd call it *dirty.*

"It's got a definite vibe," shouts Audrey over the pulsing music.

Vibe? Where does she get this stuff?

She continues, "It could use a little light. . . ."

"What it could use are fifty bottles of Lysol and a hose. This place is new?" I ask.

Veronica replies, "You should know the rules by now, Ryan. The word *new* only refers to the club's name, not the location."

"Or furniture," I add.

"Or clientele," says Veronica, pointing to a cluster of much older men who appear, amazingly enough, to actually *be* meatpackers. At least I hope that's only cow blood.

Audrey pushes us toward the bouncer. "We're with Delicate Blunder. A. Coulson, V. Wheatley, and R. Hadley."

The burly bouncer flips his sausagelike fingers through a stack of papers on a clipboard. Then he grunts and grabs Audrey's hand. She flinches a little but does well to compose herself as she realizes he just wants to stamp her hand.

The stamp is a bright red cow getting its head chopped off; little droplets of its blood spray all over my thumb.

"Gruesome, but I kind of like it," I admit.

He growls, "You ladies are at the reserved table up front. The one on the right."

Reserved table? That's a first, as is being called a lady by a man who could crush me with his pinky.

We get a massive pitcher of beer and exchange hellos with Dane's girlfriend, Molly, and Ben's parents, who sit at the table next to ours. Molly is a first-grade teacher and therefore has incredible patience—and an astounding tolerance for loud noises. Which may explain how, despite the deafening electronica, she can calmly sip a martini. Mr. and Mrs. Glover, on the other hand, are huddled together like two people facing execution.

Veronica and I prepare to sit down. Just as my butt's about to hit the seat, Audrey screams, "Stop!" She opens her purse and begins digging inside. "The place is cool, but really, should we be sitting on these?"

The chairs *are* a little dirty. Well, *foul* might be more accurate.

Audrey produces a handful of Kleenex from the tiny portable pack she keeps between her wallet and her Mace. She wads them up and vigorously scrubs at the seats. It has absolutely no effect. The dirt may actually be embedded in a fresh coat of shellac. Huh.

"When in Rome, Audrey . . ." I say.

Again, I try to sit down. Audrey grabs my arm and pulls me up.

She digs into her purse once more. She lays several tissues down on each of our seats. "For me? Please?"

Veronica and I roll our eyes at her but agree to sit down on them—in the spirit of sisterhood.

Several minutes later, and the place is really starting to fill up. How do all these fans find out about the gigs? Is there some sort of indie-rock phone tree?

I survey the room. There are women *everywhere*. Some of the faces are familiar, most are gorgeous. The band is amassing a following that is, from the looks of it, very healthy in the pert and pretty T & A department. Not surprising, really. Even with Will's classic sexy rocker persona, there's something quirky, and a little subversive, about Delicate Blunder. In other words, despite the fact that in real life they're a bunch of goofball dorks, onstage they manage to exude that special brand of bad-boy rock-star mystique that drives women to dance on tabletops and spontaneously expose themselves.

One such girl, in a black DB T-shirt, gives me what can only be described as "the evil eye." It's got to be my proximity to Veronica. In her element, Veronica comes off as quite the man-eater, and tonight is no exception. Her pink DB shirt is shredded within an inch of its life and worn braless. I have never actually been braless. I wear a bra to bed, for God's sake. Not because I have particularly large breasts or anything. But mine are just sort of *there* without the proper push and pull. Veronica's, on the other hand, are unreasonably firm and feminine regardless of the undergarment or lack thereof.

Suddenly Veronica exclaims, "Hey!"

"What?" I retort.

"I think they need us."

She points to the edge of the darkened stage, where Will's panicked face is peeking out of a door. He waves his arm wildly, motioning for us to join him.

The Triple Threat bounds into action. Audrey taps Molly on the shoulder, raises her to her feet. Then, like the gaggle of dutiful girls-with-the-band we are, we quickly make our way to Will.

He ushers us through the door and into a makeshift greenroom where they've stored dirty mops, broken chairs, and the rest of Delicate Blunder. Ben, Sammy, and Dane look ready to pass out—or explode. It's tough to tell which in the dim reddish light of the room's one lamp.

Will sputters, "I'm . . . we're a little bit . . . how do we look?"

The boys are instantaneously buried in a hail of compliments and confidence-boosting comments. And, in a freaky show of some deeply hidden motherly instinct, we all simultaneously tug at jackets, fix hair, and give hugs.

"You're going to do great!" I exclaim.

"You really think so?" Will asks.

"Are you kidding?" says Audrey. "Did you see the crowd out there? Just do what you always do."

"What's that?" Will asks, sincerely perplexed.

Audrey takes his hand and squeezes it tightly. "Play it like you mean it." She and Will lock eyes and he finally cracks a smile—a new kind of smile I've never seen from him before. Weird.

Veronica puts her hands on her hips. Oh, this should be good—Veronica's famous "Address to the Troops." It's how she began nearly all group activities in college. If it weren't for the "Address to the Troops," our apartment never would've been clean and I never would have passed a final.

She lets out a deep breath. "How many times have you done this? About a million, right? How many hours have you spent dreaming about getting a record deal? I'd guess twice as many." She paces before the boys, looking them each in the eye. "You can do this. You are on the verge of something great. It is new and frightening, yes, but it'll probably be the best thing that's ever happened to you." Their heads begin to nod, their posture stiffening already. "And you can do it. It is not only within your power: this music, your music, is in every fiber of your being. So, go out there and get it done. Kick. Some. Ass."

Suddenly the countenance of Delicate Blunder changes, the air around them seems lighter. The anxiety of the moment has been replaced by unwavering certainty. Now they're pumped. They are ready, and not just for the show—for what it could mean. Their dreams are quite possibly minutes away from coming true.

God, I miss that feeling, the buzz of knowing something spectacular is just bound to happen, just right around the corner. It's the feeling I had when I moved here. Where the hell did it go? More importantly, how do I get it back?

Too late now to be a backup singer, I suppose.

• • •

Back at our reserved table, the excitement is building. The hum of chatter and quaking pheromones, not to mention the anticipation, are all palpable. Unfortunately, I think it's all shooting out from our table. The closer it gets to showtime, the harder it is to control the shivering in my limbs. I can't tell if it's my leg or Audrey's that is tapping at the table like a jackhammer.

"Okay, now *I'm* getting really nervous," I blurt to the girls.

"You too?" Audrey looks at her watch. "Five minutes and counting."

Veronica exclaims, "We need something to take our minds off the tension. Does anybody know what this record company guy is supposed to look like?"

"Look for people you don't recognize," suggests Audrey, excited for the diversion.

Despite the limited light, I manage to spot a guy at the bar who seems new to the DB scene. I point him out to the girls.

Veronica chuckles and says, "Um, Ryan. That's a woman."

"Oops."

"It's the buzz cut," says Audrey. "Very confusing."

Okay, keep looking. There has to be someone . . .

Veronica whistles. "Who's the hottie walking in? Sign me up for some of . . . Holy shit!"

I whip my head around for the cause of Veronica's outburst.

Good Lord, please tell me this is not happening. Please tell me this is some kind of joke.

I scream. I scream like a little girl, a little rat girl. I've just made a noise that only rodents can hear.

He's headed straight for us, with just the hint of a swagger. His body tall and lithe but solid—strong arms, sturdy frame.

He wears confidence like other people wear clothes—it hangs off him like an afterthought.

Charlie.

My muscles are going rigid.

I think I may pass out.

My God, he's gorgeous. He's unbelievably gorgeous.

Oh, shit!

Veronica turns to me. "Don't panic! Things like this happen every day. Trust me, it's not fatal." Correction, it hasn't been fatal *yet.*

And just like that, Charlie is standing in front of me.

He looms over the table, looks down at me.

"Ryan?" he asks, more than a little surprised.

All right. Veronica's right. I will be calm, cool, and collected. Things like this happen every day. Plus, I am a modern woman. I am self-possessed and unflappable.

"You're not here. You're in L.A." Okay, so as it turns out I'm one of those idiots who in times of stress completely loses her mind. Good to know.

"I'm here now, actually." He stares at me. No smile, no scowl—just a stare. And, like every other time in the past, I can do nothing but stare right back. I'm such a sucker for those honey-brown eyes.

Veronica runs interference—in scary business mode. She offers her hand to him. "Veronica Wheatley. And this is Audrey . . ."

He interrupts. "Coulson. You think I could forget you guys?"

Finally his eyes wander to Veronica.

All right, what I need is a clear exit. I need a path of escape. Running and hiding happen to be two of my specialties, and they have served me very well so far, thank you very much.

I try to stand. Veronica slaps her hand on my thigh and tosses me a glare that clearly says, *Don't move.*

He points to the empty chair at our table. "Do you mind?"

I want to say, "Yes, I mind very much," but the words won't come out. Instead, Audrey replies with a bright "Sure!"

He sits across from me. He's staring again! I suddenly feel on display. The stunned silence gripping Audrey and Veronica isn't helping. Christ!

I try to smile but can only get half of my mouth to cooperate. This may be shock-induced paralysis. And I'm sitting here on a wad of Kleenex, which must give the impression that either (a) I'm too prissy to sit on dirty chairs, or (b) I'm prepared for an accident of some kind. Which, come to think of it, might not be so far off the mark.

Get me out of here!

Someone has to say something. I blurt, "What are you doing here? I mean, *this* particular bar." Seriously, I'm not intentionally going for irate psycho-bitch. It must be my brain's default mode.

"Delicate Blunder," he replies.

"Are you a fan?" Audrey asks.

"Yeah, you could say that. I'm here with Cranky Tank Records."

Veronica's eyes widen. She points at him. *"You're* the guy from the record company?"

"I am."

Veronica nods at Charlie, then gives me an elbow to the ribs. I think she wants me to participate in the conversation, but all that comes out is a stunned "What?" directed at her.

Great, now I've got him looking at me again.

Audrey steps in this time. "We're good friends of Will Monroe's, the lead singer. We've known the guys for years, since we first came to the city. Will and Ryan work together."

I push off from my chair and try to stand, but Veronica digs a fingernail into my forearm. Ouch.

I sit back down.

Veronica whispers in my ear, "You hold your head up, Ryan. You're a New Yorker now, goddamnit! You can do this!"

I try to hold my head up. If I could just think of something to say. Maybe first I should stop staring at him.

He's changed, for sure, but he's still outrageously good-looking. Why can't all ex-boyfriends get fat and bald and ugly, like they're supposed to?

He looks straight into my eyes and asks, "So, you've been here how long?"

"Four years," I reply.

"Just after graduation, then?" I know that tone of voice. I know that look in his eyes. It's bitterness. My God, he hates me.

His voice switches to a deep acerbic whisper. "So, how've you been?"

My life is flat and uninteresting—and you are fabulous. "Fine. I'm fine."

CHAPTER Eight

Cranky Tank Records is going to sign Delicate Blunder. This is one of the few things I can remember about last night.

The show passed in a haze. I do remember clapping a lot. At one point everyone was dancing. During "Sweet Agony" I think Will was singing *to* Audrey, but I can't really be sure because I spent most of the night pounding back Dos Equis and staring at my shoes. I kept expecting an anvil to drop on my head like it does in the cartoons.

When I wasn't looking down, I couldn't help but ogle Charlie. I traced the shape of his face with my eyes, trying to make it fit the snapshots my memory holds. He's more tan than I remember. There's a little scar on his neck that wasn't there before. He seems taller. His eyes seem harder, his posture not so free and easy. As a matter of fact, his whole personality is muted, a dim version of the virile and vivacious person I remember. I suppose it could be that, over the years, my subconscious has amplified his most pleasant traits. But being there next to him, it felt less like a quirk of my memory and more like time had actually made his overall presence somehow . . . smaller.

Twice during my anthropological study he felt me staring and turned to me. And twice I looked away while he glared at me.

I can't believe he still hates me. These four years, I've imagined him living a glamorous, fabulous L.A. life having easily forgotten all about me—and what I did.

After that first night at B-52's we spent nearly every waking moment together. It was a short trip from two strangers to one couple. Soon we were no longer individuals but were instead a unit, a two-headed love-monster called Charlie&Ryan. Like "Are Charlie&Ryan coming to the party?" "Did you see Charlie&Ryan today?" "Would Charlie&Ryan please report to the information desk."

We were close, and it wasn't just the sex, either. We had conversations, deep discussions. And I don't mean the kind you usually have in college, like the classic Karl Marx versus Vladimir Lenin fistfight conundrum (the intellectual's *Celebrity Deathmatch).* No, what I mean is that Charlie and I talked about everything: our families, our feelings, heartaches, embarrassments. We laughed a lot. I cried a little. Nothing was too personal to reveal. No matter how horrible or incriminating the facts, we were open and, inexplicably, understanding of one another. I'd never felt anything so close to perfect in my life. And that, as it turned out, was a problem.

The one thing I couldn't tell Charlie was that I was totally intimidated by his charm. Being on the receiving end of it wasn't exactly torture, but the fact that all that charisma was just out there . . . for anyone—it ate me up inside.

The driving force of my psychological tailspin was the demographic makeup of the university. There were three women for every man. And Charlie—(being sexy, smart, funny, tall, generally amazing in every way, etc.)—made for a high-value target. After about two months this began to make me a little, well, strange. More than strange, I became obsessed—not with Charlie, mind you—with myself.

I second-guessed everything. My clothes, my makeup, my bikini line—nothing seemed good enough. Good enough to hold perfect Charlie, good enough to compete with the roughly six thousand perfect women running around campus.

It was agonizing. I mean, this beautiful, wonderful guy would lie next to me, sleeping like a baby with his arm draped over my chest, and you know what I'd be thinking? *What is the most flattering way to position my hips? How do I lay my thighs so they look slim without looking like poseable Barbie? If I turn like this, it makes my tummy look flat but my arm looks like a Jimmy Dean sausage.* This idiotic, decidedly neurotic thought pattern didn't stop in the bedroom either. It was everywhere.

My self-consciousness and paranoia began to permeate every moment Charlie and I spent out in the world together, and was only reinforced and validated by every passing sorority girl's glance. Needless to say, I turned into a raging green-eyed monster. Actually, I was a monster in the closet. Thanks to *Oprah,* I knew that possessiveness was stupid and shameful, therefore, I kept it all to myself. My insecurity, the certainty of my inadequacy, I kept closely guarded and hidden. My heart paused its beating every time I saw Charlie talking with a girl at a party or waving to a female classmate on the street, but I never told him to stop.

Once or twice I broached the subject with him. I tried to delicately break the news that every woman in the world wanted him. Charlie didn't seem to think it was the case. It got too maddening for me to explain it to him, so eventually I just left it as my own private burden to bear.

Then, just shy of our one year mark, Charlie asked me something that knocked my already tenuous sanity squarely off its axis.

We'd spent the night before in all manner of incredibly dirty but tremendously enjoyable positions.

We were sitting on his bed eating cold leftover Thai food and watching a *Dick Van Dyke Show* marathon. I don't know why, but the thing I remember most vividly is that he was wearing red plaid flannel pajama pants with a stain on the left leg.

Weeks before, I'd slipped the pants on to get something to drink from the kitchen. I poured myself a glass of grape juice and Charlie surprised me with a behind-the-back bear hug. I dropped the glass and juice went everywhere, soaking the left leg of the pants.

I said, "Man, you'll do anything to get a girl to take her pants off."

"Actually, babe, I'd say I'll do anything to get a girl to take *my* pants off."

"Aren't you clever."

"I like to think so," he said, kissing my neck. "Now, we better get you cleaned up. You're gonna start getting sticky."

I spun around to face him, kissed him.

"I'm thinking . . . hot shower for two," he said playfully.

"All right, but I'm not falling for that 'Why don't *you* pick up the soap?' routine again."

Sitting on the bed, I stared at the stain and smiled, then shoved a blob of pad thai in my mouth.

"You're beautiful when you eat," he said to me.

"It's the chopsticks," I retorted.

Then his face went all serious. He took my chopsticks and shoved them into the pad thai, took my hands into his.

"You know I love you, right?" he said.

"Yeah. I love you too," I replied matter-of-factly.

"I was going to wait till later . . . but I don't think I can."

An inexplicable wave of fear and anxiety overtook me. "What? What is it?"

"I got a job offer." He dug inside his nightstand, produced a piece of paper, and laid it gently in my hand. "Los Angeles."

I stared at the paper, tried to read it, but the knots in my stomach were performing feats of alphabetic bondage. I couldn't make the letters into coherent words. I pretended to read it, to understand what was happening, but my eyes could only scan the page. Only three things registered: pleased . . . Los Angeles . . . you . . .

He started talking rapid-fire. "It's a great company. Major

record company. They want me. I mean, I got recruited. Better than entry level—real decision-making power. I can't say no, you know?"

"Of course not!" I agreed, my stomach feeling like a lead weight.

He took a deep breath. "I want you to come with me."

Of all the things he could have said, this was the one I least expected. "Go with you?" I replied.

"There's lots of computer stuff out there. There's the movie business, and Silicon Valley is somewhere in California, right?"

"Yeah. Uh . . ." I said weakly.

"I love you, Ryan. Please come with me?"

I almost said yes. I wanted to. I wanted to scream it and jump into his arms and never let go. But I didn't.

Instead I said, "Let me think about it, okay?"

And I did. I thought about it—every waking moment for two weeks. I imagined myself in Los Angeles, the plain, frumpy girlfriend of a music industry executive on the rise.

At our smallish college I got nervous and panicky about him, about us. I had spent months wallowing in my own inadequacy. No matter how calm the exterior, inside I was chaos. What would L.A. be like? L.A., land of glamour and perfection, home of the breast implant loan and layaway liposuction. The place where all the truly special, truly beautiful creatures in the world go to bask in each other's magnificence. I felt certain that holding myself up to those creatures on a daily basis would make me feel smaller and smaller till I finally disappeared.

While carefully examining all the possible outcomes of a

move to L.A. with Charlie, I never once told Audrey and Veronica. It sounds a bit crazy, I know. I think, somewhere deep down, I knew that as a twenty-one-year-old modern American woman I was supposed to throw caution to the wind, to be reckless and wild. I knew that for any other girl, moving to a glamorous metropolis with your fabulously handsome boyfriend would be a good thing, to say the least. I knew that Audrey and Veronica, being the supportive friends they were, would have told me that I was beautiful, and special, and not inadequate in any way. They would, without trying to, make me feel even more inadequate by pointing out that my feelings were somehow fundamentally stupid.

I realize now that I *was*, in fact, supremely stupid. But at the time my feelings were so overwhelming, I couldn't grasp the depth and breadth of their hold on the more rational parts of my brain. That's the thing about emotional upheaval, to a person in the midst of it, the emotions are as real and tangible as objects are in the physical realm. Actually, they're more real. You can shed a jacket and toss it in the closet, lose it under a pile of laundry. Self-doubt, dread, fear, confusion—these things are ever-present. There's no easy way to excise and bury them. Which is why it's so annoying to be on the receiving end of comments like "You shouldn't feel that way" or "Stop thinking that," even if they come from your best friends. It's only *after* the emotions have settled—in my case, years after—that you see the illusory nature of even the deepest, most powerful feelings.

In the thick of it, though, I was constantly at play with my imagination and my insecurities, conjuring up every possible consequence of moving to L.A. It wasn't until a week before finals that conjecture and reality collided and I made my decision.

Charlie and I went to a party at his roommate Jeff's frat house. It was the usual frat house setup: eight kegs of cheap beer, several hundred drunk people, a healthy delegation of pot dealers, etc. This setup, in case you were wondering, was my worst nightmare. Everywhere I looked was a stunning blonde, redhead, brunette. There were artists, musicians, actresses, former models, current models, and more than one *Girls Gone Wild* veteran.

Charlie went off to talk to a couple of his friends who had just been accepted at Juilliard's grad program. I left my place in Charlie's shadow, and went to the ladies' room—or should I say the frat-house equivalent: a men's bathroom with a paper sign marked Chicks and the drawing of a stick person with a skirt and enormous boobs.

When I returned, I found Charlie sitting comfortably on his throne at the center of a cool-storm, thunderous laughter and rapt attention raining on him like so many kisses. Half a dozen girls studied him, surreptitiously preening when he looked away. They flaunted their lean bodies in outfits of black and gray, like a flock of slutty emaciated crows. The guys of the group bandied about music references, the more obscure the better. They boisterously insulted each other's opinions, speaking a language of pompous musical dogma that I could not translate. And there was Charlie, their leader. His voice alone quieted the hail of tangled conversations; the crows and the sycophants alike nodded at his words of wisdom.

It felt like a trailer for the movie of my possible L.A. life. All my conjecture was confirmed—I felt tiny and insignificant. I *tried* to squeeze in behind them unnoticed, squirm my way back into Charlie's shadow without getting dragged into the discussion by such terrifying questions as "What do you think, Ryan?" But it was no use, there was no room for me there.

I backed myself into a nearby corner, watching and admiring Charlie's strength of voice, his power to persuade, his knowledge and the easy, unpretentious way he wielded it. I racked my brain, digging deep for nuggets of neglected information, for something—anything—to say. I tried to make myself *feel* that I belonged, to play the part of the girl I wished I was, but in the end I couldn't do it.

Slowly but surely I drifted away from Charlie and his group. By the end of the night I was miles away, safe—silently watching *South Park* reruns with a cluster of barely conscious potheads.

At about three, Charlie finally emerged, pink and warm from hours of laughter and inebriation. He gently pulled me from the tatty sofa in which I'd nested and walked me home.

Charlie was a happy drunk. Even when he had too much, it wasn't the alcohol that made him dizzy—his dreams did that. He could talk endlessly about the future, and that walk home was no exception.

He slung his arm around my neck, almost leaning on me. "You know what, Ry?"

"What?"

"I can't wait to get out of here."

"Me too."

"It's so close I can almost feel it. I'll get to do things my way, finally. Make music I want to make, you know? Change the system. Produce, and on my terms. Can you feel it?"

"Yep," I replied quietly.

Under normal circumstances I would have found his starry-eyed faith infectious, smiled, and encouraged it. But that night I couldn't. Halfway home it struck me—my own future was empty. *My* dreams were little puffs of smoke. They came and went, never holding their shape for very long, backed up by nothing. Charlie's, on the other hand, were solid, molded out of fact and passion.

Everything suddenly clicked into place, all the pieces fit—I was not meant for Charlie's new life. Before, I had only felt my shortcomings as they related to other people, the competition. I had imagined a million different ways in which the amorphous *they* would make me feel. But in that instant, even as his arm rested heavily on my shoulder and our feet moved in time on the same sidewalk, I could feel something even more odious: I could feel our paths diverging. I was sure then that if I followed Charlie to L.A. *I* would get lost.

Charlie and I met after his last exam, at the statue of Mozart near the music building. The sun smiled down that day. The sky was blue, the air heavy with the refreshing humidity of early summer.

Charlie practically ran me over, picked me up in a crushing squeeze.

"I'm done," he said. "College is officially over!"

"Congratulations," I said, trying not to look at him.

"What's wrong, babe? You tank your econ exam or something?"

"No, I did fine. I was . . . I think I . . . I've decided about L.A."

"Finally! Listen, I've been looking on the Internet and I think we can get a really nice place for around fifteen hundred a month. Now, don't worry. I'm gonna be making seriously good money, so you can take your time getting a job or whatever—"

"Charlie," I interrupted, "I'm not going."

"What?" he said, his face twisting in a way I'd never seen before.

"I can't . . . I can't go."

"Why?"

"I just can't."

"What do you mean, you 'just can't'?"

He suddenly looked drawn, angry. It almost made me take it back, like, "Oops. Did I say no? What I meant was, *yes.*" But instead, I reminded myself of how much harder and more painful it would be to delay the inevitable—to move to L.A. and then watch it all go to hell slowly but surely.

"I mean I just can't."

"Are you serious?"

I nodded my head forcefully.

"Let me . . . I don't get it. What are you saying? Are you saying you *can't* go or that you *won't*?"

"Does it really matter?"

"Of course it fucking matters, Ryan." He dropped his bag and paced around Mozart. *"Can't* means that either your religion won't allow it, or that the climate of Southern California will result in your actual death. *That* is *can't.*"

He crossed his arms and gaped at me. "*Won't* means that you don't care enough to go—that you . . . don't love me enough to go. Which one sounds more like what you're feeling right now, Ryan? 'Cause I can tell you which one it feels like to me."

I wanted to tell him that I would get sucked up and lost out there, that for me there was this indefinable yet somehow inevitable gloom about it. I wanted to tell him I would lose what little sanity I had. But I couldn't tell him that. There was only one thing I could do. . . .

It came out of my mouth in a whisper. "I won't."

His body went sort of limp, his shoulders slumped. He took a deep breath and looked at me with such grief, the sight of it made me want to vomit, slit my own wrists.

I realize now that what I saw in his eyes that moment was agony. I'd never, to that point, been on intimate terms with agony. It's no wonder I couldn't comprehend it. Now I know that the look in his eyes should have provoked in me a deep and overwhelming compulsion to take him in my arms, tell him that I loved him, and beg for his forgiveness.

Instead, I stood there and watched him walk away—as far away from me as he could. Until last night, that was the last time I had spoken to Charlie.

I'm not sure whether it's time, detachment, or the effect of maturity that acts as hindsight's optometrist, but whatever the cause, I have since come to understand the *real* reason I couldn't bring myself to go with Charlie. Yes, there were challenges, and yes, things could have gone horribly wrong. But it also could have been wonderful. In all those hours of exhaustive speculation, mere minutes were focused on the positive—what it would have been like if things with Charlie had actually worked out. I was scared of L.A.—scared of his dreams—and it blinded me. I never considered the possibility that instead of getting lost in L.A., I may have *found* myself there.

CHAPTER Nine

My head hurts, I'm starving, and I know the subway fluorescence is making me look as foul as I feel. My brain is like paste, thick and sticky. Thoughts come and go in slow motion. The reason? Today I semi-meticulously input hundreds of pieces of air-conditioner data:

Unit #98733 Hanover Power Frost, Twenty-first Century Central Air-Cooling Unit (with modular components)

- 37,000 Nominal Cooling Capacity, BTUH Output
- 17-inch fan plate with titanium bearings
- Patented Sound Insulated Air Flow Compression Chamber

Unit #98744 XT-4300 Special Edition Air Chiller

- 49,500 Nominal Cooling Capacity, BTUH Output
- Baked-on Powder Finish, Customizable Color
- Three-Stage Cooling Mechanism with SmartCool©

And on and on. So many stupid air conditioners. Eight hours of my life—gone. For what? Air-conditioner data, of all things. And where is all that data going? It'll get dumped in someone's hard drive and sit neglected and unused until the next round of ridiculously named 37 BTU output models goes into production. I suppose next year I'll be expected to input *that* freaking data too.

Oh, and did I forget to mention that other thing? The thing where my ex-boyfriend hates me? Yeah, paste.

I slog my body aboveground and out into the fading daylight of Greenwich Village. I try and get my bearings, look for the street signs I know should be around here somewhere, and end up being stampeded by a mob of artsy NYU students who are way too eager to get on the subway.

I hate coming down here sometimes. I mean, it is beautiful and quaint, but it's so damn hip that I feel like an interloper. I'm so uncool I can't even keep the names of the districts straight. This part of the island goes through a trendy rebirth of some sort about every six months—SoHo, NoHo, NoLita. Now someone tells me there's a SoLita.

Veronica lives down here, and not just in any part of the Village, mind you. She lives in the most picturesque, New Yorky block in the East Village. Here, a brick-clad world-class bistro for the insanely rich makes its home next to an offbeat millinery for rubber fetishists. She gets her lattes at a coffee shop/vintage store/art gallery just steps from her building, which itself is an art deco masterpiece featured in three coffee-table books (so far).

She refers to the neighborhood as "a concession to her parents," who happen to pay half the rent. Can you believe that? I think that's one of the reasons she consents to the bohemian dreamboats; she feels like she owes her mom something for all the help she gets. If only I had to make such a sacrifice.

The last two years of college I worked thirty hours a week at a video store during the school year and forty hours a week at an electronics superstore during the summer so I would have a postgraduation nest egg. The result of which is a two-hundred-square-foot closet on the uppermost Upper East Side. Veronica has zero—I repeat, *zero*—student loans and a corner apartment with six windows! The place is blanketed in creamy mustard Ralph Lauren paint and has a brown leather sofa that didn't come from IKEA.

"Hey, baby!" Veronica says as she swings the door open. Her kitchen is slathered in imported tile and cherrywood and is clean, for a change.

"Hey, Ryan," Audrey pipes in from the living room.

"I need a pair of chopsticks in my hand, like now," I say, plopping my bag on the little pass-through window between her kitchen and her living room.

"Food is on the table. I'll just get the wine," she replies.

I sink into the buttery-soft leather next to Audrey.

"You feeling any better yet? About the other night?" Audrey asks me in her most tender voice.

"What, Charlie?" She nods. "Oh, *sure,*" I say acerbically.

Veronica strides in bearing three very large glasses of wine. She crosses her long legs under the coffee table and says, "I don't think he looks that good. He really isn't aging well." She signals to Audrey with her eyes.

Audrey picks up. "Goodness, no. He looked awful."

I can't help but laugh. "Nice try, guys, but I was there, remember?"

"He was kind of an asshole, though. Didn't you get that feeling from him, Audrey?"

"Absolutely!"

And for very good reason, I don't add. Not about to spill my guts now—not when I've done such a good job of keeping it from them so far.

"Have you decided what to do if you see him again?" asks Veronica.

"Well, first, I plan to do everything within my power not to let that happen. But if by some chance I were to run into him again, I will merely handle myself with grace and dignity, of course."

"Of course," coos Audrey.

Actually, what I've decided is that ex-boyfriends are like the Loch Ness Monster: they are things of the past best left to myth and legend but that, by some sick quirk of the universe, always manage to rear their ugly heads. Nothing can be done about it. In other words, I've decided that if I ever see Charlie Cavanaugh again, I'm going to run. Run like the wind.

I take a giant bite of moo goo gai pan, and then speak while chewing. "Okay, enough about Charlie. What are we celebrating?"

"I've got news," replies Veronica.

"Me too!" Audrey exclaims, throwing her hand up in the air like she's trying to get the teacher's attention.

"Wow. Exciting," I say midbite.

Audrey turns to Veronica. "You go first."

"No, you," insists Veronica.

"No, *you*."

"For real, *you* go."

"Okay, stop," I blurt. "Veronica, you go first."

Veronica makes affected little circles in the air with her chopsticks. "Well, my boss gave me some good news today." She takes a bite of sticky rice, pausing for effect. She *so* should have been an actress. "I'm now in charge of a medium-sized deal with Iceland."

"The country?" I ask.

She nods yes.

I don't think I understand. "The whole country?"

"Yes, Ryan. The whole country."

"Excellent!" Audrey proclaims.

"Very well done," I say. But the real question is, "Cash? Use of the private jet? Give me perks."

"No pay increase or anything"—Veronica rolls her eyes—"but I do get to boss around a few guys."

She's trying to pretend it isn't important. I hate it when she does stuff like that—such a career-girl thing to do. I've certainly never been involved with any important-sounding deals with an entire nation but, if I had, you can be damn sure I would have bragged about it. I mean, who does deals with Iceland?

Audrey raises her glass. "To Veronica, Wall Street's newest überbitch."

Veronica smiles brightly and slaps her hand on her chest in mock humility. Her voice goes up an octave. "I'd just like to thank my parents, and the Academy, and his Holiness the Dalai Lama. Oh, and all the people nominated with me."

Audrey and I applaud. Veronica responds with the beauty-queen wave and tooth-whitening-cream-spokesmodel grin.

Veronica takes a sip of wine. "Okay, Audrey. Your turn."

Audrey lays her chopsticks down and adjusts her position on the couch, straightening her skirt. "Well, actually," she begins timidly, "something similar happened to me today."

"Promotion?" inquires Veronica.

Impossible. Audrey and I have jobs, not careers. We don't get promotions.

"You are looking at the newest assistant account executive at Fletcher and Roth Advertising."

What?

"Awesome!" declares Veronica. "It's about time!"

"About time?" I say, perplexed.

Veronica looks at me like I'm crazy. "The five-year plan!"

Excuse me? "You have a plan?" I ask Audrey.

"Of course."

Where did this come from? How did I miss it?

"I had no idea you had a plan. I thought, you know, you were just biding your time until the right guy came along. . . . I mean, I don't mean to sound . . . It's just . . ." I can't seem to find the words.

Veronica squints her eyes at me. "Jesus, Ryan!"

Well, what the hell? How did I miss this? I'm suddenly the only one without a plan. "I thought you *hated* your job," I say.

"I know I complain sometimes, but I don't *hate* it."

"Really, Ryan," scolds Veronica. "*I'm* offended."

"I'm sorry, okay?" I drop my chopsticks and light a cigarette. "I just thought Audrey and I were kind of going through the same things, you know?"

"You're waiting for a guy to rescue you?" asks Audrey

"No, but I thought Audrey was." I sound like an asshole. I take a long drag and blow it up to the ceiling, looking for an answer written somewhere up there. "I mean, I don't think I'd *refuse* rescuing. I don't think there's anything wrong with it," I say, trying to backtrack. Come to think of it, being rescued sounds perfect—and ridiculously unlikely. I continue, "But God, I don't have a plan! My job sucks. I thought, you know, we were in the same boat."

Apparently not, though. Apparently I'm adrift in a dinghy while Audrey and Veronica lay on the Lido deck of a luxury liner, sipping mimosas. How did this happen?

"Oh, come on, Ryan. I know we all bitch and moan sometimes, but work isn't that bad," Veronica says.

"It is for me. It really, really is," I whimper.

Audrey asks, "For real?"

Try not to cry, Ryan, you hopeless loser. I take a deep breath and throw my hands up in defeat.

"Why do you keep doing it?" asks Veronica.

I don't know. "What choice do I have?"

"Get a new one!" declares Veronica.

Who the hell is she kidding? "In this city? In this economy?

With my complete and utter lack of any real skill or experience? Easy for you to say." Even to me, this time-tested line of logic suddenly sounds more like an excuse than a reason. My head is spinning a little.

"It's not as hard as it sounds. You just need requirements. Stick to them and don't compromise," Audrey begins. "When we first got here my requirements were: One, that it be a position that would require real hands-on involvement in the business, and two, that it would be something I could get promoted out of. That's a place to start."

Holy shit! "You never told me that!" Oh my God. "My top two requirements were that the job didn't involve, one, food preparation, or two, getting naked in public." Which is why I took the first job that I got offered—Geiger.

They laugh. Audrey pats me on the back. It would be funny, except I'm not joking.

Audrey finally notices I'm the only one not laughing. "Aw, Ryan."

"But when you guys started, you knew you could do the job, though, right? You felt prepared."

Veronica chuckles. "Every day for the first three months I thought they were going to figure out I was a moron and fire me."

"Seriously?" I pose.

Veronica nods an emphatic yes.

"And you guys really like what you do?"

"I'm not completely head over heels, but I know it'll get better," says Audrey consolingly. "Even with this promotion I'm still basically an underling. But I can see the light at the end of the tunnel, you know?"

"And you will, too," Veronica says cheerily. "Though I don't completely understand what you do, I'm sure that you have a bright future doing it."

What?

"I enter data, Veronica."

"Surely there's something else? I mean, you make decisions about the data," she says, searching for something. I stare at her blankly. "You *analyze* the data?"

Again no. I shake my head.

"You just enter the data?"

"Yeah," I say, crushed.

"Oh, that *is* a problem," she replies.

"No shit!" I bite back.

My mind is racing around in circles, and it's starting to make me dizzy and nauseated. Motion sickness, or vertigo, or something caused by the abrupt disappearance of all my reference points. I am utterly directionless.

Audrey steps in. "Let's make Ryan a plan!" she says, and gives Veronica one of those looks like *Just follow my lead.*

I hate that look, and if I weren't so preoccupied considering the quickest, most painless way to commit suicide, I would tell her so.

"Excellent idea!" Veronica says in a perky, Audrey-like voice I have never heard her use. She goes to her desk and gets out a notepad and pencil.

They're trying to humor me, distract and pacify me like you would an agitated mental patient. This is not surprising, really, since I am, in fact, feeling like one.

Audrey pats my knee. "All right, Ryan, what would you do if you could do anything you wanted? Anything."

"I have no idea," I say, stubbing out my cigarette and lighting another.

Veronica is annoyed by this answer. I can tell because she's getting that little crinkle between her eyes. "Okay, Audrey. How about you? I mean anything. Fantasy job. Something you'd quit your current job to do. It doesn't have to be practical: Think fantasy occupation."

"Okay. Give me a second." She pauses and lights a cigarette. "Wow, there are so many options."

For her, maybe. The world is wide open for career girls with both direction *and* momentum in their favor.

Audrey starts up. "Maybe I would host my own show on the Travel Channel. I'd go around to fabulous places and have fabulous times and let them film me. All the while I'd be getting paid, with all expenses covered by the network!"

I have to admit, that'd be a pretty sweet gig. No, I will not let them cheer me up.

Veronica furiously jots in her notepad and chirps, "Yes! And Ryan and I could be your cohosts! It could be a show about where to go if you're young and have a limitless budget! That way we'd get to go to only the most glamorous spots."

Audrey is getting into it. "And you'd be engaged to Matthew McConaughey, and Ryan would be with Vince Vaughn!"

"Vince Vaughn?" I say. "How about Luke Wilson?"

Veronica holds up her pencil and smiles wide at me. "That, my dear, is why they invented the eraser!"

Damnit, they're making me feel better. I hate this tag-team

therapy. I have absolutely no chance to wallow in my own misery. It's just un-American, I tell you.

This sort of thing is always happening with Audrey and Veronica. They are both cursed with the gene that refuses to accept misery as a viable and comfortable mood. I think this gene is also responsible for Audrey's unflappable perkiness and Veronica's inability to accept defeat. It's sad. They've never had the pleasure of curling into the fetal position on a bed of empty Twix wrappers and watching hours of meaningless television.

I am tired and confused and a little bit lonely, but I'm glad it's Sunday and that I have some time to wallow in self-pity. It really is one of the most underrated leisure activities. Unfortunately, it's difficult to wallow when you've been infected by the unbridled optimism of your two best friends.

By the end of last night we'd come up with a lot of very meaningful career options for me.

Career List:

- Rock Star (Sheryl Crow meets Aimee Mann)
  Upside—creativity, screaming fans
  Downside—leather chaffing
- Lady Who Lunches (mornings spent shopping, afternoons spent sipping martinis and playing bridge)
  Upside—low stress
  Downside—would have to learn bridge
- Zoologist (key area of study: bears)
  Upside—communing with nature

Downside—ill-fitting khaki pants, communing with nature

- Lobster Fisherman (Maine)
  Upside—sea, sand, and New England
  Downside—allergic to shellfish
- Gwyneth Paltrow (actress/Hollywood royalty)
  Upside—killer wardrobe, trail of sexy men in wake
  Downside—perpetually shiny hair may blind unsuspecting passersby (lawsuit just waiting to happen)

Well, those are the ones I can read. The rest are something like SteeeemPip Fiterr, Inden Chhieef, Baartenddie. I have no idea.

No, I'm not *exactly* qualified to feed bears or harvest lobsters. However, failing any other options, they seem reasonable. Don't they? What's most important, they don't involve the entering of any sort of data. Except maybe zoology, because I'm sure you have to keep track of when the animals get fed and that sort of thing. And that, technically speaking, is data. But who am I kidding? I can't actually do any of these things. I don't think I can actually *do* anything.

That's not true, I can list every one of Molly Ringwald's films in chronological order. I can sing the entire catalog of Dave Matthews Band songs without once pausing to remember the words. And I enter data better than anyone I know. These things would be considered a solid foundation if I decide to become, say, a professional television quiz show contestant, but they aren't going to support anything else. I need to figure out something—anything—I can do.

Where is my fucking *plan*? My direction? I wish it would just appear. That's how it worked for Veronica and Audrey . . . and Charlie. They just knew what they were meant for. There has to be something like that out there for me, doesn't there?

Why can't there be a *Zagat Guide to Life*? They've got one for everything else. Or, better yet, why can't there be a master map like the ones they have in shopping malls? Where's my big red dot that says *You Are Here*?

CHAPTER Ten

I've been trying to come up with a plan—a real plan—for my future. Instead of diving straight into the roughly three million tons of data I'm expected to enter today, I got out a pen and paper. Unfortunately I can't seem to get past:

1. Get the hell out of here.

Not helping is the fact that, through the nearest window to my cube (seventy-five feet away), I can almost see a sliver of the dreamy blue sky outside.

Spring in Manhattan has sprung. The sunshine and warmth are nice, but I always mourn a bit for winter. The cozy, body-hiding wool wardrobe is tough to let go of. It's especially distressing when the skinny and chic break out their outrageously expensive gauzy tops and sky-high strappy Jimmy Choos. Of course, even if I could afford the waif/sun-goddess look, I could never pull it off attitude-wise. Despite the heat and sweat, in the summer months I try to expose as little skin as possible. I haven't owned a pair of shorts since I was twelve—the year puberty hit and turned my thighs to mush.

This time of year in New York does have its benefits, though. There is a distinct dip in the level of open hostility for the first few weeks of spring. I think it's the lukewarm air and the budding leaves. Central Park makes its yearly green-draped resurrection and positively swells with walkers, bikers, and lovers fondling each other in the grass. In other words, people are too busy sunning themselves to be belligerent.

Once things get hot, sticky, and smelly, the yelling and pushing go back to normal levels, though midsummer, too, has its benefits—the Hamptons. Not that I personally have gone, or ever will go. What I mean is that the really wealthy or the really wannabe wealthy scurry there every weekend. And a good percentage of the not-so-wealthy scurry off to the other not-so-fashionable areas of Long Island or the Jersey shore. This means that July weekends in Manhattan are occasionally marked by an eerie calm. Oddly, July weekends are when I feel most at home here.

I could pretend it is July, push the season, race out of here, and run naked through Bethesda Fountain.

Speaking of embarrassing myself, I finally got the courage to go back to Brock's bodega, and over the last few days I've managed to systematically purchase every one of the smashed Cupcakes, Ho Ho's, Sno Balls, and mini apple pies. Brock was very nice, he said "Hope you are feeling better" several times. He didn't, however, attempt to discourage my high-fat purchasing. I feel a little better, but unfortunately I now have a year's supply of sickly-sweet, overpriced pancakes.

"Ryan," says Betsy, wobbling near my desk. I quickly toss my "plan" under my desk. "Your evaluation sheet, dear."

"Uh, thanks," I say.

"The top one is your evaluation of Mr. Anderson, to be filled out at your earliest convenience. The bottom is a sample of the kind of evaluation he'll be doing for us."

As soon as Betsy has moved on to Will and the other cube farmers, I dive into the packet.

Shit.

Highlights of the employee evaluation form (Apparently, unless otherwise stated, I am *Blank*):

- *Blank* performs duties with care and accuracy. Comments:
- *Blank* performs duties in a timely and professional manner. Comments:
- Things that *Blank* could do better:
- Overall impressions of *Blank* and his/her future in the company:

Oh, yeah. I'm screwed.

On the upside, evaluating The Dirk will not be as difficult as I thought. His sheet is all multiple choice and true/false. Nice.

Will wheels his chair around to my cube.

"Cross your fingers that I'm not going to be here much longer. I don't think I do any of these things." A team of lawyers are, as we speak, drafting up Will's clemency from Geiger Data Systems—in the form of a contract between Delicate Blunder and Cranky Tank Records.

"Tell me about it, and I have nowhere to run," I reply.

He gives me a sympathetic pout. "Sorry."

"Sure. Say, why don't you ditch rock-stardom and stay here with me?"

"Sounds great. Hey, why don't you take a spoon and gouge out my eyes?"

Will wheels back to his cube, and I yell, "Some friend you are!"

As I try to get back to work, I notice a placid Betsy typing away, surrounded by her cat-themed knickknacks. When Will's gone, it'll be me and her and The Dirk, last of the long-term employees. Just the thought of this sends an uncomfortable chill up my spine.

My evaluation of The Dirk:

a, c, b, d, a, a, c, b, d

true, false, true, true, true, true, false, true

The questions don't really matter. I picked only the safest answers—those that make me seem most like a company-loving kiss-ass.

Tomorrow, Audrey's office is throwing her a postwork promotion party thing at a bar downtown. This means—damn the financial crisis—I must shop!

Must haves:

1. Sexy yet demure little something to wear to Audrey's get-together.
2. Something nice for Audrey's promotion/sorry-I-was-such-a-psycho-horrible-friend-and-didn't-properly-congratulate-you gift.
3. Something to distract me from my pathetic non–plan-having life.

This last one must remain secret, as Veronica said she may slowly roast me with her hair dryer if I continue to sulk about not having a plan. Apparently, I still have a will to live, because I haven't said a word about it. I can't say I'm not thinking about it, though.

I'm trying really hard not to be jealous of Audrey and Veronica's recent success. I know the envy is wrong. I mean, I should be happy for them, right? I should be cheering them on, hoping they make all their dreams come true. I shouldn't care how far ahead of me they get. But this feeling is something I can't ignore. It's not the usual kind of jealousy, that fleeting pang of wanting something you don't have. No, this is something more base, more elemental than that, almost . . . primal. It's the sensation of some previously unknown fire inside me turned up to full blast, a sort of bubbling, boiling feeling that grips every part of me. It makes my face red and my skin warm and prickly. Knowing that this feeling is, in fact, some twisted and powerful form of jealousy inspires an enormous amount of guilt. The fact that Audrey and Veronica are trying to make me feel better and support me makes the guilt even that much worse.

• • •

They've planned "fantasy shopping" before we begin the actual shopping. Fantasy shopping, you see, is the cornerstone of a good time for the modern American female. Simply put, it is a totally free, highly entertaining exercise in consumer catharsis. All one needs to fantasy-shop is one fabulous outfit, a couple of friends, and a casual familiarity with method acting.

We roam the exclusive shopping streets of New York and pretend to be wealthy, carefree women about town. That is, women with unlimited budgets, expensive taste, and very poor foreign accents.

We meet at Trump Tower and work our way through the elite shopping destinations of Fifth Avenue. On a full-day fantasy-shopping excursion the route is:

Begin at Trump Tower.
Take Fifth Avenue south.
Gucci.
Ferragamo.
Cartier.
Versace.
In front of St. Patrick's Cathedral, watch Audrey genuflect and quietly pray for God to forgive her for briefly considering a life of crime while in Cartier.
Saks Fifth Avenue.
Cross Fifth Avenue at Forty-ninth Street.
Take Fifth Avenue north. (If punch-drunk or suffering any sort of sticker shock, find the Empire State Building on the horizon and walk in the opposite direction.)
Harry Winston.

Prada.
Bergdorf Goodman.
Cross Fifth Avenue at Fifty-seventh Street.
Proceed directly to Tiffany's.

Since we're all just getting out of work, today our fantasy shopping is limited to Bergdorf's special-occasion department and, of course, Tiffany's.

Entering Tiffany's is like stepping into a dreamworld. A world in which handsome gentlemen wear ascots, tip their hats, and freely give large precious and semiprecious stones to the women they adore. In this world women wear their precious stones every day, as though they were nothing but pretty trinkets. Grocery shopping? A three-carat solitaire pendant should do nicely. Taking out the trash? Must put on the emerald-cut yellow diamond brooch.

I guess, in a way, it's the world of my father's New York dream. Unfortunately for us, since the weather's gone all toasty and ideal for travel, tourists are swarming this perfect dreamworld. There's something about plastic windbreakers and fanny packs that can shatter any fantasy, no matter how many fresh flower arrangements are involved.

"May I try this in platinum, please?" Veronica says to the clerk in her very best Helena Bonham Carter. "Gold is so unflattering to my skin."

The clerk then replaces the $10,000 gold tennis bracelet on her wrist with a $15,000 platinum one.

"I don't know, girls. What do you think?" She flashes us her slender wrist.

The bracelet is, of course, decadent and divine in every way, but Audrey and I are supposed to come to the rescue.

Audrey takes Veronica's wrist and turns it, inspecting the jewels. "I don't like it, Veronica."

My turn to lie, "It looks like something your mother would wear."

"Yes, I suppose you're right," Veronica says. She motions to the clerk, who puts it away, back to its perfect velvet-and-glass home.

"What's next, girls?" I say. "Sapphires?"

"Why not?" replies Audrey.

We glide away from the gorgeous diamond bracelets. Well, maybe *glide* is a bit of an overstatement.

Then, like three parts of the same rusty machine, we stop cold. We gaze demurely across the crowded room. As if commanded by Moses himself, the throng of midwestern families parts. A clear path emerges to the dreamiest dream section of Tiffany's—the engagement rings.

Veronica whispers, "Should we?"

Audrey and I nod a solemn yes.

No matter how single, or how attached—no matter how totally against the concept of marriage the modern American girl may be—engagement rings have a mysterious pull. It's a primitive instinct, one we're powerless to fight. The fact is, women of a certain age are genetically programmed to drool over large chunks of shiny translucent carbon.

Audrey, Veronica, and I approach the massive glass cases at a tiptoe, as if scared to rush it or to get too close. We each want one of those rings, yet are more than a little ashamed of their hold on us.

We circle the displays in silence, taking mental notes on carat weight, color, and clarity.

1½ carat, round cut, platinum setting . . .
2 carat, cushion cut, with two cabochon sapphires . . .
1 carat flawless, princess cut, bezel set . . .

These several hundred rings in front of me were created and are destined for the same purpose. Each one of them will end up on some beautiful, delicate hand. Each will be the start of something wonderful and exciting.

One will be given at a Yankees game during the seventh-inning stretch. One will be presented to a former beauty queen on her thirty-fifth birthday. One will lay in wait for three weeks, deep in a man's coat pocket, while he musters the courage to pop the question.

The one proposal I can't picture is my own. It's too frightening to consider. Actually, the thing that really scares me is the possibility that I may never get one. Trust me, I know it's silly. I mean, I'm young, right? I don't want to be married at twenty-five, necessarily. I just hope, you know, that it's something my future holds. But I've got time for all this to happen—for my life to happen. Don't I?

After spending way too much money at J.Crew . . .

"I think the ten-carat choker would look outstanding with the little Halston number you tried on at Bergdorf's, Audrey," says Veronica, adjusting her armful of heavy shopping bags as we trek back up Fifth Avenue from Rockefeller Plaza.

"Let's see . . . if I start saving now, I could afford them both in about . . . the year 2075."

"What about shoes?" I say.

"Okay, make it 2080," Audrey sighs.

"I'm sorry about the other day, you guys. I guess I just got a little freaked. Seeing Charlie really threw me, and then . . . well, my job sucks. But that's not your fault. I shouldn't have—"

"We understand," says Veronica kindly.

Audrey fingers the thin leather bracelet I bought her. "And thank you for the gift. It's beautiful." Her voice goes soft and soothing. "You know, you don't have to come tomorrow night."

"Are you kidding? I wouldn't miss it for the world. Listen, I'm over it. I'm fine." Was that convincing? They eye me doubtfully. "Well, I will be. Okay?"

Audrey pats me on the back.

Yeah, I'll be all right. Once I figure out how.

CHAPTER Eleven

I've never really met any of Audrey's coworkers. I caught a glimpse of her boss once when I picked her up for a liquid lunch last year, but Audrey likes to keep her work life and personal life separate. She'll meet them for a quick happy hour, but she's convinced that if she went out with any of them socially she'd end up getting hammered, make an ass of herself, and lose what respect they have for her. I admire that about her. I can't relate exactly, as I routinely make an ass of myself with or without alcohol, but I see the logic for Audrey.

I arrive at the bar, and on time for once. Audrey will be so proud—as soon as I find her. Friday night in TriBeCa, and I'm wading in a sea of Suits. There's enough Armani and Brooks Brothers in here to choke several thousand horses.

I peer over the short coifs layered in product (the style favored by male midlevel executives on the rise). No luck. Someone behind me tugs at my hair. I whip around—Veronica.

"Thank God, it's Friday," she sighs.

"Long day?"

"Iceland, Iceland, and more Iceland," she grunts.

"Cool."

She giggles at my sad attempt at a joke. "That was bad."

"Yeah." I go back to searching the crowd, "All right, O Tall One, can you see Audrey over the sausagefest?"

"It's fabulous, isn't it? I love a target-rich environment."

Yeah, if you're into that sort of thing. I swear, Veronica has an absolutely irrepressible soft spot for buff, driven corporate types. Get this: her favorite cheesy romantic comedies—of all time—are *The Secret of My Success* and *Working Girl.* Need I say more?

She's already scoped out a victim. She is the only person I know who actually has success with the we-saw-each-other from-across-the-crowded-room routine. The girl's got skills.

Veronica whispers, "I'm going to just—"

"Oh, I know where you're going," I interrupt.

She gives me a smile and a suggestively raised eyebrow. Then says, "Try the back patio."

I steel myself for the coming bumps and bruises and plow through the many gray-wool–covered obstacles.

I find the entrance to the back patio. The patio is wider than I'd imagined—classier too. There's a lot of restored brick and a fairly convincing copy of an Italian fresco. And real plants, actually alive.

Audrey spots me immediately. She waves wildly and rushes me at the door.

"I'm so glad you're here! Where's Veronica?"

"She's landed herself a Suit already," I say under the crush of her hug.

"That was fast." She finally lets me go. "Well, come on over. I want you to meet everybody."

She leads me to a pack of a dozen or so mostly young, mostly hip people chatting animatedly with one another. The men have their ties loosened, jackets off. The women are all as polished as they are fashionable. They smile. I smile. And I instantly feel out of my league.

Audrey turns to me conspiratorially. "See that guy over there? The one with the Heineken?"

"How could I not? He's gorgeous!" He's as metrosexual as they come, with the cocky swagger of a Mark Wahlberg and the chiseled profile of a Jude Law.

"Oooh! I'm glad you think so too. I really want you to meet him. I think you two would be so cute together."

"Audrey, I don't think—"

"Don't think. Just talk to him. He's funny and smart—"

"And a total Suit. Maybe you should introduce him to Veronica."

"Are you kidding? She'd eat him alive. He's perfect for *you.*"

"Come on." She grabs my arm and drags me into the crowd.

I plant myself at Audrey's side as she begins the introductions.

Introductions like this, especially in New York City, are not actually the casual first meetings they pretend to be. They are little interviews, auditions. Everyone in this town is looking for love, looking for a better job, or looking for any opportunity to talk about themselves with impunity. Needless to say, I do not fall into that final category.

"Ryan," Audrey says brightly, "I'd like you to meet John Dexter. He's a junior VP at Fletcher and Roth. He's the sole reason we got that new multimillion-dollar jeans account."

John gives a classic shake of the head in mock denial. This is obviously not the first time that particular compliment has been thrown his way.

I give the required response: an interested "Aaah!" and a perfunctory head nod.

Audrey turns to him. "John, this is my best friend, Ryan. She's . . ." Audrey's voice trails off. She tries desperately to think of something interesting to say about me. Her face begins to flush. I watch the pink rise from her neck to her cheeks and way up into her hairline. "She's, uh . . . in . . ."

I feel *myself* coloring, half for Audrey and half for my own growing mortification. "Data entry," I say finally.

John either senses the awkwardness of the moment or has already determined I am not worthy enough to be love-match material, because he says a quick "Nice to meet you, Ryan" and jets off to the bar, leaving behind him only the faint aroma of Cuban cigars and Dolce & Gabbana Pour Homme.

Audrey whispers to me, her face the color of an overripe tomato, "Oh, God. I am so sorry. I don't know what happened there. I am so, so sorry." She slaps her hand to her forehead, punishing herself. She pulls the hand away, aims for another blow.

I quickly stop her in midmotion. "Audrey! It's okay. Okay? Don't worry about it, it's fine." Yep. I'm fine. Nothing more, nothing less. Just . . . fine. "This is your night," I add. "Let's have a good time."

Audrey still doesn't look convinced.

"Look, he wasn't right for me anyway. I think he was wearing man jewelry under that shirt."

Audrey puts her hand on my shoulder consolingly. "Let's try this again." She takes my arm in hers and guides me to a cluster of three women, all in their midthirties, and all having that I've-been-in-this-city-forever-and-totally-have-it-by-the-tail look—fresh manicures, razor-sharp haircuts, and comfortably elegant attire with just a splash of Hermès thrown in for good measure.

Audrey runs through their names and credentials, all of which are stunning, none of which stick with me. She says, "This is my best friend, Ryan." She smiles a wide, loving Audrey smile and says, "Ryan is in computers!"

The three women let out a round of convivial "Oh"s and "How interesting"s. I play my part and smile as though they'd got it right—that my life is interesting. Audrey's infinitely pleased with this result.

One of the women, with her Hermès scarf tied loosely around her croc Kelly bag, says, "Are you in software development? Telecom . . . ?"

Audrey's face falls.

Yeah, can't really escape it. I respond, "Data entry, actually."

"She's brilliant at it," Audrey says, trying her best to be a good, supportive friend. A lot of polite nodding ensues. Unfortunately, being brilliant at data entry is like being the best shit shoveler at the shit-shoveling factory—when all is said and done, it's still just crap.

The tallest of the three ladies pipes up, "So, then, you're . . . an actress? Artist? Musician?"

I dust off my standard witty response to this sort of inquiry about my job. "I moonlight in freelance world domination plots, sold via eBay."

One of them cracks a sort of half-smile; another peers at me quizzically.

"No," I clarify, trying to curb my desire to crawl into a tiny crack in the brick paving beneath my feet. "No, I'm . . . just in data entry." Before I can take another breath, I feel a great thump in my stomach, as though I'd swallowed something heavy and sharp.

"Oh," the Kelly bag owner says. "That's . . . nice."

Well, no, actually it's not. It's awful, and suddenly makes me feel terribly small and insignificant—and, to top it all off, I'm really beginning to feel sick to my stomach.

I turn to Audrey. "I'm going to run and get myself a drink." I glance at the trio of lady execs. "Good to meet you," I say, grimacing at a new wave of queasiness.

Maybe I'm hungry or dehydrated or something.

I wade again through the throng of Suits and manage to squeeze my way through to the bar, all the while holding my stomach and trying to remember everything I ate today. Is it botulism? The dreaded salmonella? E. coli? I can't remember if I had chicken or beef for lunch—or if I had lunch at all.

I sidle into a tiny open spot at the bar near two loud and gregarious Wall Street guys. Barely out of the frat-boy stage of life, they laugh heartily at each other, the volume of their rowdy rhetoric somehow amplifying my general sense of illness. Every cry of "*What* did that asshole say?" and "I can't *fucking* believe it!" hits my head like a hammer.

I attack a nearby basket of complimentary snack mix with such voracity, the bartender looks at me askance.

"Can I help you?" he asks.

"Ginger ale," I say, slapping a five dollar bill on the bar with the hand that isn't full of stale pretzels.

"We don't—"

"Fizzy water," I say, a hail of crumbs spraying from my mouth. I swallow hard. "Anything with bubbles and no booze."

The bartender quickly fills a highball glass with tonic water and drops it in front of me. I sip slowly through the straw and try to breath deeply and regain composure.

I sip and walk, trying to make it back to the patio.

As I noisily drain the last drops of water from my glass, another massive wave of nausea grips me—every part of me—my knees feel spongy, my arms heavy. I steady myself by leaning against the grimy pine-clad wall.

What is happening to me?

Thank God, a restroom. Hanging a left, I head for it with as much speed as my wobbly legs will allow.

I lock myself in the grungy room and quickly start the tap, then splash a little cold water on my face.

Why is this happening?

Was it those insipid women from Audrey's office? Could their condescending tone be viral?

So what if I work in data entry? Big deal. I won't forever.

Will I?

So what if I don't know what I'm doing or where my life is going? What business is it of theirs, anyway?

Whatever. Who cares what they think? It's what I think of myself that matters, right? And I think I'm fine. I'm *just* fine. . . . So my life isn't perfect. So what?

I dab a wad of paper towels to my face and stare into the mirror.

"What is wrong with you?" I whisper.

Oh, great. Now I'm talking to myself—aloud.

I force myself to stand up straight, concentrate on inhaling and exhaling calmly.

After several minutes, my legs begin to firm up and my head to clear. My stomach is still unsteady, but the nausea is subsiding. I think.

I take my time getting back to the patio and arrive just as John Dexter is beginning a speech in Audrey's honor. Luckily, there's a nice little nook in the shadows for me to sit in—with a potted plant nearby, just in case the nausea turns productive.

"Well," John begins, "as you all know, we're here to celebrate the promotion of Audrey Coulson to assistant account executive." The Fletcher and Roth crew erupts in dignified applause. Audrey smiles and swats her hand at their ovation.

John continues, "Audrey, your dedication to the team through three very challenging launches has not gone unnoticed. You are calm in a crisis, levelheaded even when things are down to the wire, and never fail to make us laugh when we need it. To be perfectly frank, I don't know what we did before you joined the team."

"You made *me* miserable, that's what!" says a woman's voice.

John leads them in laughter.

He raises his glass to Audrey, who is glowing with pride. "Congratulations, Audrey, on a job well done and a well-deserved promotion!"

They clink their glasses and drink to Audrey's success, and I am suddenly seized by something raw and powerful welling up from deep inside me. The nausea returns in force. My limbs are again seized by a great weight; my head is throbbing.

The joy on Audrey's face: her cheeks are flushed with it, her head is held high, and her expression is proud and satisfied. It's pride in something she's earned, a goal accomplished, progress.

I have never felt that way. Ever.

She knew what she wanted and she got it. Every day she makes great strides . . . getting closer to what she wants. . . .

My heart pounds furiously. My hands begin to shake as a prickling sensation travels rapidly up and down my limbs. The walls feel like they're closing in. I feel trapped.

Sitting here motionless suddenly seems utterly unreasonable.

All this time I have been standing still. For *years* I have been standing still! I need to move. Now.

I step out onto the streets of Manhattan and force myself to put one foot in front of the other.

CHAPTER Twelve

One summer, when I was about ten, my parents brought me here to New York on vacation. My mother told me that if I ever got separated from them, if I ever got lost, the best thing to do was stay in one place until someone found me. "It's a big city," she said, "but one of us will find you if you're standing still."

That's what I've been doing for the last four years. I've been lost and waiting. Too scared to take a chance on finding my own way, and—hoping against hope that I wouldn't have to—I let my life sink into stagnation.

It's like I've been standing on a street corner, waiting for someone to say, "Hey! You there, Ryan Hadley! I've been looking for you. A life of love and achievement is right this way. Just go straight through chaos and confusion. (Don't worry, it'll pass more quickly than you think.) When you get to opportunity, hang a right. With a little hard work, you'll get to happiness and success in no time." I might as well have been waiting for freaking Godot.

The street lamps are dropping great pools of light on the dark and deserted streets of lower Manhattan. Without the dense thicket of investment bankers to impede me, I've just been walking. I don't know how long I've been at it. My feet hurt and my mouth is dry, but I can't stop. I think the movement is the only thing keeping me from collapsing in a heap and curling into the fetal position. I can actually *feel* the apathy and listlessness of my life rippling through me, making my hands shake and my skin hot to the touch.

How could I have been so stupid? Why did it take me so long to figure this out? It seems that everyone in this city—except me, of course—has a future all mapped out, their routes to success paved with little victories already won. They see what they want waiting for them at the end of that route and they aim for it. I, meanwhile, can't even find the starting point. And you know why? I have always played it safe, always taken the path of least resistance—the easy way—avoiding anything that scares me. I have never aimed at the things I want, because that would mean taking a risk. It would also require having a clear vision of what it is I actually desire.

I explain every little thing, try and understand it. A thousand and one opinions, a thousand and one theories to quantify and arrange my sad existence. I analyze the consequences of every action and then withdraw from anything that has the least probability of failure. Instead of saying "Fuck it" and taking a chance that I might get somewhere new and exciting, I stand still while the things I want for myself hover around me like steam from a subway grate, unable to make themselves solid. God, I'm an ass.

When I said those horrible things to Charlie—when I made him go to L.A. without me—I was just scared of taking a chance. Part of it was just textbook self-esteem nonsense, yes, but that was just a symptom of the illness. The deeper issue was something more chronic. He knew just where he was going; he had some innate sense of direction that I could not fathom. I thought that if I followed him, he would go his way—knowing, as he did, exactly how to get there—and I, having absolutely no sense of my own direction, would only fall behind and get stuck, scared and alone, in unfamiliar territory.

Ultimately, though, what good did it do me not to go with him? Here I am, four years later, four thousand miles away, and I'm still fucking lost. I've been repeating the same stupid mistakes over and over again.

And these last few days I thought I was jealous of Audrey and Veronica, but it's not jealousy I've been feeling. It's anger—at myself. That bubbling, boiling feeling is some sick subconscious recognition of my own complacency, my willingness to let life pass me by. Only now, when I see myself laboring away at a dead-end job while Will becomes a rock star, Audrey an advertising whiz, and Veronica a Wall Street wunderkind, do I finally get it. As I see them reaping rewards from the risks they've taken and moving toward the things they want out of life, it's finally clear how slowly I'm moving—so slowly, you'd need a time-lapse camera to record it.

Lost, standing still, and waiting. Something's got to give. Like now. I have to figure out what I want and get it.

I force my feet to plant themselves in the pavement and catch my breath.

Oh, shit. Where the hell am I?

I am in the middle of nowhere. I am surrounded by massive buildings, great piles of stone and metal reaching well beyond the tiny patch of black sky directly overhead. The streets are eerily vacant, not a single car or noisy city bus.

Where the hell is Broadway? Wasn't I just on Broadway?

I have no idea where I am.

I am actually, physically lost.

Right. Relax. Okay, I am somewhere in the Financial District. I stare down the deserted street left, then right. I recognize nothing. This is not surprising, since until now I have spent a total of twenty minutes in the Financial District. I stare at the nearest cross-street, hoping something about either Beaver Street or Broad Street will jog my memory.

Nope. Nothing.

Suddenly, I catch a brief glimpse of a cab slowing down at the corner and just passing out of view. I take my shoes off and, in defiance of all my better judgment, run barefoot as fast as I can in the direction of that cab.

I take a deep breath and sink into the backseat of the cab as it careens through the streets of Manhattan.

It occurs to me now that sometimes the big things in life happen quietly. All this time I was waiting for a crash, a big *something* to hit me and change the course of my life. But life-changing moments aren't all smashing into icebergs and getting mowed down by buses. Sometimes it's as simple as opening your eyes.

In midtown, the cab lurches and takes off up Third Avenue. I enjoy the feeling of motion, even with the constant bump and pitch of the uneven pavement beneath the car. Gazing past the front seat and the meter clicking away its dollar amounts, I look through the windshield and take in the vastness and the beauty of the city up ahead. There has to be something for me out there in that boundless assemblage of stone and brick and glittering brilliance. Doesn't there? Maybe one of the lights I'm seeing has its source at the bedside of a boy I'm destined to marry. Maybe this very cab has gone to and from the business I'll someday run. Maybe tonight I can finally put my life in motion.

I race up the stairs to my apartment, nearly tripping on my swollen feet and ending my life before it's even begun.

I need a plan. A real plan. Goals to aim for and meet. I need to risk it all, dive in with both feet, do something I want to do. No, do *everything* I want to do. I need to accomplish things, make something of myself.

I blast into my apartment and grab the nearest pencil and paper.

This is it—a list. Everything I want. My future on loose-leaf paper.

The future of Ryan Lorraine Hadley (in no particular order):

1. Get a fabulous job.
2. Live in the perfect New York apartment.
3. Get out of debt.

4. Boyfriend: find one.
5. Learn to ride a horse.
6. Sing on Broadway.
7. Floss daily.
8. Have hair done by famous hairstylist.
9. Learn to play a musical instrument.
10. Learn cake decorating.
11. Have a song written about me.
12. Get in shape!
13. Learn to throw pots.
14. Learn what *throwing pots* means.
15. Acquire poise and grace.
16. Kiss a movie star.
17. Own a piece of furniture I do not have to assemble myself.
18. Paint something—a portrait or still life.
19. Learn how to paint.
20. Grow herbs in the kitchen, and use them in meals.
21. Make enough money to hire a maid.
22. Learn how to walk properly in high heels.
23. Quit smoking.
24. Become a ballerina.
25. Have high tea at The Plaza.
26. Read books, become "literary."
27. Learn to speak a foreign language.
28. Get treatment at Red Door Salon.
29. Read *The New York Times* every day.
30. Do something really great for Audrey and Veronica.
31. Spend time in London or Paris.

32. Own real diamond studs; buy them myself.
33. Have a kid or two.
34. Get married (maybe not in that order).
35. Own a country house.
36. Volunteer with a charity.
37. Meet someone at the top of the Empire State Building.
38. See every piece of art at The Met.
39. Own a couture gown.
40. Become the queen of a small island nation.
41. Write my memoirs.
42. Have picture taken by Annie Leibovitz.
43. Become well versed in international issues.
44. See more Broadway shows, not just musicals.
45. Stop watching Lifetime Original Movies.
46. Take ballroom-dancing classes.
47. Live till I'm ninety in a state of utterly delicious bliss with numbers 1, 2, 33, 34, 39, and assortment of acquired skills and experiences.

Well, it's a start.

CHAPTER Thirteen

I am a new woman. I am a woman with a plan. I enter the gray-tinged cube farm and, unlike most mornings in the past, a listless mental fog doesn't take hold the moment I step into the office. I am encased in a cocoon of pleasantness. Beautiful.

"Good morning, Betsy!" I say in a singsongy way as I pass by her desk. I will spread my cheer impartially and . . .

"Did you hear?" she says excitedly.

"Hear what, Betsy?" I ask with a grin.

"Will Monroe. You two are friends, aren't you? Well, then, you must have heard! He's leaving"—her eyes widen to saucer size; she lowers her voice to a whisper—"to become a rock star."

The cube farm is all aflutter with the news of Will's success. No less than five people, including The Dirk himself, have come over to Will's cube to fawn and carry on about it. This is the first truly fun day of work I have ever had.

I know on some karmic level it's wrong of me, but every time someone passes by and asks "Isn't it great?" or "Can you believe it?" I daydream about what they'll say about me when, someday soon, I finally get out of here.

My favorites so far:

1. "Did you hear? Ryan Hadley is leaving. She got backing for her web design business."
2. "Hey, Ryan Hadley is out of here. She's invented a new email delivery system. Going to be rich beyond her wildest dreams, I tell you."
3. "I can't believe she did it! Ryan Hadley won the Powerball jackpot *and* got engaged to Orlando Bloom. In the same week!" (Work with me here.)

Will approaches, joyously waving a piece of paper at me. "This is it. The official letter of resignation."

I could grab it, cross out his name, and insert mine.

"Two weeks, then?" I ask.

"Are you kidding? Next week. It's not like I need The Dirk's recommendation. Knock wood."

He pounds twice on my imitation wood desktop.

"It's not going to be the same around here without you." I smile. "You do realize that I'm probably going to go loony."

He puts his hand on mine. "You'll get out of here too. Oh," he says with a wink, "I almost forgot. Ya'll are coming out with us tonight—all the groupies. Big celebration."

Could this day get any better? Wait. "Who's going to be there?"

"It's like I can read your mind. . . . Yes, Charlie will be there."

Uh, no. "Then I don't think so. I mean, I'd love to party with the band but . . . maybe some other time."

"Come on! We're going to some swank place on his expense account. Wouldn't a seventy-dollar lobster dinner make you feel better?"

Charlie on a plane back to la-la land would make me feel better. A seventy-dollar lobster dinner would just give me hives.

He continues, "I know you guys have history, but come on. Is it really serious enough to pass up free food?" Chalk one up for straight. Will adds, "Plus, Charlie explicitly instructed me to make you come."

"Yeah, right!" I say, rolling my eyes at him.

"I'm serious. He said, quote, 'Make sure Ryan and the girls are there. We'll make it a real party,' end quote."

Saying *quote/end quote*—chalk one up for gay.

Is that even possible? Will has never lied to me, ever. But Charlie wants *me* to be there?

"Come on," Will says, clutching his hands in prayer fashion. "We'll eat. We'll get trashed. We'll make complete asses of ourselves. It'll be like . . ."

"Every other time we go out with you guys?" I ask wryly.

"Exactly!" Will winks at me, makes smooching noises, then mouths the word *Please.*

"Uh . . . okay. I'll do it."

"You won't regret it," says Will, beaming. "Only one thing left to discuss . . ."

Who's the mind reader now? "We're brown-baggin' it today,

big guy." I pull an assortment of flattened sweets from my desk. "Ho Ho or Sno Ball?"

Maybe it's the warm spring air, but I get the sudden urge to bypass the crushing subway commute and opt to walk home instead. It's a pretty dangerous proposition, actually. Using this much energy at one time could send my body into some sort of exercise-induced shock. I have to take the chance; is it possible to lose ten pounds in twenty minutes?

I'm feeling kind of jittery; tiny waves of nervous energy tickle my stomach. Lately this feeling only strikes when I realize I've forgotten to pay a bill, or when I wake up late on Saturday morning and briefly think it's a weekday and that I'm late for work. I think tonight it must be Charlie.

Come to think of it, whenever I think of Charlie, my body responds with a semi-thrilling all-over pins-and-needles type feeling. He's the only ex-boyfriend of mine to produce that kind of lasting impression. The rare flash of recollection about other guys usually results in my getting a bit nauseated. Perhaps that's why, when things get rough, I seek solace in memories of Charlie. It's not something I do consciously, but occasionally, when the grind of the city gets too much and I'm alone and wishing I wasn't, my brain naturally clicks to him.

It starts with a smell—the smell of him. I don't mean cologne, soap, or shampoo. Not the scent of sweat or sex—I mean the essence of *him*. It's sweet, manly—indescribable really. When we were together, his smell would stay on my clothes, hang in the air when he left the room, and apparently sink into my brain when I wasn't looking.

It's got to be pheromones, like some primitive calling card or an ancient means of subliminally branding a mate. Either way, I have a sense memory so powerful that sometimes the recollection of it makes me literally ache for its return.

Yes, it's twisted, but I can't help it. And once I get to remembering his smell, a host of other things follow, tiny fragments of us: the sound of his button fly pop-pop-popping open, the little sigh he used to make when he hugged me after a long day, the feel of his hands in my hair, the taste of beer and cigarettes on his lips.

Everyone knows it's easier to digest things cut into small pieces. It's the same with memories: delving into whole events, whole days, can only lead to trouble, because for every good time, there is a bad. Like a string, I pull at the memories, one leading to the next. Unfortunately, with memories of Charlie, the string always ends outside the music building with that look on his face.

But maybe now all that can change. What if I rewrite the ending to this one? After all, he asked for me. He specifically wants me to be there tonight. Then again, he could just want to catch up. We didn't get to talk much at the show. (It's difficult to talk to someone properly when you can't look them in the eye.) Maybe it was just the shock of seeing me again that made him so hostile. I suppose he could also be planning to beat me senseless with one of those little lobster cracking hammers.

What if he wants me back? No, that's ridiculous.

But . . . let's just say, hypothetically speaking, of course, that Charlie did want to get back together. It would be a romantic story, wouldn't it? We are star-crossed lovers compelled to rekindle our previously unlucky union after years of separation and hapless, hopeless attempts at love with other people. I could have one of those sappy stories to tell people at parties. I could be one of the chosen few with a relationship worthy of envy and admiration. Not to mention, I'd have Charlie.

Why shouldn't that happen? Why shouldn't he want me back? It's been so long, maybe he really does want to forgive and forget. Who am I to stand in his way?

What if tonight I could scratch number 4 off the plan? Talk about starting this thing off with a bang. Charlie, my boyfriend again. I like the sound of that.

CHAPTER Fourteen

I am plucked, primped, rubbed, scrubbed, and scented. I've managed to conceal all that needs to be concealed, and truss up all that needs to be revealed. I am wearing my cutest black dress—the only dress I own that doesn't make me look like a stuffed sausage. All in all, I think I've done my best to fake alluring and utterly irresistible. But, since I'm not very well acquainted with this look, I should probably do a quick male-opinion poll.

I drop in on Brock at the bodega for smokes and a reaction.

Brock sees me, puts down his copy of *Entrepreneur,* and whistles. "Hot mama."

"Thank you. Thank you," I say, doing a little turn and bow. So far, so good.

"Where are you going? Hot date?"

"Sort of."

"He will be much pleased, I assure you."

"I hope so."

Brock pulls down two packs of smokes for me and rings them up. "I think you don't need matches. You are on fire already."

I'll take that as a compliment.

I walk the ten blocks to the restaurant and receive for my effort:

3 lewd remarks

2 head turns

1 proposal of marriage (Unfortunately, it was from a woman with two teeth and one shoe.)

All told, not a bad start to the evening.

Audrey and Veronica are waiting outside the restaurant for me. I attempt a casual saunter in their direction.

"Damn, heartbreaker!" cries Veronica.

"You think?"

Audrey inspects my outfit front and back. "I'd do you."

"Audrey!" Veronica and I say simultaneously.

Audrey bats her eyelashes and gives us an innocent "What?"

"Do you think Charlie would?" I say, raising an eyebrow. Audrey and Veronica are a bit stunned. I continue, "I'm going to get him back."

"Do you mean get back at him? Or get back *with* him?" poses Veronica.

"With," I reply.

"I thought we hated him because he . . . uh . . . left you to go to L.A.," Audrey tries gently.

Oh, shit. There's that damn lie again to bite me in the ass.

Crap. What do I say to that? Audrey and Veronica stare at me, not-so-patiently waiting for my response. Uh . . .

I finally blab, "I decided to forgive him."

But the girls seem to be weighing this answer against the many moments of silence that preceded it.

Veronica cocks her head to the side and inhales like she's going to say something. Her mouth opens, but she can't get the words out, so instead she just exhales loudly.

"Okay!" says Audrey. "Excellent." She nudges Veronica.

Veronica interjects, "Well, that dress is an excellent first move."

Well done—dodged the bullet. "Thanks," I reply.

Audrey gives me an air kiss on the cheek for support before turning on her heel and sashaying through the nine-foot-tall glass entrance to Blanc. Veronica and I follow, Veronica still eyeing me suspiciously.

Man, this place is even swankier than I anticipated—it's minimalist swank. For some reason, in New York, the fewer decorations a place has, the more expensive the meal. This one has white linens on the tables (all having a higher thread count than my sheets), a swarm of waitpeople outfitted by Giorgio Armani, and warm lighting that could transform even the homeliest of frogs into a prince. This confirms one of my theories about the rich and the famous—they don't actually look any better than the rest of us, they just have better lighting.

We spot Delicate Blunder at a massive rectangular table with little white wooden boxes as chairs. They look so cute in their button-down shirts and sport coats, if not a little uncomfortable. Sammy even has his hair pulled back in a ponytail. But no Charlie yet. Just the guys and Molly. A lot of hugs and kisses are exchanged before we decide who's going to sit where.

I quickly count the available boxes. Two left after the girls and I get our places. I position myself across from both empty seats. Either way Charlie goes, I'll have him in my line of sight.

Veronica catches on to my seating arrangement scheme and whispers, "Are you sure about this?"

"Absolutely."

She looks at me doubtfully.

I confirm, "Trust me. I'm good."

She shrugs her shoulders and dives into the drinks menu.

Everyone else at the table follows suit. We take turns gasping over the twenty-dollar-and-up price tags.

Sammy blurts, "I hope Charlie shows up, man, or we're gonna have to get a loan to pay the tab."

"He'll be here," says Will. He gives me a wink—like I'm the reason Charlie's coming. My stomach does a flip.

"That guy is so cool," says Dane, turning to me, "I can't believe you guys went out."

"Uh, thanks," I retort.

"No. It's that I can't picture you two together. It's not like you shouldn't have or anything. You're so different and . . ." Molly kicks him in the shin.

She tries to cover. "I don't know what he's talking about. I can totally see it."

"Speak of the devil," says Will.

All eyes turn to the door, and in walks Charlie. Talk about

stomach flipping—I feel like I've spent the afternoon giving myself the Heimlich maneuver. He breezes past the model/hostess with a swish of the head and a flirty wink. *Cool* doesn't even scratch the surface with Charlie. The word *cool* isn't cool enough. He looks every bit the modern executive, laid-back yet professional. A lightweight gray sweater, which has got to be cashmere, grazes his body like it was knitted onto him by Karl Lagerfeld himself. Irre-fucking-sistible.

He swaggers to the table and beams at us with that same radiant quality he had in college. I didn't notice it at O'Rourke's—must have been the shock.

"Hey, everyone. Good to see you." He glances at me. "There's someone I'd like you to meet."

He puts his arm behind his back and when he pulls it around front there's a woman at his side. How the hell did he do that? Who is small enough to hide behind . . . Wait a second, a woman?

"This is my fiancée, Marisa."

Audrey and Veronica gasp—audibly.

Holy shit. Oh, no. Oh, no!

Marisa, edgy and cool, wearing a thousand-dollar designer dress, smiles brightly and waves at us.

Audrey, Veronica, Molly, and I are stuck for a moment. The three of them glance briefly at me, then back to Marisa.

A deep pink color begins to spread across Audrey's face. Her eyes meet mine and she silently conveys her concern. As if on command, *my* face goes all warm and tingly.

Try and act cool, Ryan. Remain calm. Do not shout. No rat noises.

Charlie runs through everyone at the table, pointing and introducing us.

Finally, "And this is Ryan Hadley."

"Oh, Ryan. I've heard so much about you," Marisa says sweetly. She and Charlie share a look that can only mean one thing—she knows everything. She knows that I'm a horrible, mean person.

They take their seats. Brilliant plan, Ryan. Now I have them *both* in my line of sight.

And *boom*, there it is—the ice, the rock, the bling. It's got to be three carats, unquestionably a Tiffany's Lucida cut in platinum setting. A five-digit investment in Charlie's future without me. She places her manicured hand on the table, and I expect to hear a thud from the weight of it. That is a ring of class, of potential, of fancy dinners and Grammy awards.

Charlie catches me gazing at the ring. He looks me straight in the eye and smirks. It is a diabolical smile, the kind Lex Luthor gives Superman while doling out the kryptonite—retaliation made real, spite given over like a gift. Yeah, not seeing reconciliation in the cards tonight.

"Why don't we get this party started," declares Charlie.

I stare down at the menu and its many dishes with the words *Price Upon Request* where a dollar amount should be. Now that I think about it, lobster might not be such a bad idea. Maybe instead of hives, my throat will close up and I'll have a legitimate excuse to get out of here. Bonus: someone will call my ride for me—an FDNY paramedic unit.

Alas, I chicken out when the actress/waitress/waif comes to take our orders. I pick something I can't pronounce.

When the waitress leaves, an uncomfortable silence grips the table. This is the part where we're all supposed to chatter, engage in meaningless small talk. We're supposed to get to know Marisa the great. Marisa the flawless. Marisa the fiancée.

Unfortunately for me, and my now teeny tiny little ego, she is amazing. She's just like the mythical L.A. women I dreaded, only worse—not a whiff of silicone. She has unbelievably long legs and the kind of bone structure usually reserved for Greco-Roman statuary. Marisa's most striking feature, though, has to be her "rich-girl skin."

The condition commonly known as rich-girl skin occurs when, at the first sign of puberty, the wealthy female child is whisked directly to the dermatologist and put on a strict prophylactic Accutane regimen. The result is an adult who has never, in her entire life, had a blemish of any kind. The only way the average woman can mimic the appearance of rich-girl skin is to rub one hundred pounds of crushed pearls all over her body. Sadly, the effect of *this* treatment is only temporary—and incredibly messy. Veronica has rich-girl skin, but we forgive her. On Marisa, it is possibly the most annoying thing ever.

"Ryan," Marisa says, "you have such an interesting name. I have to tell you, when Charlie first told me about you, I thought for a minute he was trying to tell me he was gay."

Everyone laughs—except me, naturally.

"Yeah, I get that a lot," and I don't just mean gay ex-boyfriends.

Charlie throws me that Lex Luthor grin. "What was it you always used to say?" he asks. "It's the name of a cross-dressing junior high gym teacher. He's Ryan by day—"

"Lorraine by night," I finish. "You remember that?"

His tone sobers. "I remember plenty."

Now, that's going to leave a mark.

Veronica sees my face fall. I know because the familiar crinkle appears over her nose. She shoots out the viper look and goes on the offensive. "Marisa, did I hear you say that you work with Charlie?"

"Yes."

"So you're his secretary, then?"

Marisa chuckles. "Sometimes it feels that way." She beams at him. He smiles back at her and then eyes me like *Aren't we just the cutest couple ever?*

Veronica tries again, "You file, answer phones . . . that kind of thing?"

"No, not really," says Marisa, not catching on to Veronica's smear campaign. "Technically, my title is vice president of A and R, but A and R has gotten this bad reputation with up-and-coming artists. So I call myself director of new talent development."

"Oh" is all Veronica can marshal in response.

Nice try, though, Veronica. I do appreciate the effort.

"What is it *you* do, Ryan?" asks Marisa.

I try to speak, but Veronica gets there first. "Ryan is a genius with computers."

"Wow," responds Marisa. "I can barely turn mine on without having a little panic attack."

"You work with Will?" asks Charlie.

I nod.

Charlie's mouth opens. Here it comes. . . . "So it's really what? Data entry?"

And the hits just keep on coming.

"Yep," I say, in what approximates a cheery tone.

Charlie leans back in his seat, proud of his work. Marisa covers a rapidly developing grin with her napkin, but her smug satisfaction at my humiliation is communicated just as clearly by her eyes.

Somebody should hide Veronica's steak knife before she goes postal.

The rest of the evening goes about the same. Charlie ever so effortlessly jabs at my pride, Veronica attempts to jab back on my behalf, everyone at the table (but Audrey and Veronica of course) falls head over heels for Marisa. I mostly try and ignore it all, and concentrate instead on a stimulating discussion with Molly about the importance of art in early elementary education.

I must say, I don't hate Marisa. As a matter of fact, if I weren't so terrified by the film *Single White Female,* I might just want to be her.

Marisa is not just beautiful but possesses a veritable treasure trove of enviable qualities, which she divulges in the following choice sound bites:

Worldly: "When I was hiking through Nepal . . ."

Well Connected: "So I said to Ozzy . . ."

Edgy: "Dream duo? Joey Ramone and Joan Jett . . ."

Educated: "Fifth-century hieroglyphics tell us . . ."

Financially Independent: "My portfolio is . . ."

On my best day—like tonight, for instance—Marisa outshines me by a factor so large, it can only be written exponentially—say, ten to the hundredth power.

Dessert is served and my enthusiasm for this night of "celebration" is well past the waning stage. I'm afraid we're deep into get-me-the-hell-out-of-here territory now.

I've got to know: "When will you guys be heading back to L.A.?" I ask Marisa.

"Maybe never."

"That's great!" cheers Will.

Nightmare. Nightmare.

Trying not to sound in any way panicked or psycho, "Really? Indefinitely?"

"Yeah, corporate wanted a fresh, new, rock-oriented label out of New York. So Charlie formed Cranky Tank. Barring any unforeseen horrors, we'll be here for a very long time."

A horror is all they need, eh? Well, maybe it'll be *Single White Female* after all. If I recall, there was something to do with a stiletto. . . .

Charlie joins in, "I have very specific ideas about how a label should be run. My focus is commitment, hands-on. I want to grow binding relationships with artists." His eyes dart to me with a knifelike glare.

He takes a short breath and continues, "Too many labels these days profess loyalty and honesty but, when push comes to shove, end up really being heartless"—totally talking to me now—"cruel"—holy shit—"and indifferent. I want to be around when they need us, and not *abandon* them when things get rough."

The word *abandon* echoes through the cavernous restaurant, hovers over our table. The force of it rings in my ears and momentarily shields me from the horrible realization that everyone around me has gone silent. A great shadowy tension grips the table. I can feel their eyes on me, wondering, questioning, as all the little molecules between Charlie and I tumble about frenzied and unrestrained.

Will stares at Charlie and then back at me as my hands ever so slightly begin to shake. He looks like he's about to pounce on Charlie, lay into him. I shake my head at Will from side to side and mouth the word *No*. I am not going to let him jeopardize his relationship with Charlie in some pointless act of gallantry, especially when I don't deserve it.

Now I know why they say *cut down to size.* I feel like I've been sliced open. I have to get out of here before my guts spill out all over the white tablecloth. I can't afford to replace it.

"Wow," I say, standing up, "I just remembered that I have to get up early tomorrow. Lots of . . . data. I should get going."

I quickly gather my things.

"Congratulations, you guys. I'm so happy for you. Thanks for having me."

Don't run, Ryan. Hold it together, don't give him the satisfaction of seeing you break.

How could I have been so unbelievably stupid? Get him back? Ha! What a complete and utter idiot I am! I just want to go home. I want to curl up in the fetal position and die. Then I'm going to eat an entire Sara Lee cheesecake, wallow in my misery, and watch something uplifting—like *Schindler's List.*

First step: cab. Crying on the subway can illicit all sorts of unwanted advances. I am in no mood to be comforted by someone who has a collection of cans or speaks to himself in the third person.

I frantically wave my arm out in the street.

Come on! One lousy cab!

Shit. It's got to be the torrent of tears falling down my face. The basket case—not good cab-snagging technique.

I hear an earsplitting, two-fingered cab-hailing whistle behind me—Veronica. Audrey races out behind her.

A cab screeches to a halt in front of us. Audrey grabs me in a hug as Veronica opens the door to the cab and ushers us in.

"That guy is the biggest asshole I have ever come in contact with—and I work on Wall Street, for fuck's sake."

"Total jerk!" says Audrey.

"I have never had such an intense desire to scratch someone's eyes out," Veronica growls. "Him and his stupid Miss Perfect fiancée."

"Could she *be* more annoying?" Audrey mocks Marisa's voice, "'When I worked for Radio Free Xanadu . . .' or whatever the freakin' country. I say Radio Free this, bitch." She flips up both middle fingers.

Veronica chimes in, "What the hell was his problem? Is he off his medication or something? It's like he came with a mission. Showing up late, showing her off. It was sick and—"

"Stop!" I shout. "Just stop. It's not his fault. I deserved it, okay? I deserve it!"

CHAPTER Fifteen

By the time we get back to my apartment, I've gone through the salient details—doubt, stupidity, agony. The girls let me get into my pajamas and wash the city off my face. As I dry the cool water from my cheeks, my rigid muscles let loose and it hits me—relief.

I hadn't noticed the little cloud hovering over me all this time, but I guess it was there. A cloud of unpleasant memories all knotted up and tangled, lying in wait. I couldn't bring myself to admit to Veronica and Audrey that I got scared. Who am I kidding, I couldn't even admit it to myself. But that's all it was, wasn't it? Fear. Stupid, irrational, completely overwhelming fear. God, that's what my whole life has been about up till now.

The one thing I wasn't afraid of was Charlie not moving on. I was sure that he was better off without me. I was certain that our relationship would be only a tiny footnote in his life, an inconsequential dalliance in an otherwise spectacular existence. Silly, uncool Ryan. Ordinary, plain Ryan. How could he possibly care? How could all the distractions of the grown-up's circus that is L.A. not make up for the rejection of one ex-girlfriend? But it didn't. My God, he even has a beautiful, amazing fiancée and still he harbors this antipathy. He remembers absolutely everything and he hates me for it. Somewhere out there, on this very island, is a man who literally despises me.

I stare in the mirror at my freckles, my stringy hair, my stupid mouth that said all those stupid things all those years ago. I have to take my time. I know the girls are chomping at the bit out there—they're preparing for the grilling.

Grilling is why keeping things from your girlfriends is such a dangerous proposition. Once it all comes out, they're still not convinced you've told all. Any point of question or misunderstanding must be thoroughly reviewed, checked, and rechecked. We're women—it's all about the details.

"You were at the music building?"

"Yes."

"Outside?"

"Yes."

"And you didn't tell him why?"

"Not the real reason, no."

"And then you just let him go?" asks Audrey.

I nod.

"And you were okay with that?" asks Veronica. "You cried a lot after graduation."

"I was barely twenty-one. I didn't know which end was up. I

know it was possibly the stupidest thing I've ever done. Well, I know it now. At the time I . . ."

Audrey puts her hand on my shoulder. "We're not judging you, Ryan."

"I know. It's just . . . I feel like such an asshole for thinking I could get him back."

"You're not an asshole," says Audrey.

"Do you still want to? I mean, get him back?" questions Veronica.

"I don't know. No. I guess not. It doesn't really matter now, does it? Given the intensity and persistence of his little exhibition-o-hatred tonight, I'd say the question of what *I* want is moot. Wouldn't you?"

"Well, you broke his heart."

"Audrey!" yells Veronica.

"No, she's right. I did." I pour myself a glass of wine. "I was awful." I take a deep breath and sigh. "Whatever. It's done." No more looking to the past. No more pining over Charlie. No more little clouds hanging over my head. I have a new life ahead of me, a plan for my future. I'll let this Charlie-hating-me thing roll off my back. No big deal.

Oh, who am I kidding?

I ask Veronica to pass me my purse. I pull out my list, and add:

48. Apologize to Charlie.

"What's that?" asks Audrey.

"My life." That is, "I hope."

• • •

"I don't think I understand," says Veronica, inspecting the transcript of my life goals that I neatly typed up this afternoon when I should have been inputting data. "You're doing these things in the hopes of finding yourself?"

"No. I already found myself. Unfortunately, what I found is crap. What I need is radical change." I take a swig of wine. "Rapid execution of extreme measures."

"Whoa." She places her hand on mine. "This is a pretty long list. You know, it's going to take some time."

"I figure I can pull most of them off in a couple of months." Veronica looks at me cross-eyed. I add, "Most of them. Obviously, I'm not going to go out and get knocked up first thing." Though I did briefly entertain the idea of becoming a mail-order bride. Alas, the thriving bride trade in America seems to be largely import, rather than export.

"I think they're great," says Audrey. "And totally doable too."

Thank you, Audrey. I blow her a kiss.

"Sure they are," says Veronica sardonically. "Being named the queen of a small island nation should be a piece of cake."

"Absolutely," I play along. "At first I was thinking Jamaica. But then it dawned on me . . . *Iceland* is a relatively small island."

Veronica reluctantly gives me the smile I wanted. "Good thinking. I'll see what I can do."

"I'm not going crazy, okay? I just can't stand still anymore."

Audrey nods her head in agreement; Veronica remains skeptical.

"Plus, a lot of these things can be combined." I prop the list of goals on the wine bottle and use my cigarette as a pointer. "Get in shape, acquire grace and poise, and the ballerina thing can all be counted as one. I will become well versed on international issues by reading *The New York Times* every day. And since my first attempt at number four didn't go quite as well as I'd hoped . . ."

I feel a stroke of genius coming on. . . .

"Ha!" Got it. "We will combine reading more books with getting a boyfriend."

"You plan on cruising libraries? Barnes & Noble?" Veronica asks wryly. Then adds, "Wait a second. *We*?"

"Us. You, me, and Audrey. We research!" I'm on a roll now. "We figure out how the women in the books do it—you know, like Bridget—and then we steal their methods."

"Self-help?" questions Audrey.

"Uh, no," I reply.

Technically speaking, self-help books *are* an option, but I read *The Rules*—a gift from my aunt Rita—and felt horribly depressed for days. I kept thinking, *No wonder I can't keep a boyfriend! I tell them things about myself on the first date,* and *Woe is me, it's Friday. Even if a guy called and asked me out, I couldn't go because I wouldn't be hard enough to get.* Eventually, I got over it. That is, after I'd retired *The Rules* to a fiery grave.

I suppose we could go the more esoteric route: you know, Jung or Sartre, maybe Jong or Sontag. But, um, no. I got enough of that crap from the Birkenstock set at college. Also, Veronica might stop shaving her armpits and start talking incessantly about nothingness or vaginas. (She goes whole hog into anything that will make her seem like more of a hard-ass.)

Besides, what is it we're all really looking for? The ideal we pine for? Darcy, right? I mean, what the modern American girl really hungers for is that perfectly imperfect man who inspires that mysterious, mind-boggling, head-over-heels feeling. We want a guy who, like Darcy, is flawed enough to be interesting, yet handsome and noble enough to be irresistible. So, if Darcy is truly the ideal, why not figure out how to land *him*?

Veronica looks at me, concerned. "You get that Bridget Jones—and all the other women in those books—are fictional, right?"

"Yes. But, I think that there are tips to be had in those stories. Many tips."

"I think it sounds like fun." Thank you, Audrey.

"It will be fun. *And* educational," I implore Veronica.

"Oh, good," she responds. "The double whammy of false hope. Hey, this wouldn't have anything to do with the little Charlie reconciliation hiccup, would it?"

"Charlie who?" I bite back. "Haven't we established that he is one hundred percent totally over with and not worth the time anyway?" In other words, he is engaged and hates me.

"Ryan, I love you. But sometimes you can be so . . ." I glare at her and she stops midsentence and sweetens her tone of voice. ". . . um, rational."

"Come on, what's the harm in trying? So far, we've failed miserably on our own." I point out my dirty window. "There are roughly two and a half million straight men in this city and we can't find three?"

"My feeling is, guys are a *want*, not a *need*. They're pleasant enough when you've got one, but I don't feel incomplete just because I'm not dating someone," Veronica says emphatically.

Is she kidding me, or herself?

I try to think of something *rational* to say. I look to Audrey for some support, but she just stares at us like someone watching her parents argue about who took out the garbage last—perfectly, maddeningly neutral.

I wish I could give Veronica a list of all the concrete and perfectly plausible reasons I need a guy—the right guy. I want to tell her that I feel like I'm missing something and that something looks exactly like Mark Darcy. I want to tell her that I have a big gaping hole in my life that only he can fill. But I know I shouldn't. Self-actualized city women who read *Cosmo* aren't supposed to think like that. We're supposed to be so completely satisfied with ourselves that a man is nothing more than a pleasant distraction from our workaday lives. We're supposed to think of them as a fabulous accessory. We're supposed to be . . . Veronica.

I fail to form any valid verbal response, thus I choose the only alternative at my disposal: I pout.

Audrey hates pouting. "Ryan, I'm in. I'll do it." Well done, me.

"That's the spirit!"

Audrey and I stare at Veronica. She lights a cigarette, trying to mask the smell of defeat wafting in her direction. Change in tactics.

"I'll spot you three rounds at The Gaf," I say.

Veronica mulls this over. She dramatically flicks an ash into the ashtray, like Bette Davis. "All right. I'll do it. But don't expect me to participate in any harebrained schemes. I will not be your Ethel Mertz."

I give her a big kiss on the cheek.

• • •

Veronica Wheatley, Audrey Coulson, and Ryan Hadley—founding members of the BCSR, Book Club for the Socially Retarded. (The name was found at the bottom of the second bottle of wine.)

Despite its rocky beginning, I believe this will be a pivotal, vital part of my new life plan. If I can manage even a smidgen of Bridget's remarkable success, I'll be one hundred times better off than I am now. She goes from loser guy to winner, crap job to fab job, and so effortlessly. Surely, I can get a little bit of that?

At the conclusion of our "modern city girl" research Audrey, Veronica, and I will find ourselves transformed into veritable goddesses of city living. We will learn from the mistakes of our fictional sisters and become confident and dynamic women of the world. We'll take their tips, pointers, and methods and score great guys. Better yet, men from all walks of life will be transfixed by our feminine wiles and throw themselves at *us,* begging for just a taste of our mystery and allure. Lovely.

Veronica unbuttons her pants and leans back against my couch. "You know, we've really got plenty of time for all that boyfriend crap." She lights a cigarette and hands it to me. "I think you sometimes put too much emphasis on being attached to someone. It is perfectly normal and perfectly fine not to be in a couple."

Oh, we're back to this again. "Intellectually, yes, I know that. But really, Veronica, don't you sometimes feel just hopelessly lonely? And crazy? And like you're missing something?"

"No. I have you guys."

I try again, "No. Stuff that we can't . . . fix. You know, the stuff that only a guy can."

"You mean sex," Veronica quips.

"No, not sex. I mean, that's part of it, sure. But it's more like magic in a way. I don't know, you can't really put it into words."

Audrey chimes in, "I know that feeling, Ryan. But honestly, when you finally find the guy who gives you love and support with no strings, it won't be because you bewitched him or something. He'll be a friend, a close friend, like the three of us—only with some sex thrown in. You're still going to feel crazy sometimes. He can't *fix* you."

"Yeah, he won't *make* you better, just support you when you're feeling crazy or overwhelmed. Am I right?" Veronica prods Audrey.

Audrey nods approvingly.

"How do you two suddenly know so much?" I ask.

"I've been TiVo-ing *Oprah,*" Veronica replies flatly.

But Audrey is blushing!

I tap Veronica on the shoulder, point at Audrey.

Veronica and I lean in and stare at her. "Is there something you'd like to tell us?"

Audrey looks away and shakes her head no, but her smile suggests otherwise. She is quite possibly the worst liar in the Western World.

Veronica's eyes widen. "You're seeing someone! You sly, sneaky . . ."

I slap her playfully on the shoulder. "Why didn't you tell us?"

"Who is he?"

"When did you meet him?"

Audrey shakes her head no. "Now is not the time."

"Oh, please!" I say.

She lets out a little sigh. "I just didn't want anyone to get their hopes up. I didn't want to get *my* hopes up. I wanted to wait until I was sure it wouldn't turn into an awkward situation. . . ."

"Who is he?" I ask again.

Audrey takes a deep breath and places her hands neatly on her lap, considers it.

Veronica, impatience personified, demands, "If you don't tell us, I swear—"

"Will," chirps Audrey. "It's Will."

Say what? "You mean . . . you don't mean *our* Will?"

With an enormous cat-who-ate-the-canary grin, Audrey nods yes—while Veronica and I try to scrape our chins off the floor.

Um, I guess chalk one up for straight.

CHAPTER Sixteen

Audrey would give no further explanation on "Audrey & Will: The Relationship." No amount of pleading, begging, or guilt trips would get her to talk. And, given my own *huge*—and rather more prolonged—cover-up operation, I couldn't press her too terribly hard. But, come on. I mean, who are they, Chris and Gwyneth?

Monday, I breeze into the cube farm ready for espionage. I have to find out. I need to know. How could two of my very best friends get together without me knowing? Not to be childish, but Will was *my* friend first and he doesn't really ever see Audrey or Veronica without me. At least, that's what I *thought.*

I spot Will and walk over. Game on.

"How was the rest of your weekend, Will?" I ask innocently.

"Good," he replies.

"Oh," I say, and sit down at my computer. Come on, Ryan,

put on the pressure. Make him confess. "Uh . . ." Yeah, brilliant.

"Ryan, do you want to go out for a smoke?" Oh, Audrey must have told him that she blabbed.

"Um, Will, I don't smoke during the workday," I try. Very suddenly, I do not want to know the details of this situation. It's too . . . weird.

"*Um*, Ryan, yes you do." Damn! He's right.

"All right, let's go." Will is looking at me like I need a shock treatment, which I probably do.

On the way down, I resign myself to be very adult and mature about this whole thing. It is the most natural thing in the world—two great people getting together. Why should this particular union give me such anxiety?

Halfway to the lobby and it hits me. It feels too close. It doesn't feel like it usually does when Audrey or Will dates someone. Their relationship with each other has this annoying air of change about it—change for the dynamics of the whole group.

I light a cigarette and Will lights a cigarette, and then we stand there . . . in silence . . . watching cabs ride by.

Will starts suddenly, "I'm sorry about what happened at dinner with Charlie. I didn't know . . . I was ready to hit him."

"I know, I noticed. But listen, what happened with Charlie was . . . unavoidable." I lock eyes with Will. "I don't ever want you to risk your relationship with Charlie because of something he says or does to *me*, okay? Chivalry is dead. I'm killing it."

Will considers this; catching on that my tone is serious and I won't accept any answer but his agreement, he says, "Okay."

"Promise?" I ask.

He makes a little *X* motion over his heart. "Promise."

We both turn our attention back to the traffic. I want to know about Audrey, but how to bring it up . . . ?

Will says, "I'm packing up all my stuff today. Charlie is putting us on the fast track, I guess. They want an album out by Christmas."

Despite my mind being completely engaged in other areas, I can't stop the wave of excitement that washes over me. Something about dreams coming true—infectious joy. "Will, that's great! I am so proud of you. But so soon? Are you guys ready? Are you recording in New York or—"

"And I kissed Audrey," Will nervously blurts out, "and I'm pretty sure I really like her." That stopped the excitement wave.

"Oh." Silence . . . Mmm . . . What to say . . . ? "When did this start?" There's something!

A goofy smile perks at the corners of his mouth. "A while ago, I guess. Remember that show at The Mercury? Before all this stuff with Cranky Tank started up?" That was weeks and weeks ago! He continues, "It was cold out that night, you know? And I gave her my leather jacket for the ride home. So then I went the next day to get it back. . . . I just went to pick it up and . . ."

"And . . . ?" I prompt.

"It felt weird because I've never been around her without you there. But then we were talking, and she's really funny, you know? And then I just kissed her."

I stay quiet, hoping the silence will prompt him to elaborate so I don't have to poke him with a stick. But, alas, he's just staring at me. *He's* waiting for a reaction. A bright blue feather falls between us onto the sidewalk. I try to focus on that, give Will a chance to gather his thoughts.

Okay, Will. Continue. Any day now . . .

Can't wait. "Well, how did she react?"

"She said, 'That was nice.'" He stares at the feather.

"And?"

"So I kissed her again."

"Okay, Will. We're really going to have to speed this up or we're going to be on the world's longest smoke break."

"Then I asked her if maybe she'd like to go out sometime, just her and me. She said yes. And we did. A couple of times. Maybe more than a couple."

"Why didn't you tell me? I mean, I know why Audrey didn't, because, well, she's a great big poophead." And obviously suffering some form of mental illness, not to mention having way more self-control than I ever knew she had. "But you?"

He laughs. "I'm sorry. We're both sorry." He finally looks up from the sidewalk. "I was just . . . I was really nervous at first. I was nervous about going out with her. Not because of you or anything like that, just nervous. And I never get nervous with women!"

It's true, he doesn't. He has a way with women. Actually, women tend to throw themselves at him. So, technically speaking, he's mastered the art of taking a tackle.

Will's MO: he meets a girl and she is the smartest, funniest, most beautiful girl he's ever met. He "falls in love" with her the next day. He woos her for a week, flowers, dinner, the whole bit. She falls under his spell and turns to Will-lovin' jelly; they "date" for one more sublimely happy week. He will then, without fail, find something wrong with her. This "something" requires the "relationship" to be severed, and the girl to seek a Zoloft prescription. There is then a period of three days where Will moans that he'll never love again. On the fourth day, he begins the process anew with another woman.

We always thought this serial dating pattern was some form of overcompensation, you know, because deep down he was gay. The way men with small penises buy Hummers—the car, I mean the car.

So forgive me if I'm a little wary of Will's affection for Audrey. I know, this is where I'm supposed to be the supportive friend. I want to be, but it scares me. I hate to sound selfish, but I say, "I hate to sound selfish, but if this doesn't work out and you dump my sweet Audrey in two weeks, it'll mess everything up. I won't be able to hang out with both of you together. I'll have to decide who to invite to happy hour and who to *leave out*. Everything will be ruined." I sound so petty and mean. I'm disgusted with myself.

"Wow," he says with an uneasy chuckle, "no pressure or anything." He looks at me like I'm supposed to laugh now, let him off the hook. When my smile fails to appear, he goes on, "Ry, I don't know why, but this feels different. I can't say for sure what will happen, but I can say that I definitely want to find out where this is going. I really like her. Really."

Will's seriousness surprises me. Maybe this is the real thing. It's bizarre, but maybe they'll create beautiful, perfectly groomed little rock-and-roll babies that wear sweater sets with leather pants. Who knows about these things? Not me—as the Charlie debacle so artfully demonstrates.

Besides, I love them.

I look at his face, so sincere and hopeful. "Okay," I say, finally. "Sorry for being such an ass."

Will takes my hand and kisses it, then smiles his irresistible, lovable, bad boy smile.

I smile back. "All right, listen up. Her favorite flower is the gardenia. She loves Italian food. She has an unusual affinity for hairbrushes—owns literally hundreds. Don't touch them. She hates westerns . . ."

CHAPTER Seventeen

My first day of work without Will, and a pile of data junk has made it to the desk before me. Odd no one ever seems to actually deliver it. It's like the stuff hides out till the office is empty and then curls up in my in-box to die. Go ahead and lie there, you lifeless, useless data. I will not be tricked into burying you in your little electronic tombs. Nothing can thwart me today. I am better than you. I deserve a day to make progress on my plan and daydream of the future me—the fabulous, well-rounded, non–data-entering me to come.

Looks like getting out of debt is going to have to be my last priority. *The New York Times* is a little pricier than I'd expected. Even with new subscriber incentives, it works out to about four hundred and forty bucks a year. Not exactly economical, but not horrible, either. That's, what, roughly eight fifty a week? I'll just reduce my weekly smokes by, say, a pack and a quarter. I wanted to cut down anyway. Sadly, I think that might be the easy one. . . .

"Fifty-five dollars? For *one* half hour?" I say into the phone, trying my best not to sound poor.

"That's right," responds the sugary voice on the other end. "It's a first-class stable, Miss Hadley. The only one of its kind in Manhattan." Yeah, yeah. I know what the rent's like on Central Park West. It's just so hard to justify paying a hundred and ten bucks an hour for riding *anything*—except maybe Colin Farrell. Something tells me he's not available.

No stopping now, Ryan. Can't let a little thing like poverty stand in the way of your dreams. I inhale deeply and force out "Okay, I'll take it."

"Excellent decision, Miss Hadley. We'll see you next week."

"Thank you"—for robbing me blind.

I am going to learn to ride a horse! I can just see myself now, dashing through the Lake District on a white steed. A wisp of dust trailing behind me as I race my dashing man to our little cottage—or, should I say, the seventeen-room mansion we lovingly refer to as our cottage. Or maybe galloping bareback through the tumbleweed on my West Texas ranch. I'll be tan and tough-talkin', yet somehow soft and sexy. All the ranch hands will yearn for me. . . .

My phone rings.

I answer, "Ryan Hadley, Mistress of Circle F Ranch."

"What the hell are you talking about?" asks Veronica.

"Just signed up for horseback riding lessons."

"Oh. Hey, listen. My mom says wonderful, great, she'd love to do it, she's so excited."

"Fantastic!" I reply a little too loudly, and get a couple of odd looks from the nameless faces. "Thank you so much, Veronica!"

"No, thank *you!*"

I asked Veronica to do me a favor and put out some feelers to her mother about helping me get a new job. I know no better headhunter. Come to think of it, I know no *other* headhunter. Veronica's exact response to my request was "Thank you, God. Please, please make yourself her new project." I do what I can for my friends.

I am so kicking ass on this plan. Only a matter of weeks before I'm well on my way to greatness.

I've been to the Wheatley home many times. Audrey and I spend holidays with Veronica and her family when we're too poor to fly out and visit our own. But even after a dozen or more visits, there's still a bit of a thrill factor.

You know that real estate motto, "Location, location, location"? Well, in New York City a prime Park Avenue address is like the holy grail of locations. It means more than a nice apartment with two-thousand-plus square feet and convenient commute to Museum Mile. It means that you have arrived. You've become part of an elite class of homeowners with discriminating taste—and disposable income equal to that of a third world country. The address is more than a place; it's a lifestyle, one that is recognized the world over. Take my mom, for example. Her knowledge of New York City is limited to national monuments; in other words, she knows that the Empire State Building and Rockefeller Center are within the city limits. But when I told her that Veronica's parents lived on Park Avenue, her response was "Oh, my! Ritzy!" Of course, her next statement was "Just like on *Diff'rent Strokes*!" Anyway, she was impressed. It's really hard not to be. Especially when you're here in person.

Walking up Park Avenue, past the many grand old apartment buildings with their wide awnings and dapper doormen, it's hard not to feel a bit swept away. This part of town is so pure and open in its grandeur, so comfortable with the decadence casually displayed in every element. From the stonework and gleaming brass fittings to the slender women walking dogs and running errands in cashmere and pearls, it's all so . . . sublime.

I feel shallow for loving it so much, but I'm not about to apologize. It is way too much fun having a man in white gloves greet you by name and tip his hat as he opens the door for you. I just say "Thank you" and make my way to the elevator—with the grin that ate Manhattan.

On the tenth floor, I ring the bell at the Wheatley home. Mrs. Wheatley promptly answers the door.

"Ryan! How good to see you! How have you been?" She smiles and locks onto me in a big fleshy mom-squeeze, the billowing sleeves of her purple and green caftan enveloping me like a blanket. "We sure have missed you!"

"I've missed you too."

"Oh, sweetheart"—she takes my hand and leads me into the apartment—"Veronica told me you've been having a rough time of it lately. We'll just see what I can do to help, all right?"

We pass through the marble-laced foyer and through the gigantic formal living room. Actually, despite the sofa, chairs, and other common markers, it's not a living room at all. These walls were meant for the display of priceless works. Bright splashes of color pop off the neutral background like fireworks—Schnabel, Johns, Haring, Rothko. There's a de Kooning hanging over the fireplace, for God's sake. (A fireplace they never light, of course—because there's a de Kooning hanging over it.)

Mrs. Wheatley stops at the den and points in the general direction of the big-screen TV. "Jonah is thinking of going to graduate school in the fall. We're very excited," she says. "Jonah! Ryan's here."

I wave. He grunts and flicks his PlayStation 2 control pad at me in what I assume is a "Hello" gesture. Yep, I'm sure he's already applied to the distinguished Underwater Basket Weaving Program at Timbuktu State Online Graduate Academy.

We pass Veronica's childhood bedroom and I can't help but wonder: How did we ever become friends? She grew up in this palace, with maids, and private schools, and a trio of Milton Glaser sketches over her bed. It's a miracle she didn't turn out to be a complete snob. *I* most certainly would have.

Mrs. Wheatley and I finally arrive at her office, a room roughly the size of my entire apartment. She sits down in a comfy leather club chair and invites me to take a seat on the sofa.

"Take your shoes off. Relax." I gratefully comply and take a preparatory deep-cleansing breath. "Now," she begins, "what is your heart's desire?"

I'd love to propose moving in here and following in Jonah's carefree, slacker footsteps. Instead I say, "I really need a new job. No . . . actually, what I need is a career."

"You are in luck," she declares with a wink. "That happens to be my specialty. Did you bring your current résumé?"

I dig through my black tote and present her with the one sheet, of mostly white space, that outlines my dearth of talent and experience. She reads it carefully. This takes approximately 3.4 seconds.

"I find that a lot of people, especially in your age group, underestimate the value of early work experience in their post-college job search. Therefore, I'd like you to tell me about every job you have ever had. Leave nothing out. If you scooped poop for your neighbor's dog, I want to know about it. Got it?"

"Okay . . ." I say meekly, then quickly search the memory banks and dutifully run down everything I can think of. From babysitting my little sister to my current position as lead data-entry bitch, I give it all over. All the while hoping against hope that there's some little kernel of opportunity waiting to be explored.

"Let's go back a second to . . . Compu-Center, was it? What did you do there?"

"I turned on computers."

"I'm sorry?"

"When someone bought a new computer from the store, they would bring it to me and I would turn it on to make sure that it worked and that the software was properly installed."

"Oh," she says, tapping her finger on her jaw. "And what was it exactly that you studied in college? In layman's terms?"

"Web programming mostly, a lot of site-design work. Flash and stuff like that. I did have some real programming, coding for software. All the languages I'm proficient in are listed there at the top."

She studies my résumé again, tap-tap-tapping on her jaw. Occasionally saying "Hmmm" or "Ahhh." I don't know exactly what that means, but I get the sense things aren't as bad as I thought. "Ryan, if you were to pick your ideal job in this field, what would it be?"

I ponder it a moment, gaze languidly out the window. "Web design," I say finally. "I think web design. Nothing too complicated or intense. I'm a bit out of practice. But maybe a place where I'd get to do some things on my own every once in a while, new challenges every day. Something to look forward to and challenge me." Saying it out loud sends a wave of glee coursing through my body. What if I could do *that*?

"Well, I think you're more than qualified. You may need to brush up on some of the new technology, but otherwise I believe you are a perfect candidate for a position like that."

Hallelujah!

"Thank you so much, Mrs. Wheatley!"

She pats me on the knee. "Don't thank me till you're hired, sweetheart." She organizes her notes, putting my résumé on top. "Would you mind if I gave this a quick polish?"

"Absolutely not."

"I'll just punch it up and then get it out to the people who need to see it. Sound good?"

"Better than good! Great! Amazing!"

I slip my shoes on and stand. Mrs. Wheatley follows suit. She puts her arm around my shoulders and looks at me with a goofy, unmistakably maternal smirk. "Now, how about some milk and cookies?"

CHAPTER Eighteen

I've been reading the books of the BCSR, i.e., books in the vein of, or outright stealing from *Bridget*. You know how they go: girl meets boy, girls falls for boy, boy turns out to be a complete asshole, havoc ensues, etc. So far, the tips are few and far between. (I did learn a nice eyelash-curling trick.) But I have faith; the cumulative effect alone should cull some results. Don't you think? Unfortunately, in the meantime, they're only stirring up thoughts of Charlie. So many ex-boyfriends in these things! I compare the heroine's horror stories to my own, and inevitably contemplate the specifics of number 48 on my life plan.

I know the longer I put it off, the worse it will be. I'll get myself all twisted up in knots about it, and blabber and blubber about it with the girls till I'm blue in the face. Then, some random night, I'll run into him at a bar and spill my guts in an unintelligible drunken rant. Not a pleasant thought. I guess I'm going to have to bite the bullet and get it over with.

I've been trying to get ahold of Will for the last three hours. No answer at home, on his cell, or at Dane's house. He's not responding to email or IM. It's like he's vanished. Convenient timing, as I need Charlie's phone number. If I weren't at work and desperately wanting to postpone the whole Charlie apology thing, this would be supremely annoying. As it is, his being unreachable is just a happy accident. This is what I like to call *nibbling* the bullet. The old hey-it's-not-my-fault rationalization. Sadly, this really only works when you've exhausted every possibility, and there's one thing I haven't tried.

I dial the numbers and cross my fingers that Will has suddenly gone on vacation to an island resort with no phones or computers.

"Audrey Coulson."

"Hey, Audrey. I can't seem to get ahold of Will. You wouldn't happen to know where he is or what—"

"He's at my place," she says sweetly. Damn.

"Oh."

"Yeah, he needed some alone time to work on some lyrics. Go ahead and call him there."

"Thanks," I say, defeated.

Nibbling over.

My heart is thumping like a bass drum. I slap my hand to my chest to keep it from popping out and onto my desk.

One ring.

Maybe he won't be there. It's 12:30; he's probably at lunch. Please, please let him be at lunch.

Two rings.

He's definitely not there. Everyone answers by the second ring, right? Unless he's really far away from the phone.

Three rings.

Hallelujah. I'll get an answering machine and the ball will be in his court. If he never calls me back, it's not my fault.

Four rings.

Where's the damn answering machine—?

"Cranky Tank Records. How may I help you?" says a cheery voice in a British accent.

"May I please speak to Charlie Cavanaugh?"

"Who may I say is calling?"

"Ryan Hadley."

"Hold, please."

I could hang up now. I could hang up and when I get up the nerve some other time I could say my phone went dead. I was on my cell and lost the signal. I could . . .

"Yeah. What do you want?" he snaps. God, I hate that tone in his voice. It's the aural equivalent of a slap in the face. And man, does it sting.

"Charlie, I was wondering if we might get together. Talk a little bit."

"Why?" he snarls. *Smack.*

"I have some things I'd like to say."

"What makes you think I want to hear it?" *Smack.*

"Maybe you won't care, maybe it won't matter. But there are some things I'd like to explain."

"What *I* would like is to put all this behind me." Isn't this where the ref hands out a warning of some kind?

"Charlie, please? Ten minutes, give me ten minutes. If you don't care about what I have to say or can't stand the sight of me, you can walk away and I'll never bother you again. I promise."

Silence weighs down the phone cord as though an elephant were using it as a tightrope.

He huffs, "Fine. Ten minutes. Meet me at my office at six."

Oh, no. I've seen this episode of *Law & Order*. The ex-girlfriend gets stabbed twelve times and buried under the floorboards. "I was thinking neutral territory. Coffee? Drinks?"

He spits out another perturbed sigh. "Where, then, Ryan?"

"Where's your office?"

"Midtown."

Think, Ryan. Think. Someplace with a minimum of sharp objects. "There's a place called The Bakery. Seventh Avenue between Fifty-first and Fifty-second." They use only plastic cutlery.

"Fine. At six?"

"Great. Thank—" Click. And he's gone.

Oh, yeah, this is going to be just great. Brilliant idea, Ryan. Brilliant fucking idea.

I have combed my hair, reapplied waterproof mascara, and run through countless scenarios in my head. I'm thoroughly prepared for a guilt trip, a screaming match, and a full-out frontal assault.

I even stopped by Barnes & Noble and consulted a thesaurus.

Words I'm considering:

1. Repentant.
2. Remorseful.
3. Chastened.
4. Deplorable.
5. Formerly-lousy-chicken-shit-loser.

I cautiously enter The Bakery, scan the room like a CIA agent would in a silly B movie—with an unimpressive stone-faced imitation of nonchalance.

Thank God, he's not here yet. I order my Earl Grey and consider the seating possibilities. Let's see . . . a booth would provide distance, but then there's the looking-him-in-the-eye business. Sitting at the counter would be eye-contact prohibitive but would mean possibly rubbing elbows. Booth.

I sit, arrange my bags and myself, and wait. Five fifty-five P.M., zero minus five minutes and counting. God, this place smells good. They're baking apple pies or strudel or something. Bonus: I read somewhere that men find the smell of cinnamon soothing. Or was it the smell of Cinnabon?

Six-oh-two P.M. He used to be very prompt. But he's just getting out of work. Okay. It's okay. Wish I could smoke a cigarette in here. Damn smoke-free city!

Six-eleven P.M. Does the fifteen-minute rule apply in this situation? Should I just leave? No, he'd show up like two seconds later, curse me forever, and I'd never get the chance to come clean and apologize. . . .

The little string of bells over the door jingles, and there he is. He surveys the room and spots me. I smile as wide a smile as I can muster.

Obstinate reticence—it's pouring out of him. Everything about his body language conveys irritation and resentment.

Lock and load, sister. Just put on a happy face. . . .

"Hi," I say a little more cheerily than is called for.

"Hi." He sits down across from me, doesn't take off his jacket.

"Do you want something? Tea? Coffee, maybe?"

"No."

"I thought for a minute you weren't going to show," I confess.

"New city."

"Oh. That would be the Transportation Phase. It'll pass."

"The what?"

Commence with ice breaking. "I've got this theory about the phases people go through when they move to New York. The first phase is Transportation. Your life revolves around whether or not you know how to get from one place to another. A lot of time spent staring blankly at Transit Authority maps." He isn't screaming or hitting me, so I'll just go with it. "The second is the Huddled-Masses Phase, getting used to so many people in such a small area. Also known as the I-waited-in-line-for-an-hour-to-get-a-bagel lesson. Third is the Wow-They-Have-That Phase. This is when you're pretty confident about getting around and become enthralled with trying all the new things New York has to offer. Hungarian food, nudist performance art, porn on cable access." One half of his mouth is turning up. Was that a twitch or a smile? I choose . . . smile. "Finally, you get to the Comfort Phase; when everything settles down, and you live your life as normal." I smile at him and take a sip of my tea. Waiting for him to say something, a comment . . . anything.

He looks at his watch, holds it up for me to see. He's got a digital stopwatch function clicking down the seconds. "You have seven minutes and thirty-two seconds." Well, fuck you very much.

"Do you think we could, maybe, tone down the open hostility just a notch?"

"Why did you bring me here?"

Why *did* I? Could it be that I'm a masochist and didn't know it? I take a deep breath. "I wanted to tell you the truth . . . about why I didn't go to L.A."

"The truth?"

"That day, at the Mozart statue, when you asked me why . . . I mean, I said 'I can't' and then you asked 'can't or won't?' and then I said 'I—'"

"I remember," he interrupts.

"Well, when I said 'I won't,' I didn't mean that."

"What?" he asks quietly.

I continue: "I was afraid. Of L.A. and the women, and not being cool enough to be your girlfriend. I didn't feel smart enough, or beautiful enough, or *anything* enough, to compete with L.A. and you. I had no career plans, no idea what I was doing with my life. And you were so incredibly sure of yourself. I tried to talk to you about it, but—"

"When? When did you try and talk to me about it?"

"Tons of times, Charlie. I told you that I sometimes felt uncomfortable around your Juilliard friends, and that practically every straight girl on campus wanted you. You were the center of this perfect Charlie universe, with all that charm and magnetism shooting out all over the place indiscriminately. I was lost in it, felt inferior to it. I don't know . . . it's hard to explain, it was so stupid and irrational. . . ."

He runs his hand through his hair, then stares down at the table and begins tearing tiny little pieces off a napkin. "You should have told me . . . been more specific . . . I didn't understand."

"It doesn't matter anymore. It's all said and done. I just wanted you to know that I didn't . . . I didn't not love you. And I wanted to tell you that I'm sorry. I'm sorry that I hurt you. I don't . . . I couldn't stand the thought of you being out there still hating me . . . not knowing the truth."

He nods, but not to me. His mind is off somewhere else. He stares at the napkin, continues picking. Am I getting through or making it worse?

I add, "Feel free to continue hating me, though. I'd hate me, too, if I were you." I twist my head, look at the seconds clicking down on his watch. I gather my things and stand. He won't look up. "In case, you know, you decide to put out a restraining order on me or something . . . have a great life, Charlie." God, I've wanted to say that for so long, wished a million times that I could have before we separated. I feel the tears welling up in my eyes. "Marisa is really great. I hope you'll both be very happy."

And I make my grand exit.

Splurging on a cab. I get out my Life Plan and, with a big red marker, cross out number 48.

Well, I've apologized to Charlie. One down, forty-seven to go.

CHAPTER Nineteen

Getting together with the girls is getting harder and harder. Not for me, mind you, for them. Deal making with Iceland and assistant account exec–dom are keeping Veronica and Audrey late at work almost every night. I wanted to meet up for happy hour, but apparently women with careers are expected to work *all* hours—even those with half-price drinks. Therefore, it is now nine-thirty and, though I enjoy Bill the Bartender's company, I'm beginning to feel a little like a pathetic extra in *Barfly*.

Veronica blasts through the door. I tap on my watch. "Weren't we meeting at nine?"

"I know, honey," she says. "I'm sorry. I left as soon as I could."

"I accept. How was your day?"

"Icelandic."

"Cool," I reply with my driest, pun-filled wit.

"You know, that joke just doesn't get funny."

"Yeah."

"I'm telling you, Ryan, that damn five-hour time difference is going to kill me. We're on conference calls from eight A.M. to lunchtime, and then we spend the rest of the afternoon, and *evening*, trying to get all the work done."

"Have a Harp and relax."

"Thanks."

Through the window we see Audrey and Will crossing the street—holding hands.

"That is so freaky," Veronica whispers.

"Bizarre."

The happy couple struts into the bar, not parting their hands until Will helps Audrey take her jacket off.

"Sorry we're late," says Audrey, the word 'we're' dripping off her tongue like molasses.

"Apologize to Ryan. I just got here myself," says Veronica as she slides in next to me—so the lovebirds can snuggle.

The thought of Will and Audrey together wasn't as hard to swallow as the reality of it. They're so damn cute. Painfully, nauseatingly adorable. I can't help but stare at them, sucked into their cute little world by morbid curiosity.

Veronica breaks my ogling. "So, Will. How's the rock-star business?"

"Way more hard work than I thought. I figured getting the record deal was gonna be the really hard part. But Marisa's working us to the bone."

"Really?" I ask, very near to calm and collected.

"I basically had to sneak out. When she's not around, which is not all that much, she calls to check up on us."

"Why?" groans Veronica.

Audrey raises an eyebrow. "To make sure they're not getting into trouble."

"You're kidding!" I gasp.

"No," says Will, casually draping his arm over Audrey's shoulder. "She's like the warden or something. I don't know if it's on purpose or what, but she and Charlie are like good cop/bad cop."

Audrey does a little jump in her seat. "That reminds me, Ryan. Did you?"

"I did."

"And?" pushes Veronica.

"I'm pretty sure he'll never speak to me again," I announce.

"Whatever," says Veronica. "He's an asshole anyway."

"I second that emotion," Audrey says, raising her glass.

"I have no earthly idea what ya'll are talking about." (Will, being a boy, was not privy to the pre-Charlie apology dish.) "But I agree completely," he adds, clinking his glass with hers.

Audrey turns to Will. "That's so sweet of you."

"I *am* sweet, aren't I?" replies Will.

"You are," says Audrey, and kisses him on the cheek.

So weird. So, so weird.

Will suddenly pops up and bounds to the jukebox.

Audrey looks at Veronica and me with stars in her eyes. "I am falling so hard, you guys."

"We can tell," quips Veronica.

"Ha. Ha," deadpans Audrey.

"It's great," I say with a smile.

"We're really happy for you," agrees Veronica.

As Will heads back to the table, the first notes of Mary J. Blige's "Sweet Thing" float out of the jukebox.

He offers Audrey his hand and says, "May I have this dance?"

Veronica and I stifle giggles as Audrey accepts.

I have never seen Audrey so happy—or Will either for that matter. They are so utterly smitten, besotted by one another. They have this old-fashioned love thing going on. I mean, sometimes you'll see couples being all lovey-dovey and too cute for their own good and you can sense that it's an act, a sort of play they like to perform. I don't get that from Will and Audrey at all. They are gentle yet shamelessly passionate about one another. They touch with real affection. And it isn't that gross-out, please-just-get-a-room PDA, either. What they have is the tender minutiae.

See, for the modern American female, romance isn't something you can buy in a store. It isn't roses (highly overrated and terribly cliché). It isn't chocolate (fattening and with 74 percent chance of getting the fruit-nutty center), or balloons (please). It isn't even candles and wine. You know what it is? It's a man holding the door open for you. It's having him offer you his arm while walking down the street.

Don't get me wrong, I'm not saying that women want to be protected or coddled, or treated like fragile porcelain dolls. Well, come to think of it, Audrey might. But me? All I really want is passion displayed in a manner that doesn't involve grunting. For me, romance is the kind of simple affection the girls in the movies always get. The kind they show in close-up, or slow motion. First, second, even third dates with regular guys never seem to offer the tender minutiae—the enchanting precursor to the real life swept-off-your-feet, powerless-to-control-it, how-awesome-is-this-person sensation. I think that may be why so many women strive for long-term relationships. True, simple tenderness often comes only with time. Then again, judging by Audrey and Will, it may come only from a really special once-in-a-lifetime kind of connection.

Will tucks Audrey's hair behind her ear, softly sings the words to her in his seductive Louisiana drawl. He places his hand firmly on the small of her back. *That* is the tender minutiae.

Veronica leans over. "I think I'm gonna get going."

"Really?" I pout.

"I'm tired. And I think I'm becoming lactose intolerant." She points to Audrey and Will.

"Too cheesy for you?"

"Velveeta," says Veronica with a smile.

One beer and two songs later . . .

I get up to say my good-byes to the lovebirds. I bob and sway with the music, fluttering around them like a bee poised to sting. If I could just catch their attention for a second . . .

Oblivious.

I lean over the bar, "Hey, Bill. If they ever, you know . . . stop, tell them I went home, okay?"

He shakes his head in agreement.

I take one last look at the happy couple as I make my way out of The Gaf. If it were only that easy for everyone. If only more men considered dancing to a scratchy jukebox in a musty dive bar romantic and not just corny . . .

Thud.

I slam chest-first into something solid. A guttural "Oof" erupts from my lungs as the wind is knocked out of me. Ouch.

It's not the door, not a wall . . .

Two strong hands grip my shoulders, struggle to keep me upright. "Charlie?" I croak.

"Are you okay?" He actually seems concerned, hasn't let go of my shoulders, even though I'm clearly standing on my own steam.

"I was just leaving," I blurt while desperately trying to squeeze around him and out the door.

"Hold on. Wait right there. I was hoping you'd be here. Don't move, okay?" he says breathlessly.

I've never been very good at disobeying direct orders, especially when they come from devastatingly handsome men.

Charlie crosses the room to Will and Audrey.

Audrey roars, "Busted."

Will tries to play it off. "Charlie! What a surprise! What are you doin' in this part of town?"

"Marisa sent me out to find you. Dane thought you might be here."

"Shit. I'm sorry," grovels Will. "I just wanted some time to—"

Charlie stops him with a wave of the hand. "You're preaching to the choir, man. I'll tell her you, uh . . . went for an inspirational walk."

"That'll work?" asks Will.

"Yeah. If she asks, just give her some bullshit about the creative power of the skyline at night, or something like that."

"Okay," Will responds skeptically. "Thanks."

"Don't mention it," replies Charlie. "And I mean that." He whispers, but not low enough, "I wasn't here."

Charlie turns back to me. Behind him I see Audrey mouth the words *Are you okay?* All I can do is shrug my shoulders. I have no idea.

"Would you mind sitting with me for a minute?" he asks.

I know I should say "I'll give you ten," but instead I slide into the window booth.

Charlie orders two drafts from Bill. He watches me like a hawk. I guess he's making sure I don't bolt, which I'd like to. He impatiently drums his fingers on the bar, as if to accelerate Bill's pouring. Bill resents being hurried and hates tapping of any kind on his bar, which makes the pouring even slower.

Finally, Charlie carefully places a beer in front of me. He sits down. "You still like Guinness?"

I shrug while my head bobs in what approximates an up-and-down motion.

Charlie gazes out the window at the people meandering to and from other bars and restaurants, absentmindedly tracking their movements with his eyes. He inhales slowly, holds it in, releases it slowly. Some form of meditation? What are we doing here? He rubs his hands together, like someone trying to start a fire with two sticks. I don't know what that means. That is a totally new gesture, never seen it before.

He takes a nervous gulp of his beer—consuming roughly half of its contents—then gently places the glass back on the table. "I wanted to apologize . . . I've been really, fucking . . . cruel and unusual to you." He looks around, nervously runs his hand through his hair. "I was . . . I didn't . . . I'm not proud of how I've been acting to you." He takes another deep breath and goes completely silent. He rubs a finger down his glass, wiping away the bits of Guinness foam that have slipped down the side of the glass.

I've never seen him fidget like this; he was always so unflappable, so calm and collected. This behavior is kind of freaking me out. "Charlie?" I ask softly.

He looks up at me. "What you did—back then—it fucked me up . . ." Ouch. A hard knot forms in my throat; I take a sip of beer to try and clear it. He continues, "I felt things for you . . ." He stops himself and collects his thoughts. "I was really pissed at you, for a very long time. So, when I saw you again—"

"You don't have to explain. I understand. I know that you can't forgive me. I wasn't—I'm *not*—asking you to forgive me. I just—"

"Could you answer a few questions for me?"

Scary. Scary. "Sure," I say, in what approximates an easy tone.

"When we were together, did I *do* something? Something that made you feel bad?"

"No, never. You were . . . great, Charlie. Always."

"So, it was, what? Self-esteem or something?"

I take a deep breath and consider what to say. "That was part of it, yeah. But it was mostly that I didn't know what I wanted. I felt lost, and I thought I'd only get more lost if I followed you. But it wasn't *you.* It was my own . . . stupidity and shortsightedness."

"Huh," he says, going back to staring at his beer.

"For what it's worth, Charlie," I say bluntly, "it fucked me up pretty good too."

Charlie looks up and his eyes connect with mine. I feel like he's examining me, measuring and calculating something. I see—it's so insufferably clear—how hurt he still is. But I think—I hope—I also see the first signs that he's softening.

"Okay, I have an idea," he says suddenly.

"What's that?" I ask, matching his lighter tone.

He offers his hand for me to shake. "Charlie Cavanaugh. I think we went to college together."

I want to ask if this means he forgives me, but I know that would be greedy of me. Besides, I'm pretty sure the answer would be no. Even so, I can't stop a weak little smile from forming. "Ryan Hadley." I shake his hand. Oh my God, I remember that hand—soft, warm, capable. I jerk my hand away, play it off by grabbing my beer.

"Friends?" Charlie asks.

What does he mean by *friends*? He would be neither a "can-we-just-be-friends?" friend, or a "we're-better-off-as-friends" friend. Those I understand. Those are amicable and civilized arrangements that require only two things: one, avoidance of the "friend" at all costs; and, two, the odd awkward hello at parties. This thing with Charlie, though, could mean anything. Would he expect me to call him with random dinner invites like I do with Will and the girls? As his little introduction implies, does it mean that I'm just supposed to ignore all our history and pretend like we've just met? Or is this, perhaps, a simple I'm-ashamed-that-I-was-mean-to-you-so-I'll-call-you-a-friend-to-make-myself-feel-better kind of thing?

Any way you cut it, this has real disaster potential. But I can't really say no, can I? *Can* I? Oh, what the hell. "Friends."

CHAPTER Twenty

I've got to tell you, this Life Plan thing is the shit. Not only do I have something to look forward to every morning, but it now appears that I am hater-free—in the non–hip-hop sense, of course. Though I don't know what this new friendship with Charlie will entail, it seems an awful lot like a clean slate. Even if he hasn't completely forgiven me, at the very least, it feels like closure on the old unpleasant memories and an end to his all-out assault on my pride. I was really taking a pounding there for a while—not fun.

This, however, is fun. *The New York Times* arrived at my building sometime in the predawn hours. Thus, I am now enjoying my tea and Froot Loops with a healthy dose of in-depth world-class reportage. Very grown-up. Well, I do feel a bit like a little girl wearing her mother's slip and pretending to be grown up. But, close enough.

Important international issues I've become apprised of:

1. Julio Iglesias is considering a European tour.
2. A former soap opera star has been arrested in Amsterdam. (It begs the question *How does one get arrested in Amsterdam?* Isn't *everything* legal there?)
3. George Clooney is redecorating his house in Tuscany.

Now, I admit these matters are not, say, on the UN's current agenda. But I perused the world-news section and the print was so small and the pictures so gory—not at all conducive to Froot Loop consumption. Not to mention, you can't discount Julio Iglesias's influence in the Latino community. He's practically an ambassador to the world. Okay, yes, my mother happens to be a fan.

In any event, I can now finally be counted as one of those very New Yorky–seeming New Yorkers who carries the *Times* curled under their arm while getting on and off the subway. Actually reading it on the subway is another matter altogether, as my commute time usually doubles as naptime.

Stop the presses: Betsy has a new hairstyle. The jet-black (truthfully, almost blue) color of old is now a very flattering nutmeg brown with subtle auburn highlights. Soft layers lightly sweep her shoulders, and the skillful application of razor cutting frames her face beautifully. She looks at least ten years younger and ten pounds lighter.

Could she be taller? She seems taller. Then again, she's sitting down. New chair?

"Betsy, you look amazing!" I declare, entering the cube farm.

She looks over her nose demurely. "Thank you."

I pause in front of the desk, poised for the traditional effusive elaboration.

She looks at me, perplexed. "Is there something I can do for you, Miss Hadley?"

"Uh, no," I say briskly.

Who is this strange creature in Betsy's orthopedic shoes?

I squeeze into my cube and shove the *Times* into my big black tote. It would be silly to keep it under my arm all day, though I'm sure there are people who do. It is a very easy prop to master. The only drawback is the rather unsightly grayish smudge developing under my right pit.

On the data menu today: magazine subscription telemarketing returns. It appears that some people actually say yes to those teenagers who offer two-for-one subscriptions to *Field & Stream*. Amazingly enough, quite a few of these suckers are from New York City. I'm not aware of any major fields or streams in the triborough area, but there must be quite a few.

Seven hours and twenty three minutes left. . . .

I can literally feel the days getting longer. The sun seems to be hanging on, eking out every last drop of warmth before the night takes over and turns it all back to cool again. This is the perfect setting for horseback riding in the park. I can just see myself clip-clopping along the bridle paths through dappled light, gazing up at the spindly branches of trees doing their best to bloom. Peace and tranquillity amid the city's chaos, a short reprieve from my own mental rat race.

I arrive at the stables precisely on time, dressed for rough riding. Well, I'm wearing things I think it'll be easy to get the horse smell out of. Anyway, I'm ready for this important step in my plan. I will master horsemanship and be a woman of class and sophistication, a woman who is down-to-earth yet unmistakably refined.

I wonder if Marisa rides. She probably does. I bet she's from one of those families that invests in Thoroughbreds and makes yearly treks to the Kentucky Derby. She probably had one of those childhoods where the question "Daddy, can I have a pony?" was answered with the rapid acquisition of a pint-sized white stallion, complete with pretty pink ribbons in its perfect mane.

What the hell am I talking about? Who cares about Marisa? Focus on the task ahead, Ryan.

The receptionist looks up from her *Us Weekly* just long enough to see me approaching the desk. She says, "Ryan Hadley?"

"That's me," I reply.

She points over her shoulder. "Go through there and wait for your instructor."

I step tentatively through a set of double doors, into a wide cobblestone aisle. The heady cocktail of horses, hay, and leather fills my nostrils—sweet and raw. I suddenly feel out of place, like this may be a mistake. It's all so unfamiliar. Funny-looking tools, straps, and metal things hang from the walls. I think this is how one of the *Texas Chainsaw Massacre* movies began, a young woman alone in a room full of seemingly innocuous junk that turns out to be the stuff of torture.

Just as I'm about to bolt, a very chic and very tiny woman approaches me with a wide, generous smile.

"Welcome, Ryan. I'm Sherry," she says. "I'll be your instructor."

I was kind of hoping for a strapping young cowboy, but I guess she'll do. I introduce myself and shake her hand.

"Follow me," she says.

We head up a steep wooden ramp as Sherry begins a well-rehearsed speech on the history of the riding school. I try to listen, but then I hear horses. Horses on the second floor; I have never seen anything like this. We enter a wide central corridor that separates two rows of stalls. I peer in at one of the horses. Typical, it turns out there are *horses* in this city with more luxurious accommodations than mine. Sherry leads me up another ramp to yet another level. These horses have a triplex!

We get to the middle of the corridor and Sherry stops. She waves her arm over and around a stall door, presenting it like she's one of Barker's Beauties on *The Price Is Right.*

"This is Starlight; he'll be your horse!" she says in a tone appropriate for speaking to third-graders.

He is beautiful, the color of caramel, with a white stripe running from between his ears to the top of his nose. His great big eye scans my face, up and down, side to side.

"Go ahead," Sherry says, "get to know each other a little."

I reach in my bag and pull out three large knobby carrots (been sitting in the fresh veg drawer at the bottom of my fridge for three weeks). "Are these okay?"

"Perfect. The way to Starlight's heart is through his belly." The little twinkle in her eye as she says this freaks me out a little.

I offer a carrot to Starlight, holding it by the very end, keeping my fingers as far away from teeth as possible.

Sherry exhales a startled "Ooh!"

She grabs my hand, puts the carrot in my flat palm, and then shoves it in Starlight's face. He takes it gently, as if to assure me he's not going to take my hand off with his snack. I carefully pet his muzzle—I've seen them do it in the movies—and he seems to like it. Well, he's pretty much just standing and breathing, but I'm going to assume that means he likes me. Who knows, I may just have a talent for this, taming the great wild beasts of the animal kingdom. Maybe I'm a female horse whisperer, a modern-day Snow White with an innate gift for frolicking joyously with wildlife.

"This is great," I say.

"You two are getting on like a house afire. I think we can move on to the next step."

"Riding! Yes, let's," I say, somewhat *like* a third-grader.

"Not quite." Say what, little lady?

Sherry opens the door to the stall and ushers Starlight out into the corridor. She positions me on one side of Starlight's head and she moves around to the other. Starlight doesn't need any poking or directing. He leads *us* down the ramps and back to the room with all the strange tools. Without a word from Sherry, he stops in the middle of the cobblestone aisle. Something tells me Starlight has made this particular trip more than once. Maybe I'm not quite the horse whisperer I thought I was.

"All right, here we go!" Sherry exclaims.

Sherry explains the tools, leather straps, brushes, and equine equipment scattered around the room. She has me brush Starlight for about ten minutes while demonstrating how to saddle up, what a bridle does, how a bit and reins work. She calls it "tacking up."

And just when I think we're getting somewhere, and Starlight is about as sedated by Sherry's voice as I am . . .

Sherry says, "Well, that's about all our time for today."

"But I haven't gotten up on the horse yet!" Oops, was that whining?

"Patience, Ryan. You have to learn these things before you can learn to ride. We might be able to get you up on Starlight for a bit next time." Patience? I'm on a mission, damnit!

I consider telling this aperitif-sized Sherry exactly where she can stuff her "patience," but instead I say, "Uh, okay," and try not to scowl.

"Shall we make another appointment for next week?" she asks.

"I'll be here." I'm going to ride that horse if it kills me—or bankrupts me. I was hoping I could become a horsewoman of class and sophistication in four lessons or less. Any more than that and I'll be a *homeless* woman of class and sophistication. My budgetary constraints are, after all, compounded daily by Visa.

I fork over my fifty-five bucks and schedule my next lesson. I know I shouldn't, but I feel a little gypped. I was hoping to kick off my plan with a galloping start. What I got instead was to experience firsthand the boring parts of the movie *Seabiscuit*. The bright side? I've never felt so close to Tobey Maguire.

CHAPTER Twenty-one

Big Saturday planned. No hangover to speak of and I haven't watched a single Lifetime Original Movie or *E! True Hollywood Story*. And I have flossed twice today already. Excellent. Of course, my lack of hangover is directly attributable to a lack of friends.

Yesterday, Veronica went straight from work to bed, which I found out when I called and woke her up at about eight P.M. She plans to spend all of today in a bubble bath.

Audrey and Will now spend their limited free time canoodling with one another. Actually, Audrey called what they plan to do this weekend "hanging out," but I do believe there will be a fair amount of nooky involved.

So, here I am. Working on the plan. Alone. But it's really all right, right? I am an independent woman, a modern woman. I am perfectly happy and satisfied doing things all by myself. I think. I can't really remember the last time I tried. But I've read all the how-to guides on the subject that they offer in the magazines—how to eat in a restaurant alone, how to go to a movie alone. Unfortunately, they don't have one for how to go to the Met alone. Whatever, I can do it. I can.

Dressed and ready for a day at the museum . . .

Comfortable walking shoes. Check.

Guidebook. Check.

Lunch money. Check.

Cell phone. Check.

I guess I should be going now.

I could maybe wait a *little* longer, right? What's the hurry? The art's not going anywhere.

I should probably wait till after lunch, save money.

Surely it couldn't hurt to watch just a *teensy* bit of Lifetime. . . .

I reach for the clicker, my finger almost to the ON button and *buuuuuuz* . . . an alarm? I jump back from the remote control.

Buuuuuuz . . . *buuuuuuz*. It's the front door, Ryan, you asshole.

Thank God, someone's here! I knew Veronica couldn't soak that long. I hold the button to open the main door, then run out to the stairwell.

I lean over the railing and scream down, "I knew you couldn't resist me! You run out of bubbles?"

A male voice calls up, "What?"

"Oh, shit, I'm sorry!" I yell down. "I thought it was for me.

You must have hit my buzzer by accident. Sorry." Embarrassing. Embarrassing.

I race back toward my door.

The male voice says, "Ryan?"

I turn around and it's Charlie. "Charlie?"

"I seem to be getting this confused, amazed, slightly frightened reaction from you lately. It's making feel a little like a stalker," he says with a wary smile.

"I'm sorry." I plaster a congenial sort of look on my face. "Hiya, Charlie. What brings you to this part of town?"

"That's a little better . . . I guess." He continues, "I hope you don't mind, Will gave me your address."

I shrug my shoulders, but I think he was expecting some kind of comment. I'd just really like to know what he's doing here.

He takes my silence in the manner it was intended. "I was hoping you might be able to show me around some. Give me a New Yorker's firsthand tour of the city?"

"I don't know if I—"

"I thought, with your theory about the phases and everything . . . and we could, uh, test the new friendship treaty."

"Where's Marisa?"

He stiffly shifts his weight from one foot to the other. "Wedding planning." He forces out a little chuckle. "Evidently, the groom's job is to hand over his credit card and show up sober at the appointed date and time."

Visions of Marisa chatting over croissants with Martha Stewart herself. No, it would have to be someone cooler than Martha. Ah . . . sipping iced tea with Colin Cowie. No, no.

Even cooler, edgier, sought after, and chic—Preston Bailey. Yep, Preston Bailey and a grand discussion about the benefits and drawbacks of orchid arrangements at a New York fete. Don't ask me how I know so much about New York wedding planners. This stuff just accumulates, okay?

As I drift back to reality it occurs to me that a heavy awkwardness is threatening to swallow all the oxygen in the hallway. This thing with Charlie feels strange, strained. I don't know that I can tolerate an entire afternoon in this state of unease. I feel like I'm standing here with a stranger, all jittery and uncomfortable in his presence. But it's just Charlie, right? And I did agree to be friends. Though I hadn't expected our friendship to be the go-ahead-drop-by-unannounced kind. Even so, what could be the harm?

I say, "Okay. I'll do it."

He lets out a sigh. Had he actually been holding his breath? "Great, good."

We both just stand outside my door . . . waiting. For what, I don't know.

He speaks up first. "Should we go? I mean, are you ready now, or . . ."

"Oh, yeah. I just . . . need to grab my keys." I slip into my apartment. Do I have him wait outside, or invite him in? It would be stupid to have him standing out there, I guess. "Uh, do you want to come in?"

"Sure," he says brightly.

As I search for my keys—which I could have sworn were right here on the coffee table, but have now vanished—I see Charlie furtively taking in my humble abode, letting his eyes casually scan every piece of multipurpose furniture, the building's few elements of prewar charm.

It suddenly hits me: Charlie Cavanaugh is standing in my kitchenette. Of all the people in all the world that I've ever imagined standing in my kitchenette, he was not one of them. Well, to be honest, I typically imagine only one man in my kitchenette—Rocco DiSpirito . . . making me the perfect gnocchi . . . in nothing but a teeny tiny little apron. But Charlie? Never.

The sight of him here, surrounded by all my things, his hands self-consciously in his pockets—staring at me.

Oh, God, he's staring at me. I think I'm staring back.

A great wave of nervous quivering shakes my midsection. I look away and pretend to dig through the sofa cushions.

Charlie speaks up, almost timidly. "Is this . . ."

I look up. He's pointing to my four measly walls.

"Yep, this is it. The whole shebang." I get up from crouching beside the sofa.

He desperately tries to hold back laughter, his face almost beet red from the effort. "It's . . . cozy."

He's trying so hard not to laugh. I crack up, and he follows suit.

Between cackles he says, "No, it's really . . . I think my sister had a dollhouse this size."

I practically roar with laughter, tears streaming down my face.

He gets control of himself. "Seriously, it's nice. Really."

"Yeah, yeah," I say, regaining my breath and wiping the damp from my face.

And, like a magic wand has been waved, the air is clear and all the awkwardness is gone. We're just Charlie and Ryan again. No stupid grudges or guilt trips. No more jitters. Just two friends, plain and simple.

We step out onto the street and I turn to him. "What's your pleasure?"

"I don't have a clue."

"Well, I was planning on going to the Met today. Does that sound all right for a start?"

"Sounds good."

We make our way west and then south along Lex in almost complete silence. The one great thing about being on the streets of this city is that there isn't ever really silence. Sirens, horns, the low hum of thousands of people talking at once always fill in the gaps. It's a warm and breezy spring day, and everyone is out enjoying it, so the noise level is even higher than a typical Saturday. Not that Charlie would notice the silence between us anyway. I can see that he's still taking in New York, trying to wrap his brain around it and somehow get ahold of it. Gazing skyward, stopping when the blinking sign says "Don't Walk," reacting almost viscerally to the lack of personal space. Honestly, I find it sort of refreshing.

"It takes a while," I say as we cross Lex at Eighty-fourth, "but eventually it all sinks in."

"Or you sink into it," he replies.

"You make it sound so sinister."

"No, I don't mean it like that. It's just, I adjusted to L.A. so easily."

"More exposed flesh, and fewer bodies," I say only half joking.

"You think people there live in their bikinis?"

Yes. "No, what I meant was that it's much more relaxed, right?"

He nods vehemently. "Exactly. Relaxed. Of course, it's also superficial and phony. One of the reasons I wanted to come here was to get away from all that. Have a more authentic life, you know?"

"Oh, my God, authentic? That is so L.A.," I say in my best Valley girl impersonation.

He smirks at me, knowing it's true. "Seriously, Ryan. New York is so . . ."

"Fast. Big. Scary. Real."

"All of the above."

"It may sound like bullshit right now, and it may take longer than it did in L.A., but you'll get it." We stop at Fifth Avenue, waiting for traffic to clear. "You'll get it and you'll love it here. I know you, Charlie; you were meant for this place."

His eyes lock on mine and I suddenly feel that was too personal of a thing to say to an engaged ex-boyfriend whom I haven't spoken to in four years.

I quickly disengage the eye contact, turn to face Central Park and the massive Metropolitan Museum of Art. "Dar she blows!" I am such an ass.

We wade through the people hanging around outside the museum, and it's as if everyone has just decided to couple. Without warning, all the cute and cuddly couples of Manhattan have converged on the Met. They're strolling hand in hand, browsing the wares of starving artists who have set up stalls along Fifth Avenue. They're lounging and having picnics on the steps. They are *everywhere*! I try to ignore them, and manage—by breaking into a near sprint—to make it into the building safely.

Charlie and I make our "donations" and get our little metal clips with their sophisticated little M's.

I say, "Now, if you don't mind, I'd like to focus on Egypt. I kind of have this goal, a small goal for today, part of a larger goal, within the framework of an even larger . . ." Shut up, Ryan. "Anyway, I know it's not flashy, but I wanted to do Egypt. Does that sound all right to you?"

"Sounds fascinating," he says, with only a hint of sarcasm.

"All righty, then." I try and bolt for Egypt before the questions start occurring to him. According to my guidebook it should be dead ahead. . . .

"What's this larger goal? The largest one?" That's it, that was the question I was hoping to avoid. Me and my big mouth.

Somewhere between the Outer Coffin of Henettawy and the Seated Statue of Hatshepsut, Charlie manages to force me to tell him all about my Life Plan. I have to say, he's worse than the girls when it comes to needing details. But, amazingly enough, he seems to be genuinely fascinated.

"Admirable," he says while glancing at the Heart Scarab of Hatnofer.

"It *is* beautiful, isn't it?"

"I was talking about the plan, Ryan. It's a good plan."

"Oh, thanks."

"Yeah, plans are good," he says, though it's tough to tell if he's talking to me or to himself.

"I've always heard they were good," I reply, trying to keep myself from laughing.

"The important thing is not to get too wrapped up in it. Don't let ambition take over your whole life. That's one of the reasons I left L.A."

"What is?"

"People there get so wrapped up in success, everything's about making it to the top. It's all anyone ever talks about."

"I appreciate the advice, and I'll keep it in mind. But, seeing as I've spent the last twenty-five years actively *avoiding* success, I think a little time devoted to it might be healthy. Besides, I don't think what I'm doing exactly qualifies as ambition."

"If you're aiming for something, it's ambition."

I don't know what to say to that. I guess it *is* ambition. I'd never thought of myself as an ambitious person, but maybe now I am. I want to say, "Thank you, Charlie. That means a lot to me." But it seems silly and would probably make things awkward. So, instead, I stare at Charlie as he inspects an ancient hieroglyph and marvel that I'm here with him.

Charlie walks ahead. "You always did like to organize things. You always had a system or a theory for everything."

"I did not!" That may qualify as mock shock.

"Ha! Remember that time we went camping in the mountains?" How could I forget? One fire, one tent, one sleeping bag. Bliss. "And your notebook of survival skills?" he continues. "Three pages on how to survive a flash flood? Like we'd have the time to consult the manual while trying to keep our heads above water."

Now there's that *Worst-Case Scenario Survival Handbook*; totally missed the boat on that one. "I admit, the flash flood info may have been overkill. But if you were bitten by a rattlesnake, I would have known exactly what to do."

"Rattlesnakes don't even live in that part of the country, Ryan."

"Please, those things are always turning up under people's porches."

I continue my stroll through Egyptian history, taking time for every hieroglyph, every wooden sculpture, every coffin. It's all starting to blend together, seem fake, like an exhibition of *Cleopatra* memorabilia at a low-rent Planet Hollywood.

A little statue catches my eye. It's about two feet tall, maybe more, made of stone. A man and woman seated on a bench. The description card says, *Yuny and his wife, Renenutet.* A husband and wife sit next to each other, facing forward. Almost exactly like old pictures of dead relatives that my mom has in a special box at home. They sit stiff and upright, but you can tell there's something between them, that they are a unit. Renenutet has her arm gently resting on Yuny's shoulder. It's so sweet and so telling. . . .

"The tender minutiae," I say under my breath. They had it even then.

"What?" Charlie says. I had no idea he was right behind me.

"Nothing," I reply curtly.

"No, what did you say?" he presses.

"The tender minutiae," I repeat. He tips his head sideways

ever so slightly, scrunches up his eyes. Man, how could he possibly *still* be making that face? I continue, "The little things that people do when they love each other. Like Rene-whatever-her-name-is there. See how she tenderly touches Yuny's shoulder? And like Will and Audrey in the bar the other night, you know? The tender minutiae."

He makes a thoughtful "Mmmm" and studies the statue. I continue on through the exhibit. Alabaster cat, Sphinx of Amenhotep III, a bright blue hippo—I march past them all in a desperate attempt to reach the Temple of Dendur before he thinks of probing further.

I pretend to be fascinated by a fountain.

Charlie sneaks in behind me and says, "Did we do that?"

"Did we do what?"

"The tender minutiae."

What the hell? What do I say to that? Of course, you idiot. Now shut up and look at the art. No, that won't work. "Yeah."

"Like what? What did *I* do?" he asks.

Is he looking for tips to use on Marisa? "You want me to draw you a diagram or something?"

"Just show me," he says.

I glare at him, but he can see there's no malice behind it. He gives me a good old-fashioned buddy-buddy poke in the arm.

I give in. "Fine."

I lead him into a great limestone structure, an actual Egyptian building plopped in the middle of Manhattan. A trio of men in funny headgear do their "Walk Like an Egyptian" dance on the wall.

I say, "Sometimes, when we would walk into a room, you'd

put your hand on the small of my back to guide me in the door."

"Like this?" he asks. He puts his hand ever so gently on the small of my back. Oh, my. All five fingers touching. I suddenly wish I were wearing a gauzier top. Must move away before I explode.

I take a quiet, calming breath and continue. "Sometimes you would absentmindedly, sort of, rub my arm with the back of your finger. Mostly when you were talking to people or . . ."

He rubs my shoulder, slowly up and down, just like he used to. "Like this?" he asks.

I can only close my eyes and bow my head. I think I may pass out. I think this may be a good time to stop. He stops first.

"Anything else?" he asks.

I probably shouldn't, but what could be the harm? Just one friend helping out another, right? They're tips . . . for Marisa.

"Sometimes you would tuck my hair back behind my ear."

Charlie positions himself directly in front of me, closer than is really necessary. He slowly brings his hand up to my face and pauses, for just a split second, as his fingertips graze my cheek. His beautiful, incredible honey-brown eyes are sucking me in. He gently brushes a section of hair off my face and pushes it, ever so softly, around my ear, his index finger tenderly tracing the outline of my earlobe and following the line of my neck to my collarbone.

"Like that?" he asks softly.

I can feel the moment building, a tension between us. In another lifetime this is the moment when we would have kissed. I can physically feel it, like my refusal to lean in for it is somehow breaking the laws of nature. I feel the moment, and I can tell he feels it too.

And then, just as quickly as it came, the moment passes. All the tingling nerve endings go back to neutral.

"Yep," I say matter-of-factly, "just like that."

CHAPTER Twenty-two

I somehow manage to wrangle a liquid/light-lunch meeting out of Audrey and Veronica so that we may have the first, and last, meeting of the Book Club for the Socially Retarded. Actually, I lured them in with hints of the strange museum incident with Charlie.

"Was it, you know, sort of romantic?" asks Audrey, adjusting the cheap umbrella over our patio table.

"It was weird, and then it wasn't. And then it was really awkward in a whatever-happens-I-gotta-get-me-some-more-of-that kind of way."

"So he was hard-core coming on to you?" asks Veronica.

"That's the thing," I say, tapping my knife on the bread plate for emphasis, "I don't know. I mean, it doesn't make any sense. Does it?" The girls shake their heads in shared bewilderment. "Lacking any further evidence or a rational explanation,

I'm going to assume it was an effort to obtain tips. Girly tips . . . for Marisa." Time to change the subject, the real purpose of this meeting. I'd like to get this BCSR business concluded. Plus, every time I think about what happened at the museum, I get that stupid all-over tingly feeling, which I then have to tame and suppress. I shouldn't feel anything for Charlie but friendship. He is engaged. He is in the past. Therefore, "Speaking of tips, the BCSR, what's the verdict?"

Veronica looks down guiltily. "I got through the first half of the first book, Ryan. But I'm just so damn busy!" Just a twinge of dishonesty in that last bit.

"You didn't like it," I say, cutting to the point.

"Not even a little," she confesses.

"And you, Audrey?"

"I liked it a lot, but I really didn't have time to read more. The new jeans campaign, and Will and everything." That I believe. "I'm sorry, Ryan."

I try to put on an admonishing glare, but it's no use. "They didn't have any useful tips anyway."

"No?" asks Veronica.

There were trends but no tips. I say, "I've read four and I am not an inch closer to getting a boyfriend."

The only hard facts to come out of my extensive modern-city-girl research are the three categories under which, according to the books, every man in the world can fit. They are as follows:

Category 1: Mr. Bait and Tackle

Modus Operandi—Supplies female with massive quantities of alcohol, typically cheap domestic in the bottle or in plastic cup from keg. Demonstrates feat of strength such as lifting heavy object (often the girl herself, sometimes household appliance). Woos girl with war tales of football, hockey, or other bloody sport. Takes her to her place where he fumbles with female undergarments, inserts himself for three seconds, flips over, and begins snoring.

Identifying Marks—Hulking manly frame, scar from aforementioned contact sport, and fraternity tattoo.

Best Defense—The modern American female can avoid encouraging Mr. Bait and Tackle in one of two ways. Option one: Change topic of conversation to politics, the stock market, or marriage. Option two: Say the word *tampon*.

Category 2: Mr. Flaming Loins of Lust

Modus Operandi—Supplies female with massive quantities of alcohol, typically smartly chosen wine, or chic microbrew. Demonstrates keen knowledge of the English language and deep passion for sophisticated prose. Woos girl by sharing a deeply personal sob story and/or by revealing his "deep, dark secret" (often something to do with the great American novel or white picket fences). Takes her to his place, where he lights scented candles, delicately undresses and caresses her, inserts himself for three seconds, and whispers sweet nothings till he can flip over and begin snoring.

Identifying Marks—Degree in English or Philosophy, chic expensive eyeglasses that scream studious and avant-garde, and perpetually lit cigarette.

Best Defense—The modern American female can easily avoid encouraging Mr. Flaming Loins of Lust by one of two methods. Option one: Refuse to swoon over "deep, dark secret" or sob story, simply nod, or say "Mmm" in response. If you find yourself saying "Awww" or offering concerned advice, you're done for. Option two: Buy him a shot. Mr. Flaming Loins of Lust is a lightweight.

Category 3: Mr. Bond My Stock

Modus Operandi—Supplies female with massive quantities of alcohol while demonstrating aptitude for all things financial. Woos girl by planting fantasy of fancy car, house in Hamptons, and Saks charge account with no preset spending limit. Flashes expensive watch and bulging wallet casually so as to draw attention without looking intentional. Drops sexy Wall Street lingo like so much fiscal Spanish fly. Takes her to his place, where he plays light rock on three-thousand-dollar stereo, fondles, prods, inserts himself for three seconds, and mumbles something about having to get up early before flipping over and beginning to snore.

Identifying Marks—Immaculately tailored Armani or Brooks Brothers suit, clean close shave, and wallet bulge noticeably larger than another certain bulge.

Best Defense—The modern American female may easily avoid Mr. Bond My Stock altogether by not frequenting bars that have a ridiculous cover charge and/or velvet rope.

In short, the result of my tireless research is an introduction to a class of men who have carefully designed courses of action by which they subtly work their way into a woman's pants with as little effort as possible. They all have an intense fear of telephonic communication and/or basic human kindness, and all routinely succeed at their mission to seek out and conquer unsuspecting, heartbroken, and vulnerable women between the ages of eighteen and thirty-two.

These female heroines all fall prey to a member of at least one category. They are crushed by his callousness and, as a result, engage in an excessive amount of male-bashing and tedious overuse of the words *spunky* and *zany.* Of course, eventually, the heroine uses the knowledge gained to forge a fulfilling and healthy relationship with the tall, dark, and handsome superman who has been conveniently lurking just under the radar in the guise of her lifelong best male friend.

I would discount the whole lot of these fictional men if it weren't for Audrey. She has, in fact, dated a classic Category One—the Soccer Player. And she managed to miraculously find the perfect boyfriend right there under her nose—Will. Oddly enough, this isn't doing much to quell my disappointment. I wanted hard facts, results. What I got is a useless system of bad-boyfriend classification.

Audrey is delighted by her resemblance to the fictional modern city girls. "You see, Ryan. I told you. All you have to do is wait. The right guy will just turn up. That *is* a tip." Veronica and I look at her askance. "It worked for me," she says triumphantly.

She and Will have openly declared themselves "boyfriend

and girlfriend." Thus, Audrey is now an expert on relationships, whether we like it or not. If I didn't love her so much, I might just dive over our grilled-chicken salads and throttle her.

"I just had a thought," muses Veronica. "What if he already turned up?"

"Who?" I ask, genuinely intrigued.

She squints her eyes at me. "Oh, I think you know who."

"You mean Charlie?" I chuckle.

Veronica raises an eyebrow and takes a long gulp of her Harp.

"You're crazy."

"I don't know," adds Audrey. "She could be right."

I roll my eyes at them. "Hello! Engaged. To a goddess." I should add something like "I don't like him anyway" or "I don't want to be anything more than friends"; unfortunately, I can't make the words come out. Charlie has changed, no doubt about it, but he hasn't changed enough to erase all the old feelings I had for him. I have felt them ebb and flow ever since the museum. But it doesn't matter, does it? He is engaged. To a goddess.

"Not a goddess," says Audrey.

"I have to disagree."

"No, really," repeats Audrey knowingly, "not a goddess."

"Just spill it already!" demands Veronica.

Audrey wiggles in her seat, setting herself up to drop a bomb. "The guys . . . the band, uh . . . how should I put this? I'll just say, they seriously dislike her."

Very pleased by this, Veronica drawls, "Reeeally?"

Audrey continues, "More than the stuff about checking up

on them, she's starting to, uh, not-so-politely suggest what songs they drop from the album. She's trying to talk them out of 'Sweet Agony,' for goodness' sake!" It is, by far, their best, sweetest, sappiest, girl-drool–inducing song.

"Bitch!" declares Veronica, an unlit cigarette dangling from her mouth.

Audrey nods in agreement and lights a cigarette of her own, very proud of herself and her inside information.

Veronica's eyes go wide. I can almost see a little lightbulb flash to life over her head. "Steal him, Ryan!"

"Are you insane?" My volume makes the guy sitting behind Veronica jump. I lower my voice. "I haven't had a date in, what, six months? And you think I'm going to be capable of stealing the boyfriend of a high-class almost-goddess? You've got to be crazy!" Oops, forgot something. "Oh, and that would be wrong. Morally wrong." It would, wouldn't it?

CHAPTER Twenty-three

Control yourself, Ryan! Control yourself! My heart is all aflutter and I have the unbelievable desire to scream "Yes!" at the top of my lungs. But I'm sitting in my cube. Maintain calm, Ryan.

A little "Yip!" escapes from my subconscious and right out of my mouth. I smack my hand over it to prevent any further outbursts, and stick my head over the cube wall to make sure no one heard the last one. I slowly sit back down and take a long, cleansing breath.

Mrs. Wheatley got me interviews. *Three* whole interviews. Over the next three days I will take extra long lunches and find the key to my future happiness. One of these positions is my ticket out of this hellhole. It will mean financial independence, and a meteoric rise up the ladder of success. I can feel it.

• • •

I spent all of last night modeling outfits. Well, I don't know that *modeling* is entirely accurate, as I was the only one who did the looking. But Audrey and Veronica were my virtual stylists, of course. They answered important questions like "Is a blue button down too casual if I wear my trusty Doc Marten Mary Jane's?" and "Are you sure my red pencil skirt doesn't look too wintry?" Five short hours later I had three outfits set aside, each a clever blend of business casual and corporate chic.

Outfit One: red fitted Gap Favorite Tee, black wide-leg pants in linenesque semi-floaty fabric, with red modern pointy-toed loafers.

I walk into the corporate headquarters of Kepler-Koto International feeling very confident and secure in my abilities. By the time I reach the human resources department on the eighth floor, I feel ready to crawl out of my skin and die a slow, lingering death as a pile of floppy flesh. Excellent beginning.

Kepler-Koto is a very staid environment. There's a plethora of tasteful furniture, the kind bought at an office furniture warehouse ("Two cases of framed art free with the purchase of seventy waiting room chairs").

I make my presence known to the HR secretary and take a seat in an uncomfortable chair next to four men—grown men. They must be here for another job. They're much older and have the look of career coders—pasty white skin, slightly creepy bug-eyed faraway look.

Precisely fifteen minutes after I arrive, the HR secretary calls my name and ushers me into a tiny office with an expansive view of a brick wall. A slender, very attractive woman stands up from behind her desk, shakes my hand, and introduces herself as Diane, head of human resources. She tells me that she has extensive experience in web-related database development so I shouldn't feel that I'm talking to a novice. I think she means to reassure me; it's not working.

I sit down and mentally prepare myself for the interview: Please, Ryan. Whatever you do, don't fuck this up.

Diane flips open a file and gives me a wide, comforting grin. "You have an impressive résumé for someone so young, Miss Hadley. And Kepler-Koto is always interested in promoting diversity in their coding department."

I smile and nod my head as if I know what she's talking about. *My* résumé, impressive? And, uh, coding? What happened to web design? I continue to smile through the silence.

Should I be saying something here?

"Yes, well," Diane begins again. "Let's get down to specifics, shall we?"

"Perfect," I say.

"Could you describe your particular experience with Oracle8*i* and Oracle9*i*?"

With what? What is she talking about? "I'm sorry?"

She squints a little, pauses, studies my ever-increasing tension. "You *do* have experience developing Oracle stored procedures and packages?" I shake my head no. She tries again: "Developing Unix shell scripts?"

Very quietly, so that she may not hear me, I say, "No."

She flips through her papers again. "You have a thorough knowledge of html, xml, and Java?"

A little too excited, I say, "Oooh, yes. Yes, those I have!"

"But no Oracle or PL/SQL?"

Okay. It is a bad sign when you get lost in the interview, is it not? "I'm sorry. Oracle I'm familiar with, insomuch as I know it exists. But the PL . . . I don't have any idea."

Diane stands up abruptly. "There must be some sort of mix-up. We're looking for a senior oracle application developer."

"Uh, do you have any entry-level web design positions open, by any chance?"

She opens the door and, with her eyes, strongly urges me to leave immediately.

"Thank you for your"—the door slams in my face—"time."

So, then, I probably shouldn't be printing up any Kepler-Koto business cards.

Outfit Two: white button-down with nerdy-chic charcoal gray sweater vest, black knee-length mini with kick pleat and comfy black Doc Marten Mary Janes. Very geek-chic: she-wears-a-pocket-protector—and-nothing-else kind of vibe.

The outfit goes perfectly with the image of the company—that is, according to my research. I did a little digging to make sure that this firm actually *does* web design. They do, thank God. No repeats of the last interview. In fact, I will never think of the last interview again, except in recurring nightmares, of course.

I am on time and looking good. Everyone waiting to interview is my age. Actually, everyone in the company seems to be my age. It's all very casual and hip. The many desks are outfitted with *Star Wars* action figures, LEGO cities, and the like. It practically oozes creativity and fun. This would be a really great place to work. I can just see myself flirting coyly with the nerdy-cute boy in the cube next to mine. Lovely.

As my name is called, I say a little prayer to Saint Jude: "Please, please. Don't let me fuck this up."

Whoa, mama. Cute-boss alert. A handsome, barely thirty-year-old stunner shakes my hand and offers me a seat and a beverage. I accept the first, decline the second—don't need to spill anything on myself or develop hiccups in the middle of an interview.

Cute Boss lowers the volume on The Strokes song currently playing on his iMac. He leans back in his chair, flings his flip-flopped feet on the desk, and says, "Stagger me."

His words have the same effect on me as, say, being gored in the belly by one of those bulls from Pamplona. I try getting clarification, "How do you mean?" I ask timidly.

"Impress me"—he skims my résumé, finds what he's looking for—"Ryan."

Oh, God. I can feel the blood draining from my face—away from my brain and pooling somewhere between my twitching right shoulder and trembling right hand.

I tell myself to dazzle and amaze him with my sharp wit and deep understanding of web design and programming. What actually comes out of my mouth is a word-for-word breakdown of my old résumé, the one that was so *dazzling* it got me into Geiger-freaking-Data Systems. Way to go, Ryan!

Cute Boss spends a moment tapping his right flip-flop against the bottom of his foot. Finally he says, "Tell me about the last full life-cycle project you worked on"—he skims my résumé again—"Ryan."

"Software coding or web programming?" I ask.

"The software."

"Well, I did some in college, but it was really more of a workshop type arrangement. Small projects with specific goals."

"No integration/regression testing?"

"Planning, designing, and a bit of preliminary code construction."

Cute Boss slides his feet off the desk and stands up. It appears they're looking for someone with more than what I've got.

He shakes my hand hurriedly. "Thanks for coming in. We'll be getting back to you within the week." In other words, thanks but no thanks, L-O-S-E-R.

I say my good-byes and try not to notice all the laughing and goofing-off going on among the workers, try not to feel completely crestfallen at having been rejected by a place so awesome.

Outfit Three: springy yellow shirtdress with kelly-green Prada knockoff pumps and matching handbag, a sort of low-rent *Sex and the City* style.

I can already sense doom on the horizon. It's coming, it's only a matter of time. A dark cloud looms over the HR office, lightning ready to strike me down as I enter.

I cannot sit through another hopeless meeting, just waiting for the other shoe to drop. I cannot bear to look into the eyes of the interviewer and know exactly what she's thinking: *You, Ryan Hadley, are not good enough.*

The usual hellos are exchanged, but before I even sit down I ask, "I hope you don't mind me asking, but . . . what is the exact title of the open position?" (Were this an interview training course, this would be the point at which the instructor would rap me across the knuckles with a ruler.)

The interviewer looks at me, perplexed, her brow deeply furrowing. She checks her paperwork and answers, "Senior web programmer analyst, specialization Java, .NET, and Visual Basic."

Yeah, I can't do that. "I'm going to save you some time here and leave immediately. But first, would you mind if I take that copy of my résumé with me?"

The stunned interviewer hands me the paper and watches wide-eyed as I march right back out of the office.

I wander over to Bryant Park, buy myself a big, juicy, calorie-drenched hot dog, and settle into an empty bench.

Just as I suspected, this résumé is complete fiction. Mrs. Wheatley has managed to turn my data-entry experience into data warehousing and database development. I suppose to the uninitiated it would seem like a mere title boost, but they're actually completely different animals. She's also made my limited experience with coding and programming from college sound like I'd written the source codes for Yahoo! or something.

Now, intellectually, I know that somewhere in this city is a job for me. Nothing fancy, just a small, low-pressure web-design gig that I can grow into and out of. And, though my brain has processed that these disastrous interviews say more about Mrs. Wheatley's skill at job placement than my own potential in web design, my heart doesn't seem to have gotten the memo. My heart keeps forming the word *failure* and whipping it back and forth between my ears.

No. I absolutely refuse to get mired in this. I will sit here and eat my street-vendor dog, which only tourists and detectives in gritty TV crime dramas are supposed to eat, and feel bad. But when I step out of Bryant Park, I will leave this grievously unfortunate week behind me.

Done.

CHAPTER Twenty-four

"Oh, dear. That's too bad," says Mrs. Wheatley through the hiss of her cell phone line.

"Yeah. The thing is, the person whose résumé . . . I mean, on paper it looked to them like . . ." Oh, spit it out, Ryan! "Mrs. Wheatley, I think we need to be looking for something more, you know, entry-level."

"Of course, Ryan. This market is a little tighter than I'd anticipated, but I'll keep plugging away. Give it time."

For someone who's jump-starting their life, I seem to be doing an awful lot of waiting. Rapid execution of extreme measures? Easier said than done.

The pile of data cramming my in-box tugs at my stomach. Or could that be last night's curry? I better just suck it up and get to it. Today miniature dollhouse furniture, tomorrow . . . the world!

Or, at the very least, the state.

The county?

Oh, who am I kidding? I'd settle for one measly city block.

Only one thing I ask, the next time you see miniature furniture at the teeny tiny miniature furniture showplace, remember this. Remember the ridiculous amounts of data propping up Item #46734, 1/16th scale Georgian Armoire with Hand-Painted Interior, SKU #G786500912. Say a little prayer for me and my numb fingertips.

Item #46735, 1/16th Scale Portrait of Lord Byron in Gilded Oval Frame, SKU #G7864000932.

Item # . . .

"Ryan?" I nearly jump out of my seat. Betsy leans into me; her hair smells like bubble gum. "It's time," she says in a low and gentle tone.

My God, she sounds like a prison guard come to escort me to the death house. "Time for what?"

"Your evaluation, dear."

Oh, shit. Dead girl walking.

The short walk across the office seems to take an hour. My legs are stiff, I have to concentrate on moving my feet. Right. Left. Right. Left.

I really cannot afford to get canned right now. I still haven't found another job. And, goddamnit, I have a horse to feed!

As I weave through the aisles of cubes, all the nameless faces do double-takes. I see the worry in their eyes. Actually, their eyes are more glazed over than worried—miniature furniture.

I knock on the wall of The Dirk's lair. His office is really a cube, too, except his gray burlapish walls are over six feet tall and there are four of them.

"Come in," I hear from behind the panels.

He sits behind his desk, palms resting on his pleather desk mat. His blue-gray suit is almost the same color as the walls. It makes his head look like it's floating in midair, his too-wide tie keeping it tethered to the desk.

I sit down across from him. My knee bumps against the metal desk, causing a rumble of fake thunder to echo through the office.

"Ryan Hadley"—he opens a slim green folder, flattens it neatly on the desk—"you've been with us for nearly four years now?"

"Yes, sir."

I just called The Dirk "sir."

He smoothes the comb-over. "Let me start by saying, as I'm sure you already know, we've decided this year to initiate a friendly evaluation process. It's an informal-type thing, you see. I merely review the quality of work and so on and so forth and make a determination of quality and whatnot, so that adjustments can be made."

I may eventually need clarification on the "so on and so forth" and "whatnot," but "All righty." Wow, smooth.

"I'll get right into it, then?"

"Absolutely," I say. No time like the present. Bring on the pink slip, mister.

"I am delighted to tell you, Miss Hadley, that you are the number one employee in our unit."

"Excuse me?"

"Your work this year, as I'm sure is the case in all the previous years as well, has been exemplary and right on target. You perform your duties with dedication and professionalism. You get your data in on time and with little hassle." If that's true, it was purely by accident. "Overall, I'd say you are the model employee."

I stare at his pasty face, agog. He smiles his brightest—and it must be said, creepiest—smile. I think he's serious. Oh, my God, he's serious.

A high-pitched cackle worms its way from the deep recesses of my stomach and out through my mouth at a volume that could be considered dangerous. I can't stop it. My eyes water, my stomach aches. I cannot stop laughing.

The Dirk gives an uncomfortable laugh of his own.

I finally contain myself—at least, enough to lower the volume and wipe the tears from my face.

The Dirk stands up and offers his hand. "Congratulations, Miss Hadley." I shake his clammy hand, but I don't think I should stand up. All the blood has rushed to my face. I can feel it glowing like a Christmas tree.

How is this happening?

The Dirk takes his seat again. "Now, I'm sorry to say that we can't, at this time, offer you a raise or bonus or anything of that sort. But then, I assured the boys upstairs that you were a very agreeable, easygoing sort of young woman—"

"I'm sorry. Upstairs?"

He gives a chortle. "Naturally. The administrative sector, sales and client management, that sort of thing."

I have never given a single thought to "the boys upstairs." I guess I knew they existed, but I've never actually seen any in person. I suppose I always pictured one old guy behind a massive mahogany desk, plotting complex stratagems of torture for those of us down in the farm. "Let's give them fourteen days of baby bumpers, followed by eight days of telemarketing returns."

"These people know about me?" I ask, trying to keep down a second wave of laughter.

The Dirk's smile widens, thrilled to be the one to give the good news to the poor silly girl. "Miss Hadley, they made you employee of the month!"

He stands. "Now, as I said, there is not at this time any monetary compensation, you see, for this honor." He's staring at me; I force myself to follow his lead and stand. "However, the boys upstairs wanted me to tell you that you most certainly have a future here at Geiger Data Systems."

Well, now, isn't *that* a lovely thought?

He escorts me out of his office.

I walk beside him, trying to catch my breath. On the way, I grab a handful of tissues from the Kleenex box of a gangly pubescent coworker whose name I think is something like Donna. Lana? I dab my eyes and try to pull myself together.

The Dirk stops, turns to me, then shakes my hand again and says cheerily, "You never know, Miss Hadley, you could be sitting behind my desk someday!"

"Oh" is the only thing I can think to say.

He calls out across the room, "Betsy!"

Betsy appears from behind a cubicle and claps her hands like someone commanding their dog off the sofa.

Suddenly, I'm surrounded. The cubes empty and everyone crowds around in a semicircle.

"Ladies and gentleman, your employee of the month," The Dirk announces, and begins clapping. A halfhearted round of applause stings my ears.

A flash of light blinds me momentarily.

I want to run, but the *Twilight Zone* nature of it all is making my feet like lead, melting into the floor.

Betsy's hands reach for the wall behind me. A shiny new wooden plaque hangs next to the office's one dusty fake ficus tree. In gold letters it says *Data Entry Employee of the Month.* She slips something behind a little glass plate mounted on the plaque.

Fuck. A Polaroid of me, with *Ryan Hadley* scrawled in the white space under my face. There I am, mouth open, eyes bugging out of my head, face all pink and damp. Immortalized for all eternity, or a month—whichever comes first.

I, Ryan Lorraine Hadley, am the finest in data outsourcing.

Out across the office, I scan over the multitude of cubicles, through the bank of windows, to the building across the street. Suddenly, the absurdity and humor of this incredibly embarrassing moment shifts to something different. I am struck by a profound . . . something. . . . I think it's sadness.

The emotionless faces of my coworkers glare back at me, their hands smacking together in time. They don't know me, and I don't know them. *I* am a nameless face. I'm no different than them. They hate this place as much as I do. There is no company pride here! They're clapping for themselves, for a surprise three-minute break from the monotony.

How many offices like this are there in this city? How many people sit in their cubicles wishing to be whisked away by some man/woman/sweepstakes/acting gig/big miraculous success? Waiting for something—anything—to change? I am no different than any of them. Me, the number-one-fucking-employee at Geiger Data Systems.

Betsy shoves a paper cup into my hand, something pink and fizzy. Mmm, virgin fruit punch with just a splash of 7-Up.

The Dirk raises his glass of punch and yells, "Speech!"

Oh, I guess that means me.

What I want to say is something like "Disperse, you ridiculous automatons! Rise up and revolt while you can! Get out of here while you're still young and your dreams are still tangible!" But that might seem ungrateful. Let's see, what else could I say? Maybe "I am doing my best to get the hell out of here. Hope you all get out of here too." No.

Mind blanking. I can literally feel the brain cells hiding. I take a deep breath and let it out slowly. "Thank you for the punch and cookies. This was . . . surprising."

The Dirk, Betsy, and the rest of the cube farmers stare at me expectantly. The silence is ruffled only by the high whine of gusting winds whipping across the high-rise's windows.

"Uh . . ." I continue, "this is . . . nice. Thank you."

I put the paper cup to my lips and drink as slowly as possible.

CHAPTER Twenty-five

I've managed to recover from the shock—I mean, the *honor*—of being named "The Finest in Data Outsourcing." If nothing else, I know I've got a paycheck coming for the next few weeks. But I can't shake the feeling that this transformation of mine is creeping along at a snail's pace. I mean, shouldn't I have accomplished something? Anything? Am I ever going to get out of here?

"Data-entry bitch Numero Uno! I've come to rescue you from your hellish existence," says the lovely familiar voice of Will. "For approximately five minutes."

"What are you doing here?" I exclaim. "It's so good to see you!" I hop up and give him a hug.

"Ryan, it's only been a few days."

"It's good to see you *here*!"

"Had a bad week, I take it?"

"See Exhibit A." I point across the room to my plaque.

"I saw. But hey, look on the bright side. You're very photogenic."

"Thanks," I say acerbically. "Do me a favor?" I grab a notepad and scribble nine words on the page, hand it to Will. "Say that to me."

He glances at the page. "You know this already."

"Yeah, I just like to be reminded every once in a while."

He reads: "You don't belong here. You are better than this place." He smiles. "Better now?"

"Almost."

"Well, I think I might have just the thing to seal the deal." Will puts his hand behind his back and produces three perfect Hershey bars.

"The man brings chocolate! I love you!"

The first has a little note taped to it: I recognize it as Audrey's personalized notepaper. It says, *Feel better. Things will work out. Hugs and kisses, Audrey.* So sweet.

The second bar has a Post-it slipped under the brown Hershey wrapper. It says, *Greetings from Iceland. Hope Björk here can cheer you up. I love you! Veronica.*

"She called you Björk."

"I'm flattered." Will holds up the third Hershey bar dramatically and kisses it before handing it over.

"Aw, thank you," I say.

"You know, that's now been kissed by a rock star. You probably shouldn't eat it. You should seal it in plastic and sell it on eBay in a few years."

I hold it out in both hands as if it were some sacred artifact. "My God, you're right," I tease him. "Forget a new job. This candy bar could be my ticket to financial freedom."

"Sure, you mock me now," he says, shaking a finger at me.

I invite Will to take a seat on my desk. I plop down next to him, dig into my candy. I could use a quick chocolate-induced serotonin boost.

"Speaking of rock stardom, how did you . . . ?"

"Escaped. I hid a pickax under my pillow and made a crude rope from the horsehair stuffing of my sleeping mat."

"Is she really that bad?"

"You have no idea." Will surveys the cube farm. "Am I gonna get you in trouble?"

"Who, me? The finest in data outsourcing?"

Just as I finish the sentence, The Dirk approaches my cube. Shit. I don't care, I'm not getting off my desk.

He smoothes his comb-over and attempts a smile. "Hello, Mr. Monroe."

"Hey," replies Will in his best James Dean.

The Dirk turns his attention to me. "Miss Hadley, have you completed the Sarfatti Waste Management account?"

Didn't even know I had it. Could that be why my in-box seems to reek? "No, sir. Almost," I say with a smile.

The Dirk backs up two steps. "You know, Miss Hadley, you'll have to work at it if you want to stay on top." He points to the ghastly Employee of the Month plaque across the room.

"Yes, Mr. Anderson."

The Dirk pauses uncomfortably, like he's trying to decide whether or not to walk away. He fidgets a little, then pulls a piece of paper from his pocket. He nervously clears his throat and says to Will, "Would you, um . . ."

Will tries to hold back the silly grin threatening to take over his face. He grabs a pen from my desktop and quickly autographs the slip of paper.

"Thank you," says The Dirk as he scuttles back to his lair.

Will and I burst into fits of laughter.

Yesterday was my second horseback-riding lesson—and another great waste of fifty-five bucks, if I do say so myself. Spent ten minutes grooming Starlight under the expert direction of Sherry, who sipped tea and chatted incessantly about something called "dressage." Next, spent fifteen minutes trying to heave my massive and, as it turns out, unwieldy ass into a saddle. Once finally sitting atop the horse, spent five minutes learning how to hold the reins. Really, horseback-*riding* lesson is a bit of a misnomer. It does, after all, imply movement.

Tonight, however, is a different story. Tonight is my first ballet lesson. It will drain another fifty bucks a week from my already aching check card, but it's worth it. Poise and grace. And, though the lessons are to be taught by a woman named Vera at Vera's Park Slope Academy of Dance in Brooklyn, I do believe they will be life altering. How could they not be?

Isn't ballet how all the lithe women of the world attain their litheness? Isn't ballet the ultimate synthesis of refinement and physical prowess? The ballet studio, regardless of its status as the last bastion of the leg warmer, is a place where elegance is honed. I could definitely use some honing.

• • •

The bright mirrored dance studio is an encouraging sight. It has well-worn wooden floors, an old upright piano, and a long row of three-tiered wooden barres on the back wall—just like *Fame*. Okay, I know it's cheesy, but I loved that show as a kid. Not to mention *Flashdance* and *White Nights*. God, I remember forcing my mom to make a bootleg VHS copy of that goofy Mary Tyler Moore movie *Six Weeks*, the one where her daughter is a ballerina with cancer. I watched it over and over, cried every time.

Since I'm the first one to arrive, I drop my bags in the corner and do my best to warm up. Stretching has never been a particularly easy thing for me. My body's default state is somewhere between inflexible and rigor mortis. But I do my best to limber up the legs.

Suddenly, as if a great Playskool gate has been opened, the room swells with eight-year-old girls and their mothers. A dozen fresh little faces flit and flutter in front of the mirror, with their precious chignons and various combinations of pale pink and black ballet wear. Black tights, pink leotard. Pink skirt, black leotard. I'm an extra in a bad Degas.

Vera had told me on the phone that the beginner's class would be mostly kids, but I hadn't realized what a spectacle it would turn out to be. I'm wearing workout leggings and a fitted T-shirt that, according to the girl at Lady Foot Locker, will wick away all moisture. Though roughly five years old, these items have been worn only twice: a costume party, and one failed attempt at jogging around the Reservoir in Central Park. This, and the fact that I've got about two feet in height and seventy pounds in weight on each of my fellow classmates, makes me quite the center of attention. I watch the mothers eyeing me. I see them counting heads and realizing that I am not, in fact, the very young mother of a student but a student myself. I could quietly slip out—except that I prepaid. Oops.

I continue to stretch while the tiny ballerinas go about comparing each other's Danskin gear. Behind a cluster at the door I spot a young boy of about ten but even shorter than the girls. He's rail thin, even in baggy sweatpants, but with a sort of presence. I can't really explain it. The girls part for him to pass. He finds an empty spot about five feet away from me. What do you call a male ballerina, a ballerin*o*?

The place goes quiet and I get a first glimpse of the woman who will change my body and whip me into shape. My very own guru of beauty, polish, and agility—Vera of Park Slope. She is slender and carries her body with the nimble self-possession of a dancer—but, I have to say, she looks an awful lot like a soccer mom. I don't know why, but I'd imagined someone a little more rough-and-tumble. A scraggly, tough-as-nails former chorus girl who'd shout a lot and reprimand you with piercing eyes.

"Welcome to the first class, everyone." A voice like cotton candy velvet. "I'm Vera."

Vera takes command and ushers the mothers out of the room. She smiles and has us introduce ourselves and tell why we want to take ballet lessons. The girls all have names that end in a *y*. Their reasons for joining the class vary slightly, but all involve *American Idol*, *Star Search*, or something they call Nutcracker Barbie. I sincerely hope they mean the Mattel toy and the Christmas ballet.

So it comes down to me and the little boy. Panic is firmly

planting itself in my chest. I have no idea what to say. Something like "I'd like to have the body of Gwyneth Paltrow and the posture of Audrey Hepburn, please." Or maybe "My life sucks and I thought this would help."

The boy says, "I want to dance."

The girls giggle, whisper to each other.

My turn. "My name is Ryan Hadley. I joined the class because . . ." Okay, think of something. I blurt, "I watched *Fame* as a kid." Vera gives me a big warm smile, but no laughs from the peanut gallery. Several of the *y*'s screw up their eyes in confusion. I realize it wasn't exactly Letterman-worthy, but a little something would be nice.

Vera speaks up, "*Fame* was a television show in the 1980s, everyone."

The *y*'s let out a flurry of understanding ohs and ahs. I hear someone say, "She was *alive* in the eighties? That is *so* old." Thank you, thank you very much.

Vera lines us up in a row along the barre, and illustrates positions one through five, and the correct way to change position. She holds each pose for an incredible amount of time until she's sure we all have the idea, then walks around perfecting our technique. "Back upright, as if you were being pulled straight by a string through the top of your head," "Fingers loose, with the thumb and middle fingers slightly inward," "Strong legs girls, strong legs." To me, her advice is generally "Shoulders back, eyes forward."

It is an hourlong ballet drill session: repeat, repeat, and repeat some more. I'm beginning to think maybe you have to be eight years old to appreciate this teaching technique. At that age you're used to being told to do things more than once. For example, has the command "Eat your vegetables" ever been complied with after the first utterance? Not in my house.

Vera claps her hands several times and announces, "Performance time!" Say what? "Ballet," trumpets Vera authoritatively, "is an art that must be shared to be appreciated. You do want to dance in front of people, don't you? Your parents? Your friends?"

Nope. Not even a little bit. The *y*'s and the lonely ballerino cluck their high-pitched and unmitigated enthusiasm.

"Well then," Vera goes on, "we have to get used to sharing our talents with others. As with the steps themselves, the act of performing also requires practice."

It's official: Vera is the Devil.

Vera takes a roll of tape from her bag and places a strip of it on the floor in the middle of the room. Thankfully, she begins at the other end of the line with the *y*'s.

Each of the elfin *y*'s displays her brand of the basic positions. Some show a real talent for it; others haven't quite mastered the use of their own limbs. Predictably, there's a fair amount of snickering at mistakes, and a roar of giggles follows each loss of balance. So, when it's the ballerino's turn, I cross my fingers for him. It must be really humiliating to be the only boy—almost as humiliating as being the only twenty-five-year-old.

He gets through one and two with ease and, I must say, a certain amount of style. But a long, lingering pause follows position three.

Come on, you can do it. Right foot turned out twelve inches in front of the left, right arm in front, left arm by your ear. Come on, ballerino!

The *y*'s begin to stir; they mutter little insults between them. A surge of mumbled giggles echoes through the studio. The *y* who's laughing loudest turns to me with a devilish sort of smirk. So, being the mature and sophisticated adult I am, I stick my tongue out at her.

He finally remembers fourth position, and does fifth with aplomb, holding it until Vera says, "Thank you."

This means only one thing—time for me to fake an ankle injury. Oh, come on. It always worked in gym class.

"Way to go," I whisper to the ballerino as he gets back in line.

"Hey," he whispers, "ignore them."

"Huh?"

"Pretend like they're not there."

I manage to stammer out a little "Thanks."

Ignore them. Pretend they're not there. His words swirl around and around in my mind as I walk slowly to the mark on the floor. He wasn't nervous at all. He went out there and did his thing.

Ignore them. Pretend they're not there.

The sea of *y*'s are just aching to laugh at me, I can see it in their beady little eyes. I mean, the beady little eyes of those that aren't twirling their hair or picking their noses. The others, though—the others are ready to pounce at any little misstep I make.

Vera says, "You may begin."

First position . . . ah, right . . . heels together, arms how? *How?* Low circle! Done. Transition, and . . .

Second position, heels facing one another, feet shoulder

width apart, arms . . . it rhymes. Wide and to the side! Transition and . . .

Third position, feet turned out but together, arms wide and to the side. I am so kicking ass. Transition and . . .

Fourth position, feet turned out right in front of left and arms . . . Oh, shit. The mothers are coming in. They're creeping in slowly and quietly, but the mothers are watching me. What the fuck? You couldn't wait two more minutes? Arms, fourth position. Is it right up, left down? Left out, right up? The *y*'s rattle their cages, whisper to one another. I feel my face go all hot and red. I glance quickly over to the ballerino, who is gritting his teeth and has his right finger pointed at me and his left pointed up. Ah-ha! Right arm out front, left arm by your ear. Hallelujah, thank you! Transition and . . .

Fifth position, feet turned out heel to foot, low circle with the arms and done! I dash back to my spot in line.

"Thank you," I whisper.

As I catch my breath, I'm already dreading the next class and my next "performance." Maybe I should quit while I'm ahead.

CHAPTER Twenty-six

Spent a leisurely afternoon touring the Greek and Roman art section of the Met, and have come to the conclusion that it will take a decade of Sundays to see everything. Yet another downturn in my plan for speedy transformation. So far, I have spent all of five minutes on a horse, bombed three job interviews, embarrassed myself in front of a roomful of eight-year-olds, and grossly underestimated what a year's supply of flat Hostess Cupcakes looks like.

I take a detour on the way home and stop by Brock's for some sugar therapy. (Yes, I did eat all three candy bars. So sue me.) I pick up too many smokes and too many calories, but I earned them, damnit!

A hazy spring evening descends on the city, and I desperately wish I had someplace to go. Number 4 on the Life Plan is dangerously close to the back burner these days. What can I do?

How can you find a boyfriend without prowling for one? And I have no one to prowl with. Audrey has no need for prowling anymore, and Veronica is all Iceland, all the time.

Sadly, I don't know any other guy-snagging technique but the pack method; Audrey and Veronica are such excellent bait. Plus, prowling with them means two people to talk to in case of meat market man-drought, and two backup Mace canisters in case of weirdo stalker types. Of course, in this arrangement I usually get the leftovers. But then, I'm one of those crazy people who enjoys the day-after-Thanksgiving turkey sandwich more than the actual turkey dinner.

Halfway through *Center Stage* and my phone rings. I want to let it ring and finish watching the bulimic ballerina screw up her relationship with the cute caterer, but curiosity gets the best of me.

"Hello?"

"Ryan, it's Charlie. Listen, I've got a problem."

"Does it involve a dead hooker?"

"No." He laughs.

"Bail money?"

"No."

"Spies, drugs, or federal law enforcement?"

"No."

"Okay, then, shoot," I say finally.

"It's my computer, I can't get it to do . . . anything."

"What kind is it and what are you getting when you turn it on?" I say quite professionally, if I do say so myself. "Any error messages?"

"I've tried the tech help over the phone. I still can't make any sense out of it." He takes a long, loooong pause. "Do you think you could come over and take a look at it?"

My turn for the long, loooong pause as I wait for the sky-rockets-in-flight feeling to dissipate. "Sure, okay."

Turns out Charlie lives in the West-freaking-Village. Only one of the most expensive areas of Manhattan, with its low-rise brownstone and brick apartment buildings and their 1880s charm and sophistication. Artists and yuppies, so many artists and yuppies. It's the perfect place for perfectly cool Marisa to live. I'm sorry, does that sound bitter?

I hit the fabulous brass buzzer by the fabulous white tag that reads *Campanella/Cavanaugh* (fabulousness implied). Need I add, it is one of only *four* little tags for the whole building.

Charlie's voice comes through loud and clear. "I'll be right down."

In a matter of moments he opens the door and leads me into the—you guessed it—fabulous lobby. It's an odd arrangement that I've never seen before: one neat row of brass mailboxes and four large doors, two on either side of the room.

Charlie approaches the second door on the right and pulls it open to reveal an elevator. Oh. My. God. Private keyed elevators—why didn't I think of that? Maybe because, having never seen one in person, I thought they were a figment of some ambitious real estate broker's imagination.

I get into the elevator and try not to look overwhelmed by the staggering luxury of Charlie's lifestyle. I'm feeling a little dizzy with it, or could it be the cologne he's wearing?

"Did you have any trouble finding the place?" he asks while fighting to fit the elevator key in its slot.

"No, not at all." I just followed the champagne cracker crumbs left by all the wealthy young fabulous people.

We reach the fourth floor, Charlie slides back the elevator door, and I literally gasp. It is, quite possibly, the most awesome apartment in the history of apartments. A bank of slender floor-to-twelve-foot-high-ceiling windows, arched doorways, a wall of built-in bookcases, pressed tin ceiling. Is that a plasma TV? I can't take it all in. Thankfully, Charlie doesn't notice—or ignores my complete lack of composure at the sight of it.

"Come on in," he says, closing the elevator door behind me. "The computer is over there." He points to a sleek mahogany desk across the room. I consider asking him for a map.

"Hey, Charlie? When you live in New York, and you have an impressive apartment, it's customary to give a brief tour and show it off." Was that rude?

"Oh, sure!" he says agreeably.

He walks into the center of the massive living/dining area and spreads his arms wide. "This is the living room." Damn, men. I need details! Where on earth did you find a ten-foot-long suede sofa, Charlie? Are those vintage Eames chairs? How long did it take you to find lampshades in that shade of cream? I almost wish Marisa were here—almost.

It's staggering what four years can do. I remember Charlie and his roommate Jeff's apartment in college as being very, well, male. If I recall correctly, the central decorative elements were old multicolored Christmas lights, a world-class collection of beer cans, and a single poster of Gillian Anderson surrounded by candles in shrinelike fashion. This place is so sleek and untouchable, so put together. He obviously lives here, though. Hanging over the fireplace is an insanely large black-and-white photo of him and Marisa prancing on some beach.

Charlie disappears behind a wall—oops. Should probably follow.

"This is the kitchen," he says. Sub-zero fridge with transparent doors, very eating-disorder–friendly. That explains a lot.

He leads me through a wide hallway, points to a room, and says, "Bathroom." He walks a little further and says, "Master bedroom and a bathroom through there." He then turns around and heads back down the hall, opens a door, and says, "Guest bedroom in here." Damn you, crazy man! I want to see the master . . . the guest bedroom. The guest bedroom is Charlie's. A pair of beautiful guitars are displayed in the corner. A poster of the first live show Charlie ever promoted is framed and hangs on the main wall; it's the same one that was tacked up over his bed in college.

"This is your stuff," I say without thinking.

"Yeah, my junk doesn't go with the rest of the place. So I get a nook." He's smiling, trying to play off the Aren't-women-funny? routine, but I sense more than a little bitterness just below the surface. He turns around and goes back to the living room.

I follow right behind. "This is the computer?"

"Yeah. You think you can save her?"

"I'll see what I can do."

"Great. I'll be in the next room. Yell if you need anything."

"Okay."

My first impression of the laptop is that it should be in a museum. This sucker is about two steps above a Commodore 64. You'd think with all this money he could invest a little in a new computer. I suppose it shouldn't surprise me, men sometimes form very personal and sentimental bonds with their hardware.

I push the ON button. No response.

First things first: check the battery.

It appears to be in properly, but may not be charging. Okay . . .

Next, check the plug. You would be amazed how many people fail to check the plug when their computer acts up. The plug into the laptop itself is in right. How about the one to the wall . . . ? What is . . .

Uh, is that a top-of-the-line, three-thousand-dollar laptop tucked under the bookshelf by the desk? What? Why is there a shitty old clunker on *top* of the desk?

Charlie calls in from the kitchen, "I was just going to make some dinner. You want to stay?"

Oh. My. God. Did he ask me here for dinner under the guise of computer repair? Did he hide away his brand-new, no doubt fully functional laptop to complete the ruse? Could this possibly be happening?

Uh . . .

Footsteps approach on the immaculate antique hardwood floor. I spring up and pretend to be inspecting the old computer.

Charlie comes over, wiping his hands on a dish towel that's

draped over his shoulder. "I'm throwing some dinner together. You want to stay?"

"I . . . uh . . . Sure!"

He points to the computer. "How's it going?"

"Does Marisa have a laptop you could use, or . . ."

"No, she keeps hers at the office." Holy shit. "Problem?" Charlie says nervously.

Should I expose him or play along? I choose . . . "Well, Charlie, we did all we could. She suffered massive internal injuries that, I'm afraid, were too extensive to repair. She's led a good long life. It's time to let her go."

Charlie wrings his dish towel in mock frustration, dabs an imaginary tear from his cheek. "If you say so."

He smiles, and I smile back. And for a split second I think he knows that I know what's really going on. Luckily, we pretend not to notice.

Charlie bounds in bearing two enormous plates. "Charlie's famous three-cheese baconburgers." He jerks to a stop. "Oh, man. You do still eat meat?" he asks.

A really dirty response lies heavy on the tip of my tongue, but instead I just say, "Yep."

He looks around the room with uncertainty, approaches the dining table, then quickly turns away. "Would you mind if we ate in the living room?"

"Not at all," I say, heading in that direction.

"The dining-room chairs are so uncomfortable and—"

"It's cool, Charlie."

Just as my rear is about to sink into the sumptuous suede

sofa, Charlie shouts, "No!" I jump up and away from it, as if it were on fire. He composes himself. "Marisa doesn't like any food on the couch. Truthfully, any kind of sitting on it, food or not, makes her jumpy." He forces out a grin, but it's awkward—almost pained.

Charlie places the food on the coffee table and claims two large floor cushions for us to sit on—an indoor picnic. The floor is warm and the night sky floods in through the windows. We're too low for a skyline view, but behind the church across the street the Manhattan light pollution makes for a dreamy glow. This would be picture perfect except . . . I get the sense Charlie eats like this a lot. He has a system: cushion on floor, sit, cross legs, arrange plate and utensils. His movements are effortless yet deliberate, like a ritual repeated so often that it's become instinctive. I don't know why, but it makes me a little sad.

"You're so different, Charlie," I say, with more pity in my tone than I'd intended.

"How?" He points to my plate. "Dig in."

You're strung too tight, your personality's all boxed in. I can't really put my finger on it. Better make something up. "Well, you live like a grown-up, for one."

"Nah," he says, shoving a french fry in his mouth. "It's the money. Easier to fake it." He takes a swig of beer and continues, "Honestly, I kind of wanted to rough it, you know? Do the real New York experience. Get a little one bedroom with bars on the windows, and simplify. Like you did."

"Please, I can only *dream* of a bedroom with an actual door."

"If it helps, in my experience, getting the door is a lot more fun than trying to keep it." Charlie gazes down at his plate, idly whirling a fry in ketchup.

"Good to know," I reply, but he suddenly seems distant. To pull him back, I change the subject. "Do you like what you do? I mean, I know the money's good, but . . . ?"

He lifts his head. "I love it. I love everything about it. The music, the people, the dealing. Everything. It's what I'm meant to do, you know?"

"No. You lucky bastard," I joke.

"Oh, come on. How's the Plan going?"

"Way too slow."

Charlie takes a moment, swallows a bite of burger. "It isn't a race, Ryan."

"Says who?" I retort. "Look at you. This place, this job you love." Not to mention the perfect fiancée, who I currently want to pretend doesn't exist. "It's the same with Veronica and Audrey. My God, look at Will. He's almost a friggin' rock star. I feel like everyone's moving up, and I'm still lagging. You're all getting somewhere, you know? I'm trying, but I just don't feel like I'm getting anywhere." I may be getting carried away here. Better just shut up.

"Nobody's keeping score, except maybe you. And there's no finish line. I'm not saying don't have goals, but don't spend your life chasing some unattainable ideal. You've got to be happy in the moment, be present for every bit of your life. The good *and* the bad. . . ."

What a SoCal new-agey thing to say. A goofy grin spreads across my face.

He catches my amusement, laughs. "Okay, so I spent too much time in L.A.! But seriously"—his tone softens—"did you ever think that maybe you're just different? Special?" He locks eyes with me, and I am powerless to resist. "Maybe it'll take longer to find that great job, great apartment, great—"

"Boyfriend." Holy shit! Did I just say that out loud?

"Yeah," he says quietly. "Maybe the struggle will make it that much sweeter when it happens. Just live your life *your* way, Ryan. Nobody's gonna leave you behind."

The silence is deafening. His eyes are fixed on me with such intensity that I feel I might break under the weight of it. I should leap across the coffee table and kiss him, allow myself to melt into him and surrender. But I'm scared. No, beyond scared—I'm petrified. What if I'm misinterpreting his meaning? What if I'm just so easily sucked in to his hypnotic eyes and gorgeous lips and strong arms that I *think* I'm getting the kiss-me vibe from him, but he's actually not giving it? He might actually be giving it. Holy shit.

But what if he's not?

Have. To. Say. Something. "You should really be giving seminars. Or have a talk show. You're better than Dr. Phil," I say with a smile.

And he laughs, a howling, effervescent Charlie laugh. There he is. My first real glimpse of the old Charlie—*my* Charlie.

"I don't think I'd classify it as the end of civilization as we know it," I say.

"Mark my words. If things continue like this, it'll mean the end of all rational thought. There won't be any room for creativity or experimentation or . . . soul," Charlie replies, brandishing a clenched fist to emphasize his point.

"We're talking about Justin Timberlake here, Charlie, the guy can't pick out his clothes without a team of stylists. You think he's got some evil master plan?"

Charlie raises an eyebrow, gives me a sly smirk. "You have a crush on him, don't you?"

"I do not!" I say half believably, half guiltily. Charlie stares me down, knowing it's a fib. "So I appreciate his skills on the dance floor," I admit.

"Do you own a CD?"

I make a face and roll my eyes. "I've downloaded one or two tracks. . . ."

Charlie lets out a triumphant "Ha!" then smiles and points at me.

"Only the duets with legitimate rap artists! I swear!"

"Shorty, you so fine!" Charlie mocks.

"Shut up!" I laugh, bury my head in a floor cushion. "He's cute, okay? What can I say, I'm a sucker for blondes." Oops. Freudian slip of some kind. Basically I just said, "I'm a sucker for *you*, Charlie."

Charlie springs to his feet and begins an impressively lame beat-box attempt while imitating the semibreakdance moves of J.T.

He flails and gyrates. He busts out the running man and I lose my shit, laugh so hard my stomach aches. I really should start doing sit-ups or something.

"What *are* you doing?" an agitated female voice demands

from across the room. The shrill echo terminates my laughter like a head-on collision.

I whip around to see Marisa standing in the elevator with an armful of shopping bags. She glares at Charlie, studies me. I am exposed, caught doing something sordid and shameful. Naked, miserable, sleazy.

"Oh, hi!" Charlie says, a gossamer-thin veil over his panic. "Ryan and I were just catching up."

"And it required visual aides?" she bites.

"Something like that," he says.

I want to get up and dive for the elevator, but I know it would make things worse. A quick exit would only amplify the weird adulterous vibe that seems to be radiating from my general vicinity.

Charlie blurts, "I could use some ice cream. Any takers?"

What the hell is he talking about? Ice cream?

"Yeah," says Marisa, putting her bags on the floor.

Charlie disappears into the kitchen, and Marisa struts to the sofa. She lounges casually, embraced by its downy suede perfection. I try to sit up straight, contemplate getting up and sitting in a chair. I feel like a defendant on *Judge Judy* with Marisa filling in on the bench, looming above me on her comfortable throne. Bringing myself to her eye level may constitute contempt of court.

I should break the tension with some good old-fashioned modern American female chitchat. You know—mascara, highlights, exfoliation. "I love your jeans," I say in as easy and friendly a tone as I can summon. "Earl?"

"Yeah. Thanks." Here's where you're supposed to tell me

where you got them, Marisa. What a great deal they were. An anecdote about the crazy salesgirl. Anything!

She resumes her silent appraisal of the situation, letting her eyes dance over the messy dinner plates on the coffee table, my shoes and purse in a little pile by the fireplace. I can see the wheels turning in her head, constructing all sorts of lurid explanations.

I want to tell her that we really *were* catching up, that we really *hadn't* done anything wrong. I would, of course, leave out the little bit about her fiancé luring me here with tales of a broken laptop. But who am I kidding? It wouldn't come out right.

Let's try this again, "Your shoes are fabulous."

"Thanks. Christian Louboutin."

"Oh. Nice." For four hundred bucks.

Charlie calls from the kitchen, "Babe?"

"Yeah?" Marisa and I *both* yell back in unison.

Holy shit. Holy fucking shit. Did I just do that?

Marisa turns back to me. As if in slow motion, I see the vengeful scowl form on her face—fury, shock, and irritation.

Holy shit. Holy fucking shit. My body says, *Dive! Dive! Torpedoes in the water!* Recover, Ryan. Recover!

I let out a strained and uncomfortable chuckle. I knock my fist against my head in the universal What-a-dunce! sign. Marisa doesn't seem to get it.

"I . . . I'm . . . he was talking to you, obviously." I squeeze out a weak smile.

Marisa's viper look blows Veronica's right out of the water. It is so insolent and penetrating, I feel like I'm being physically assaulted.

In one swift motion I slip my shoes on, gather my bag, and stand. She doesn't break her glare for even a moment.

From the corner of my eye I see Charlie walk back from the kitchen, but the force of Marisa's stare pushes me straight into the elevator.

I stutter, "It's not . . . I'm sorry I . . . I'm just going to go now," and then hit the DOWN button several thousand times.

CHAPTER Twenty-seven

"I should've said something like 'You can glare at me all you want. I made a mistake. I'm sorry, but I want my ice cream . . . bee-otch.'"

"I don't know what I would have done in that situation," says Audrey sweetly. "I think you handled yourself pretty well."

"I ran away, Audrey. I always run away. It's a pattern I'm beginning to think I need to address. I either run or I hide, or both. And it's starting to get on my nerves."

"Mine too," says Veronica, bounding into the room.

Fifteen floors up, in a high-tech Wall Street conference room, Veronica is in her element—very much the bitch-on-heels. We're ostensibly here to help her prepare for an important Icelandic presentation.

"Thank you for your warmth and understanding, Veronica," I say sarcastically.

"I'm sorry. I promise we'll get through the Charlie-slash-Marisa the Wicked situation after the prep, okay?"

I begrudgingly nod in agreement. Audrey and I take our seats at one end of the long glossy table. Veronica drops two massive folders in front of us.

Audrey flips through her folder. "What is it we're supposed to do?"

"Just quiz me." Veronica takes her post at the other end of the table, clutching a remote control for her PowerPoint presentation. She stretches out her neck and shoulders like a prize-fighter prepping to take on Tyson. "I've highlighted the most important bits, but anything is up for grabs. So hit me at random." She gets serious. "Let me remind you again, you cannot discuss anything you hear tonight with anyone."

"Vee vill kip your secrets, comrade," I hiss.

"Da," Audrey agrees.

Veronica pleads, "I'm serious, you guys."

I inspect my folder. The charts and graphs look like abstract pop art. The reports, gibberish. I recognize the words as English, but only every third word or so means anything to me. I tell her, "Not a problem."

After many beers on my part and much pondering and analysis on the parts of Audrey and Veronica, we came to the conclusion that I am, in fact, a big fat coward. Well, Audrey called it "seeking a place of comfort and stability," and Veronica called it "the natural consequence of a perfection-centric society." In any event, a consensus was reached. Not that I really needed The Gaf Summit on Gutless Wonders to figure it out. I've been feeling the effects of it more and more acutely lately. When I first saw Charlie again, my first instinct was to run. When I walked into the stables for my first lesson, danced in front of the *y*'s—all I wanted to do was get out of there. Running away from confrontation, from any risky situation, is my usual MO. If there is even the slightest possibility of embarrassment or awkwardness, I am gone, regardless of the *good* that might come out of the situation if I didn't run.

I've done pretty well lately with not actually bolting, but if running and hiding are out there as an option, it's only a matter of time before I pull a classic Ryan cut-and-run routine and retreat again to the safety of stagnation. If that happens, my plan, instead of being a way to get my life moving, will be a place to hide. I'll have the I'm-not-done-yet excuse to shield me from failure. I'll have the option to say "This part of the plan didn't work out" as a convenient cover story for chickenshit behavior, for conceding to fear. If I really want to become all that I say I do, quitting cannot be an option. The run-and-hide method of dealing with, well, everything has to come to an end.

Addendum to The Future of Ryan Lorraine Hadley:

49. No quitting.
50. No running.
51. No hiding.

I am resolute, I will not compromise.

It feels like someone just snatched my security blanket and shredded it into a million tiny pieces.

• • •

In a desperate attempt to have fun while complying with Marisa's demand that Delicate Blunder never leave their residences for anything not band related, Will and Ben have organized a party at their apartment tonight. This will be the first real test of the no-running-from-confrontation amendment to my plan. We'll see how long it takes before I collapse into a pile of slush like the Wicked Witch of the West. You see, Charlie and Marisa are definitely going to be there. In Will's words, "We can't *not* invite them, Ryan. I am so *so* sorry." But it's okay. I will triumph in the end. I hope. Man, if there were ever a time when flying monkeys would come in handy . . .

Nothing would make me happier than never seeing Marisa again, ever. But Charlie? I'm getting used to seeing his face. Getting to like it, in fact. For those few brief moments the other day when I could see my old Charlie, I fell right back, not in love really, but I fell into . . . extreme like with him again. However, having no grasp on his true feelings or intentions, I absolutely refuse to obsess. Oh, and there's that other minor issue—the colossal rock on somebody else's finger. I am really not the "other woman" type.

Dearest Saint Jude, give me the strength to resist his magnetism. Depolarize me, just for tonight.

Will and Ben live on the fringe of Hell's Kitchen—not that being on the fringe means any improvement in living conditions from the heart of Hell's Kitchen. It only means that Will can, in good conscience, tell his mother he lives in the Garment District without technically lying. Will's mother is a dainty, sweet southern belle who would, according to Will, promptly swoon and die if she knew her son lived anywhere with the word hell in its title.

The apartment itself isn't *that* terrible. Though, I must admit, it could be featured in a Scorsese film without much fussing by a set decorator. It's a fairly large, grungy old bachelor pad, decorated in a style I like to call "early Salvation Army." It's coated in olive green and burnt umber—Nixon chic. Ashtrays outnumber cleaning tools four to one. And adding to its charm are innumerable bits of band equipment, mike stands, amps, Ben's huge drum kit, and an impressive collection of lost guitar picks lodged in every possible crack and crevice. Needless to say, the vibe at a Will and Ben party is similar to that of a bad rock-umentary.

I arrive shortly after eight, fashionably early. Audrey greets me at the door. The distinctive, pungent aroma of Lysol overwhelms me as I walk into the kitchen. I can't help but stick my nose in the air, sniff like a dog.

Audrey sees this and explains, "I know. Great, right? I had Ben on all fours with a scrub brush."

"Audrey, you dirty girl!" I say playfully.

"Like Mr. Clean, Ryan. Not like Ron Jeremy. Ooh, only one more thing to do. I'll only be a second." She flies out of the kitchen, leaving me to my own devices.

I stick my beer in the now completely organized and sanitized fridge. I bet she even has . . . Yep, bags of ice in the freezer. I wonder what Will thinks of all this?

I pop open a Red Stripe and wander into the tidy living room, the furrows of recent vacuuming still fresh on the deep-pile goldenrod carpet. Will and Ben lounge on the sofa watching MTV2, a new pastime they're both enthralled with—culling ideas for their own video.

Ben exclaims, "Ryan, do you think we'd look tougher in a big silver box or, like, onstage in some dive?"

"I don't know." I mull it a second. "The dive probably. A big silver box could read a bit boy band, don't you think?"

"Ha!" Will shouts, sticks his finger in Ben's face.

"Thanks a lot," Ben mutters wryly.

"Anytime," I reply.

Ben gets up to change. Audrey's still on God-knows-what sort of domestic mission.

"You do realize you're hosting a party with cocktail napkins and coasters?"

Will gives me a huge smile. He scans the room for eavesdroppers and whispers, "I hate to admit it, but I'm kind of diggin' it."

I gasp in mock shock.

"I know," he says. "Bizarre."

Audrey breezes into the room. Will pats the sofa. "Come here, baby. Sit down and relax. The place looks great."

She winks at him and complies, steals a sip of his beer. Will gives her a peck on the cheek, drapes his arm over her shoulders. Audrey puts her hand on his knee. They are so comfortable, so easy—like they've been sitting like this for years. Damn, they're cute.

It takes about thirty minutes for Will's apartment to go from the quiet, almost eerie preparty waiting period to the dull roar of twenty-plus people doing their best to get completely hammered. Neighbors, Delicate Blunder's day-job friends, and the token weird old guy mingle and meander, shouting at each other over The Clash. Naturally, Veronica and I, as world-renowned life-of-the-party types, are camped out on the sofa, pounding down beers and chain-smoking.

"Do you think they'll show?" she asks between drags.

"Who?" I say stoically. Veronica rolls her eyes at me. I shift my gaze in the direction of the front door. "I don't know. I . . ." Damn. Marisa struts out of the kitchen, Charlie close behind.

"Fuck 'em," says Veronica. My only reply is a long drag of my cigarette. She adds, "Stick to your guns, Ryan."

Easier said than done, I'm afraid. An uncomfortable wooziness washes over my vital organs.

Marisa surveys the room, like a jungle cat marking her targets. Over her shoulder, Charlie does the same, though with much less calculation. His eyes land on me and he waves. Marisa, attuned as she is to any sudden movements, catches him and, without hesitation, turns her attention to me. It's official: I am no longer hater-free. In fact, I get the distinct impression that I am lunch.

I may not be able to run, but I don't have to be an easy target, either. Like other helpless wild animals doomed by their inferior position in the food chain, I will attempt to shield myself in the middle of the pack. I drag Veronica off the couch and into a round of defensive mingling.

Several pointless party conversations later—the superiority of Chicken McNuggets over other chickenlike meat products; the state of Christina Aguilera's abs; what if pencils had never been invented?—and my mingling has turned into a reconnaissance mission. The party has built to a fever pitch. The place is practically overflowing with people, and there's enough music and alcohol for Veronica and me to go unnoticed in a corner of the room. For the last hour we've done nothing but observe Charlie and Marisa.

"I'm actually getting to like this Ethel Mertz–ish sidekick thing," Veronica declares.

"I'll get Will to sing 'Babalu' for you later." I turn my eyes back to Charlie and Marisa. "Man, she is on him like glue. Very expensive, shiny, tall, thin glue."

Marisa has perched herself on or near Charlie all night. Currently, her perfectly round buttocks are half on, half off Charlie's left thigh, her right arm draped over his shoulder. She is deep in conversation with Molly while Charlie listens in.

"He seems pretty disinterested, don't you think?" I ask Veronica.

"I don't know," Veronica replies thoughtfully. "See how he's leaning into her a bit there?"

"Yeah, but his legs are facing the opposite direction. The legs are the giveaway." Several years ago I memorized a *Cosmo* article entitled "Breaking the Secret Code of Your Man's Body Language." "Look at Audrey and Will," I add. "Both with legs crossed, both turning in *toward* each other. You see?"

Veronica nods in agreement, then points back to Charlie and Marisa. "But look, he's playing with her hair while she talks to him. What does that mean?"

"Maybe there's something in there."

"Like horns?" asks Veronica.

"Ooh, he's smiling at her, see? That looks like a real smile, doesn't it?"

Molly leaves the chair across from Marisa's and, as has been the trend of the last hour, another partier swoops in to take her place. It's like people keep an eye on the seat, waiting breathlessly for an audience with Her Esteemed Royal Highness Marisa the Wicked—her throne, Charlie's lap.

Marisa adjusts her position and squeezes in next to him on the chair. She looks up to Charlie, kissing him tenderly for a moment or two. I cringe a little, look away in a desperate attempt to wipe that particular image from my memory banks.

"The kissing seems genuine," says Veronica.

I mean to say, "Yeah, it does, doesn't it?" but it comes out something like "Uh, grrr." I quiet the inner turmoil and ask, "So you think they're really in love, then?"

Veronica takes another look at the happy couple, then turns back to me. "It's hard to tell with such a short observation period. But, overall, I'd have to say"—she puts a consoling hand on my shoulder—"yeah."

The secret wish I had that Charlie was somehow reinterested in me has been completely shot to hell. He's barely acknowledged my presence and has made no effort to talk to me. He's glanced at me and smiled a couple of times, but that's it. Although, it must be said, he's spent much of the evening with at least one part of Marisa strategically draped over him. The La Mer–enhanced glow of her flawless skin is quite blinding. Perhaps being in such close proximity to her, his vision has been impaired?

Yeah, right.

My heart sinks. "I must have been imagining things."

• • •

I've avoided this long enough. The crowd is thinning, and Veronica's already made her way to the sofa with Will, Audrey, Charlie, and (cue sound effects of impending doom) Marisa. I approach in random fashion, the harder to track my true destination. Stop at the fridge, stop at the CD rack, and finally park myself on the radiator under the window, directly behind Veronica's chair.

Charlie catches me. "Hey."

"Hey," I say back. This elicits a sharp quiet from the peanut gallery.

Veronica picks up the slack and says to Will, "So, when are we allowed to hear the new songs?"

"We'll have a demo in a couple of weeks," replies Will.

"Why not tonight?" she says. "You're all here."

"You could do it acoustic," cries Audrey enthusiastically.

Will shakes his head. "I don't know if we're ready."

"Not true," says Charlie.

"I'm with Charlie," agrees Marisa, throwing her arm around his shoulder. Marisa gives me a quick glance and a tip of the head as if to say, "See, he's mine." What a freak.

"We wanted to get you guys into a couple of small venues to work out the album," Marisa says. "It doesn't get much smaller than this, does it?"

"I'll ask the guys. Maybe we'll do it later," replies Will.

Marisa takes a long pull of her beer and says, "Speaking of small venues and the demo: Will, we really need to get moving with the promo stuff. Photo shoots, start thinking about cover art, get a website up and running."

Did someone just say *website*?

Audrey reads my mind. "Website?"

"An official site, for fans. Tour dates, backstage pictures, a place to buy T-shirts. The usual," Marisa replies. "These days, a website can hit before the band does."

"I can do that." Did I just say that? I suddenly seem to be the center of attention—must have been me.

Will gets excited. "Really?"

"Yeah. Absolutely, yeah!" I say, getting a little excited myself. I mean, God. I totally know these guys. I know all about their music, the stories behind the songs. I know their image and I know web design. Holy shit, this could totally rock. "I could do a Flash site, even, something sexy and cool yet not too intimidating to someone who hasn't heard the music. I could do samples of the album—not enough to bootleg. Have you seen the Agent Provocateur site? It has a story. Yours could be something like that: a bit interactive—narrative, even. I mean, without you guys in lingerie, of course—"

"Whoa, calm down," interrupts Marisa in a sour, condescending tone. "We might need someone a bit more . . ." She fixes her gaze on me. I wonder . . . which insult will she choose? ". . . experienced. Perhaps a *professional*?" Ah, an oldie but goodie.

I say, "Of course, but I—"

Marisa turns to Will. "I've looked into a couple of small but very hip, very cutting-edge, extremely talented design firms." That bitch just cut me off. I cannot even believe it.

Veronica's about ready for a catfight, head down, eyes up, her foot tapping on the floor like a hammer. I put my hand on her arm to steady her. Everyone else just goes quiet.

Marisa, quite deliberately, threads her fingers through Charlie's.

Charlie, just as deliberately, unthreads her hand from his and gets up, saying gruffly, "I need another beer."

Marisa's face goes slack for a moment, but it so quickly returns to a serene yet conceited smile, I'm not sure anyone but me noticed. Did he just get up because Marisa was insulting me? Is that possible?

Marisa resumes courting Will like I'm some nuisance she's managed to swat away. "I've worked with several West Coast groups that would do an amazing job too. I think we should check out their work and decide on something soon."

In other words, "Fat chance, Ryan, you big dope." My God. Here I am in a corner. Even if my pride would let me, I have nowhere to run. I'm just a big fleshy lump for Marisa to stomp on. All my ideas, so quick to burst to the surface at the *hint* of doing the website, march slowly back to their dark and lonely caves deep in my brain.

My face grows hot and red. Audrey throws me a soft, silent, comforting smile, but it doesn't help. The more Marisa's insolent, disgustingly refined voice chatters on, the more I want to slap her around. Lucky for her I'm a sissy. Oops, I mean a pacifist.

No! No. I will not let this happen. I can do this, damnit. I know I can build this website. No, it's more than that: I am the perfect person to do it. I don't care how much more experience these so-called superhip, cutting-edge, *amazing* firms may have. I. Can. Do. This.

CHAPTER Twenty-eight

Marisa can kiss my ass. With or without her permission, I am building this site. I do not kowtow to self-involved psychobitches—anymore.

First things first: make sure I've got the software.

I've already emailed about a dozen quasi friends for their assistance. Quasi friends, you see, are more than acquaintances but not quite real friends. Quasi friends exchange Christmas cards and hang out when they happen to run into each other at a bar. There are no standing arrangements between quasi friends, but they're always available for quid pro quo favors. My quasi friends are all techies from college; in fact, several of them are still *in* college—the ten-year plan. Now, roughly 75 percent of all programmers secretly wish they were hackers (the other 25 percent actually are). As such, programmers are always willing to jaunt briefly on the wild side and dupe illegal copies of expensive software for their friends and family. Twelve requests made, and I'm sure to get at least eight responses.

Next, I went out and bought one of those huge sketch pads that you see people scribbling on in Central Park. Also purchased an industrial-sized kit of colored pencils. I think I actually heard my Visa screaming as the clerk rang up the total. But what the hell—no pain, no gain. With these I will scratch out some ideas for the site that I can show Will and the rest of Delicate Blunder. I will dazzle and amaze them. That is, if they can get over seeing themselves as stick figures.

Finally, I have scoured the Internet searching for inspiration. I've checked out every possible band site—fan, official, even the stalker-esque. I can totally do this. I am certain of it, because most of the ones I saw seriously bite.

I arrange to meet Will at our favorite lunch spot, one of the many midtown eateries with generous afternoon beer specials. I skip out of Geiger early and find the perfect table at The Hairy Moose.

I can't believe how nervous I am. It's odd to be so freaked out about getting together with Will. But what if he says no? What if he's too afraid of Marisa to take a chance? What if he's scared that I'll screw it up and that, in turn, will screw up our friendship? Yes, I've given this a little thought.

Okay, relax. Wipe out the doubts, Ryan. You're just meeting a friend for lunch, to discuss an idea. An idea that could be the beginning of everything you have ever wanted. No pressure or anything.

Will swaggers in, looking very much the rock star. He's got a new haircut courtesy of Marisa and Mudhoney (the SoHo salon, not the band), and a pair of shades that rival Tom Cruise's *Risky Business* Ray-Bans in their sheer unadulterated cool power. The album hasn't even been recorded, and he's already catching the attention of strangers. The female patrons of The Hairy Moose track him with their eyes, and it's not the usual flirtatious interest that any cute guy gets. It is, quite clearly, the restless curiosity of women wondering, *Who is that guy? He has to be somebody*. Amazing.

"Hey," he says, sitting down across from me.

"Hey," I reply, not knowing exactly how to broach the subject. Probably best to just get down to it, right? "Will, I have a proposal for you. You and the band, actually." I pull my big sketch pad from under the table and flip it open to the first page. "I think I'm the perfect person to do the website. I have a million ideas of how it could go, and no one knows you guys better than I do. I'm sure there are plenty of firms that could do a nice job, but I can make it great. A real extension of the music and Delicate Blunder's philosophy and image—"

"You're absolutely right," he says with a smile.

"I am?"

"Yes. We discussed it, and you are not only the number one choice but the only choice."

"We, as in . . ."

"The band, Ryan."

"You're kidding?" I say. He shakes his head. He's not kidding. "Don't you even want to see my lame drawings? I spent so much time on them," I joke.

"Ry, you can do anything you want with the site."

This is all too easy. "Tell me the truth. Are you guys doing this because you think I'm the best person to do it, or to screw Marisa?"

A sly grin creeps across his face. "I'm not gonna lie—we *are* looking forward to pissing her off—but that's mostly a bonus. You're it. You're the one. You got the job. Oh, except we can't pay you."

"I didn't expect you to. Honestly, I'm doing this as much for me as I am for you, you know?"

He reaches across the table and gives me a big Grandma pinch on both cheeks. "Baby, you're the greatest," he says goofily.

"You are such a dork," I joke. Ha! I got the job. I am going to build the Delicate Blunder website. What if I fuck it up? "Man, I hope I can really pull this off."

"Don't spaz out on me," Will replies. "Look at me, Ryan. I have no tattoos, no part of my body has been pierced or branded. I come from a family of bankers and debutantes, for Christ's sake. Not exactly Ozzy, you know? The only reason I made it this far is that I wanted it bad enough."

"Yeah?"

"Yeah," he says with a smile. Will stands, leans over, and gives me a big sloppy wet kiss on the forehead. "I gotta get back to the cell before roll call. Good luck . . . not that you're going to need it," he adds.

Oh, I'm going to need it all right. Ideas are one thing; now I have to do it.

CHAPTER Twenty-nine

I have relinquished my title as "the finest in data outsourcing," in more ways than one. I handed over the scepter, crown, and embarrassing Polaroid to a worthy successor—Betsy. Betsy seemed genuinely touched by the recognition and, having been tipped off by a "top secret" memo, even had her new boyfriend on hand for the "ceremony." It was actually kind of sweet. If I weren't so completely preoccupied with the DB website I might have felt the shame of my own less-than-gracious acceptance of Employee of the Month a little more acutely. As it is, I clapped with the other nameless faces and did my best to convey genuine admiration for Betsy's unseating me. Of course, I also repeated the words "Please don't let me be here for the next one of these," over and over again under my breath. Toward that end, I've begun the web design in earnest.

I got responses from nine out of twelve quasi friends, and as a result am now eagerly awaiting the arrival of roughly ten thousand dollars in bootlegged software, for which I will pay the handsome sum of zero dollars. Well, my ex–lab partner Robin is getting the use of my floor as her quid pro quo. She plans to spend spring break in the city. All things considered, a brilliant beginning.

Brilliant might have been an overstatement. It took me a week of thinking, twenty-four/seven–type thinking, to get it all straight in my head. I got excited about, and then quickly dumped the many thousands of too-gimmicky, too-sleek, or too-pretentious ideas. I mean, I think I'm a relatively creative person; I have no problem using my imagination. But I'm not exactly an artist. I do think, though, that I have pretty good taste. So I trust that wherever my creativity leads I will be able to separate the wheat from the chaff and make the best of it. I have accepted, however, that truly unique and startlingly brilliant are beyond my reach. For DB I decided instead to go with classy, simple, and cool. Sounds easy, right? Not so much.

I have spent the last three weeks busting my ass. I mean that both literally and figuratively. Most days were fully twenty hours of work, with biweekly excursions to meet Sherry and Vera—my very own tyrannical twosome. My sorry, flabby behind can't keep up with all the trotting and pliés. Over our last three lessons Sherry has relentlessly scolded me (in thirty-minute installments) about "the bounce," her label for the interminable and violent thumping of my backside up and down in the saddle. "Use your thighs to steady yourself," she yelled over and over. The problem? My thighs have been twitching since Vera decided to drill us on the grand plié. "Think of yourself as an elastic band," she cooed, "like a curly spring you push down, down, down, and then pop up!" More than once I wanted to pop *her*. The result of all this "improvement"? My lower half now resembles an impressionist painting in shades of lavender and green. The many hours I devoted to building the website were spent with ice under my butt and a heating pad between my legs. Not attractive, but then, I haven't had time to see anyone, anyway. Between Geiger and my in-house web design outfit . . .

Grand tally of friendly human interaction:

1. Saw Will for approximately seven minutes when picking up candid photos to use on the site.
2. Received gift of sustenance from Audrey and Veronica, in the form of a tuna sandwich on rye and an enormous plate of brownies.

Important Bits of News Exchanged:

a. Audrey and Will are apartment hunting—together.
b. Veronica has single-handedly conquered Iceland.

3. Obscenely frequent visits to Brock's for caffeine and nicotine supplements.
4. Three phone calls from Charlie. One on a Monday, a week later on Wednesday, and this week on Tuesday.

I don't know what to make of his calling so much. I only actually answered the phone on his final call, and then he just wanted to ask me directions to the place where everyone was meeting for happy hour. I provided him a detailed description of landmarks, and made him write down the subway stops and line changes. He said, "See you there." To which I responded, "I'm not going." I gave some lame excuse about working on my plan and having too many lessons to go to, as he and Marisa are on website information blackout. His response didn't involve the heaving sobs of disappointment that I was hoping for. He said, "Oh, okay. Thanks."

One of the unexpected treats of nonstop work on the website is that I haven't had time to think about Charlie. Well, I have *occasionally* slipped into daydreams of him and me sipping tea by the fire in his beautiful apartment. The two of us lounging carefree in ratty old T-shirts, playing Scrabble. Together again as the two-headed Charlie&Ryan love-monster ("Would Charlie&Ryan please refrain from heavy petting in public?"). But, all in all, fewer all-over-tingly images of Charlie than there would have been had I not been so otherwise mentally engaged. A really nice break.

Actually, this whole thing is nice. The project, the work, being busy and unreachable. Even the pain of Sherry and Vera's torture has been enjoyable, in a decidedly sick and twisted way. Frankly, just sticking with my lessons through all of this has been a victory of sorts, but there's more to it than that. Being in control of a horse—even one as docile in temperament as Starlight—and forcing my body to move in ways contrary to its default state of inertia and inflexibility have given me a great deal of satisfaction. Though I can't exactly pinpoint the specific changes the lessons have made in me, I have a general sense of accomplishment that somehow lightens my general load. It makes the chaos of a hectic schedule somehow easier to grin and bear.

I mean, I've been running around, whizzing home from Geiger with real excitement. When I'm not actually doing the work, I'm thinking about it—sitting on the train, racing from my stop to my building. Sometimes it's the technical stuff, but mostly I fantasize about how everyone will react to it, the pleasure I hope it will give them. And, in those moments, I am satisfied.

I've gotten a taste of the gratification, the serenity of usefulness and productivity. At last I understand that smiling sigh that Audrey and Veronica let out at the end of a hard day. I am finally, thrillingly, in motion. The physical pain of my classes, and many long hours in web-land, are proof of it. My aching head and throbbing thighs are only blissful souvenirs of progress.

I think the site might be done. As it is my first fully functional, non–lab-project website I can't really be sure. I keep polishing and repolishing the elements. Testing and retesting. I want it all to be perfect, smooth . . . special. I think it really might be.

I give up the ghost, shut down my computer, and wander into the kitchen. Need Count Chocula like air.

The front door buzzer rings out its loud, irritating drone.

"Delivery for a Ryan Hadley," cracks the voice through the intercom.

"I'll be right down," I say, trying not to sound too excited—which, of course, I am.

The words *I got a package! I got a package!* loop around my head in singsongy fashion as I race down the stairwell. It's probably only a care package from my parents. However, there is a chance that within its overly bubble-wrapped interior lies cold, hard cash or, at the very least, candy of some kind.

I throw open the big blue door and am greeted not by a UPS man but a bike messenger with frizzy red dreadlocks. And he holds not a large craft-paper–wrapped box but a thin manila envelope. Oh, no. This can't be good.

There are only three possibilities:

1. A credit card company is desperately seeking what little available funds I have.
2. The IRS has suddenly decided to audit single women between the ages of twenty-five and thirty who own more than ten pairs of shoes.
3. I am being sued for something.

The messenger holds out the envelope to me. I put my hands behind my back.

"What is it?" I ask.

"I dunno," he says indignantly. "You gonna take it, or what?"

I lean over, peer down on the envelope. My name, my address. The return address label says *Cranky Tank Records.* Shit. My stomach turns, blood drains from my face—Marisa.

The messenger shoves the envelope at me; the corner of it pokes my ribs. "I've got, like, seven other deliveries to make, lady. You gonna sign for it?"

I've got my hand on the big blue door, ready to push my way back into the building and race up to the safety of the fifth floor. I could do it. I could . . .

If it weren't for stupid 50 and 51. Damn me and my stupid plans! No running and hiding—brilliant, Ryan.

I let out a great huff of defeat, sign the messenger's papers, and take the cursed envelope.

CHAPTER Thirty

I gingerly place the envelope on the coffee table, as I am now certain it contains an incendiary device of some kind. I sit on the sofa and stare at it.

I attempt, by relying on my limited knowledge of the film *Carrie*, to psychically will it out of existence.

Doesn't seem to be working.

Okay, I can stay perched here hovering over it for all eternity, or I can just open the damn thing and be done with it. Let's see, I've got Diet Coke, cereal, and cigarettes to last me roughly three days. . . .

Oh, screw it.

I flip the thing over and slowly bend open the metal fastener, lift the paper flap. With a pair of crusty chopsticks I spread the envelope open and carefully slide out the single sheet of paper resting inside.

Charlie's handwriting. Graceful looping *O*'s and beefy *C*'s twice the size of any other letter. Under his very sexy, um, stately Cranky Tank letterhead it says, *I am invoking Article 218 of the Hadley-Cavanaugh Friendship Treaty: If you can't beat 'em, join 'em. Be downstairs on your stoop at precisely 7 p.m. Charlie."*

Holy shit.

It has taken me three hours to prepare for this . . . thing with Charlie. Do you know how hard it is to choose the proper outfit for a possibly (hopefully) semi-illicit meeting with a questionably platonic (hopefully adulterous) ex-boyfriend? Try it sometime, I dare you. It's unbelievably nerve-wracking. In the end I chose flirty circle skirt, high-heeled retro Mary Janes and thin cotton sweater that always "accidentally" slides off my shoulder.

I step out into the balmy Manhattan evening and make a brief attempt at leaning seductively against the concrete railing. Judging by the cross-eyed glare from one of my buildingmates, probably better to sit on the steps like a normal person.

A smile keeps creeping out across my face, no matter how hard I try to curb it. I light a cigarette so as to seem casual, and scan the sidewalks for any sign of Charlie. Any minute now he'll walk around the corner. Maybe with flowers? Maybe he'll bring me peonies (though they're not yet in season), remembering that they're my favorite. Maybe he'll . . .

"Miss Hadley?" says a man standing by a gunmetal gray Town Car.

"Yes?"

He quickly opens the rear car door and stares at me. "Something wrong, ma'am?"

I think so. Something is very wrong. For a start, chauffeured cars simply don't pick me up. "That car is for me?" I say, astonished.

The driver's face lights up. "Yes, ma'am."

"Oh. Okay," I say tentatively, and subdue the wave of nausea rumbling through my belly.

I slide into the luxurious leather seat and the driver closes the door gently behind me. So far, this is the most exciting night I have ever had in New York.

The driver, Tom, as a little sign on the console names him, puts the car in drive and careens down the side street toward Third Avenue.

"Uh, Tom?"

"Yes, ma'am?"

"Where are we going? If you don't mind my asking."

"I'm sorry, ma'am, but Mr. Cavanaugh insisted that it be a surprise."

"Oh. That's fine." Correction: this is the most exciting night I have ever had in my life.

Tom brings the car to a stop. Just as I was feeling easy in the glamour . . . A ride down Fifth Avenue on a Saturday night in a chauffeured Town Car can do that to you.

Tom flies out of his seat and races to open my door. As I step out, he hands me a small envelope: "From Mr. Cavanaugh."

"Thank you," I reply. He tips his hat at me and runs back to the driver's seat.

In an attempt to get my bearings, I look, as I always do, for the street signs. Thirty-fourth and Fifth Avenue. Why does that sound so familiar?

Oh. My. God.

I lift my eyes skyward. . . . Yep, there it is. In all its massive, elegantly phallic glory—the Empire State Building.

I rip into the envelope with all the self-restraint of a two-year-old. Inside, another note from Charlie, and an observatory ticket. The note reads, *86th Floor*. I feel my face go all flush, and my feet guide the rest of me into the building of their own volition.

I make it to the elevator and, though I should be nervous, I'm not. Not at all. Even the bustling and bumping of the tourists can't wipe the silly grin from my face. But damn if this elevator isn't the slowest in the universe.

As the doors finally open and the tourists disperse, I search for Charlie's face. I calmly drift out onto the promenade.

Charlie leans with his back to the vast expanse of sky and clouds, hands in his pockets, waiting for me.

Well, I've now met someone at the top of the Empire State Building. Cross off Number 37.

"Hi," I say to him. This is my second-choice greeting. The first would be a little too brazen, I think—tackling him and ripping off all his clothes in a fit of unfettered lust.

He runs a hand through his hair. "Hi. You surprised?"

"Are you kidding? This kind of thing happens to me all the time. Last week a bored billionaire friend of mine gassed up the private jet and flew me to Paris."

He smiles that irresistible Charlie smile. "I figured, if you *have* to ignore my advice to take it slow, and absolutely insist on getting this plan finished, the least I could do is help."

"I appreciate it."

Charlie takes a glance over his shoulder, then back to me. "You wanna stroll?"

"Sure."

He holds out his left arm for me to take. Heart melting. Knees wobbly. I am losing it here.

We gaze out over the city so massive, yet so tiny from this distance. The sunset causes great black streaky skyscraper shadows to dampen out entire city blocks. All of Manhattan looks orange and black, a wild warm glow washing away the mess of it all. The haphazard clusters of buildings seem tucked under a sheet of mango-colored linen. It takes my breath away.

Charlie steers us clear of the field trippers and whining families to an area next to the railing, overlooking Midtown, Central Park, and well beyond.

I am quickly mesmerized by the dancing flicker of millions of bathroom lights going on and office lights going out. Cabs zooming this way and that, like yellow bugs scurrying aimlessly through a maze.

Charlie breaks my silent urban reverie. "It's pretty incredible what people can do. Isn't it? I mean, here was this little island with nothing on it. And now there's this."

"Correction," I say. "A couple hundred years, millions of people, a few trillion dollars, and then this."

"Yeah, but still . . ." He smiles.

I recognize that awe-inspired expression. "Look at you! It happened, didn't it? You got sucked in," I kid.

"In more ways than one." He turns his eyes to mine and looks into me, deep and penetrating; the intensity, once so familiar, now makes me want to scream. A wave of frustration, the natural outcome of insincere emotional restraint, forces me to look away.

After a moment he asks, "Can I ask you something personal?"

I hate that question. Has anyone ever actually said no to that question? "Sure."

"The reasons you didn't go to L.A. . . . all that stuff. Are you over it?"

How am I to respond to that? Damnit, Charlie, you're engaged. We're supposed to be friends, and nothing more. If I fall for you again, I could be crushed.

The tension grows in our little corner of the promenade; a mushroom cloud of confusion, swirls of dusty old memories rise over my head.

"You think too much, Ryan," he says finally.

"Oh, really?"

"Just answer the question. Are you back in the dogfight, zooming through the straightaways, taking on the courtroom?"

What the hell is he—Oh, got it—the dork. "Tom Cruise-ian psychology?"

He gives me a wry chuckle.

"You're on to a whole new brand of crazy, you realize that?" I respond.

"Answer the question."

I let out a reflexive sigh. "I think so." I'm not sure that's exactly true, but for now it's the only answer I've got.

I desperately want to ask him a question in return. I want details of his love—or lack thereof—for Marisa. The words are right on the tip of my tongue, ready to spring out onto him. But no sound comes out of my mouth, only a puff of flaccid hot air. So I return to staring at the darkening sky, the brightening skyline, and pretend not to notice that Charlie's arm is grazing mine.

Tom opens the car door and ushers Charlie and me in with aplomb.

"This was great, Charlie. Thank you."

He raises an eyebrow and declares, "Oh, we're just getting started." He leans forward. "Tom, next stop, please."

CHAPTER Thirty-one

The car pulls into a darkened alley off Forty-ninth Street; it looks a tad like a set from *The Sopranos*, but I have yet to see a single baseball bat, and no one has offered me anything I can't refuse.

The only light comes from a sputtering halogen bulb over a set of battered steel doors, the words EMPLOYEES ONLY stamped across them in large white letters.

"Here we are," says Charlie. Tom opens the car door.

I have no idea which part of my plan this is. I don't recall a single goal involving an alley.

Charlie gives me a sly smile and bangs his fist on the letter O in ONLY—two knocks . . . pause . . . one knock . . . pause . . . three knocks. The door creaks open, behind it a semifamiliar face. Someone from college, maybe? Charlie shakes hands with mysterious door guy and he quickly leads us through a dimly lit series of hallways and stairwells.

We walk through another wide doorway; the sound of my shoes echoes and bounces around—a hardwood floor, cavernous space. It has a musty smell, and paint, and . . .

"You ready?" asks Charlie.

"I don't even know where I am."

He takes my hand to guide me through the darkness. This is good enough, the holding-my-hand part is really all I need. Should have put that in the plan.

He turns to face me. All I can see are his eyes.

"We're at Forty-ninth and *Broadway,*" he says calmly.

"What?" I yelp.

He calls out, "Steve!"

A whirring sound, several loud clicks, and the whole place lights up in a wave.

I am in the middle of an enormous stage in a Broadway theater. Velvet curtains, orchestra pit, a towering balcony section. Behind me is an intricate set, a Victorian parlor.

"Holy shit. How did you . . . ?"

"I'll tell you later," Charlie says, "but we don't have a lot of time. I picked a song for you; I hope you don't mind. Something I think you know all the words to."

"Huh?" I really need to get some new material.

A voice cries out from somewhere in the distance, "Ready to go?"

Charlie gives the thumbs-up sign. Says to me, "Break a leg." He runs off the stage, then darts up the aisle and takes a seat at the end of the fifth row.

A spotlight strikes me in the face like lightning, a throbbing bass line rumbles over the empty seats.

Is this Delicate Blunder?

Oh, my God, it is. It's "Slant." Okay, I do know all the words. Okay. So why do I feel like I'm going to pass out? Thank God this song is fast and furious, and that Will doesn't sing so much as scream the words.

I clear my throat and get ready for the first verse.

Here it comes.

Will's voice cries out through the theater—without Will present. A little creepy.

My voice comes out like a murmur.

I'm really not *trying* to be quiet about this. But the spotlight is so bright, and the room so incredibly large . . .

Charlie beams at me from the fifth row, motions for me to up my volume. He does a little dance in his seat, points at me, and slings his signature infectious enthusiasm.

So, I give the chorus everything I've got: *"Cracked it open / Open wide / Why'd you do it / It's not mine / Mind your places / Place your bets / Best behavior / Slanted depths."*

I scream, shriek, and wail my way through the song. I gyrate, I dance, I make faces which seem appropriately rock star–ish.

Finally, the last word from Will (and me), the last strum of Dane's guitar.

I did it. I can't believe I actually did it. I just sang on Broadway.

Charlie and Mysterious Door Guy clap. Charlie hoots and whistles, does his best imitation of a roaring crowd.

I bow to them, wave, and blow kisses to my imaginary fans.

Holy shit, cross off Number 6.

• • •

"Hungry?" Charlie asks as we streak through the streets of Manhattan.

"Starving!" I reply a little too zealously.

Charlie and Tom share a glance through the rearview mirror, and the car speeds up.

This is all so covert and spectacular, being whisked to and from these fantasies by this handsome, amazing guy. I've got to say, I'm getting a vibe from him and it is not *Back off, I'm taken.* But I don't know exactly what it *is*. He's sitting more toward me than away from me, laughing at my stupid jokes with more affection than friendship really requires. I have the deep desire to rest my head on his lap like I used to, to touch his face, to test him somehow—understand the true nature of this silly treaty, and his feelings for Marisa. But I cannot, for the life of me, summon the courage.

Charlie guides me into the bustling bar and grill with the careful, delicate placement of his hand on the small of my back. A tiny moan escapes my lips before I have the chance to stifle it.

Charlie whispers to the terminally preppy host and slips him a bill of some impressive denomination. Almost immediately, a slender waitress leads us to an intimate back-corner booth. Sitting down, I try to gather my emotions and my strength. I suddenly feel like I'm falling.

The very air in here seems dyed in muted tones of amber and honey, coating everyone with a mellow, healthy glow. The carnal aromatic mixture of champagne, roses, curry, and cinnamon swirl effortlessly, dangerously, in and out of my body. This place is a minefield of aphrodisiacs, scored by silky smooth Ella Fitzgerald ballads. I could get lost in this little booth with Charlie. I could get lost and never want to be found.

I have to understand what's going on inside that mind of his—before I get in too deep.

I wait till the orders are placed. . . .

Step one, smash hazardous sexy vibe: "So, Charlie. What's new with you?"

"Nothing, really. Work's going good. The album is coming along. I've got guys out scouting for new talent."

Step two, bring up The Wicked: "And Marisa?"

Charlie twitches a little before answering, "Fine. She's fine."

Step three, remind him he's engaged, see what happens: "Have you guys set a date?"

"For?" he asks, genuinely puzzled.

"Your *wedding*."

"Oh, right. No. Not exactly." Very interesting answer, indeed. Good answer.

Step four, attempt suggestive subtext: "It's good to keep your options open. Especially in this city, amazing and strange things happen all the time. You could be all set on one thing, and then *boom*—something better comes along."

"Uh-huh," he grunts matter-of-factly while staring at the door. No suggestive subtext in return, damnit.

"Have you two decided on a honeymoon yet?"

"We were thinking about the Bahamas, but I think Marisa's changed her mind to Italy."

"Sounds exciting. I've never been."

"Neither have I. But Marisa speaks Italian, so . . ."

Of course she does. "Oh, that's nice."

He nods.

This is not going anywhere. Step five: yell, scream, demand answers. Okay, maybe not.

Soup, salad, and salmon pass with increasing confusion on my part, and increasing agitation on Charlie's. I mean, he's participating in my nonsensical chitchat, but he fidgets through it, disinterested. He has not-so-surreptitiously checked his watch three times, and stared at the front door for approximately twenty-seven of our forty minutes here. The tap-tap-tapping of his thumb on the table is about to drive me insane. It is painfully obvious that he wants this to be over as soon as possible. I have no intention of disappointing him.

Our dirty plates are cleared from the table and Charlie shakes his head as if responding to some disturbing internal question.

"Do you want a drink? How about a drink?" he mutters.

"I don't—"

He shoots his hand up and motions to the waitress. "Excuse me!"

The waitress flutters on over to the table, "Yes?"

"A Manhattan, please. Very dry." Charlie looks to me.

"Same," I respond to his silent command for a drink order. A Manhattan is perfect. All the whiskey you need to get completely hammered, without the shame that accompanies ordering a bottle of Jack Daniel's.

The waitress scuttles away on her stiltlike legs.

Charlie goes back to staring at the door.

"Charlie, are you okay? You seem really . . ."—*Loco*— ". . . distracted."

Still looking at the door, "I'm sorry. I, uh—" His countenance changes; all the knots in his face and body melt away. He smiles a broad, easy, Charlie smile.

Okay . . . that was an almost schizophrenic emotional shift. I turn my head to see what might have caused it, but before I can fully turn around, Charlie taps my hand with his. "I've got to take a leak. I'll be right back."

Right. It's now abundantly clear to me that Charlie is a completely different, completely neurotic person. I'm sure he and Marisa have a beautiful lithium-laced future ahead of them.

The Manhattans arrive, and I rip into mine with real modern-city-girl verve—to hell with the cherry.

Charlie races back to the table, takes my hand, and pulls me to my feet. "I've got one last surprise for you tonight. I know that your plan said movie star but, contrary to popular belief, not everyone in L.A. lives next door to one." He's talking so fast I can hardly keep up. Wait, did he say *movie star?*

"What?" I say, my voice cracking. My hands start to shake, my heart to beat at a pace of roughly one thousand times per second.

"He's been in movies, but he's mostly known for TV. We met at a party in Brentwood when I was living in L.A., and then one of the bands I worked with was on *SNL* a couple of years ago. He's a really great guy, and my sister thinks he's cute, so—"

"*SNL*? As in *Saturday Night Live*?"

"Jimmy Fallon."

I gasp with such a force, I almost swallow my own tongue.

"Okay," Charlie continues, "take it easy. It's just one kiss."

"You want me to kiss Jimmy Fallon?" I yelp. The other restaurant patrons stir in their pretty little booths.

Charlie whispers, "It was on your list."

I whisper back, "I didn't think I'd ever . . ."

"Well, now's your big chance. He's back there by the phone, outside the ladies' room."

I stammer, "I don't understand, how did you . . . why would he—"

"We're always running into each other at industry things. The last time I ran into him, I just asked him if he'd do it. It didn't take much convincing, actually. I described you and told him about your plan, and he thought you sounded great so . . ."

"Holy shit, Charlie!"

"I know!" he says excitedly.

Charlie pulls a tube of Binaca from his pants pocket, says, "Open up." I do, and he gives me a double squirt of spearmint.

I give him a big false grin. "Anything in my teeth?"

"No, you're good," he replies.

"My hair? Makeup?"

"You look beautiful." He spins me around to face the restroom hall, positions himself behind me with both his hands on my back, ready to push. He puts his chin on my shoulder and whispers, "Go get him, tiger," then pats me on the butt like I'm some third-string quarterback getting thrown in with the starters. He gives me a nudge, and I tiptoe toward the restrooms.

Okay. So I am going to kiss Jimmy Fallon, cutest *SNL* cast member in the history of *SNL* cast members.

Okay, right. Goals for the next several minutes: do not giggle uncontrollably, pass out, or vomit.

He leans against the phone booth staring down at his shuffling Converse "Chucks." As I move closer, his head tips up slightly to monitor my approach. I try to look as non-psycho and friendly as possible, but I'm afraid that the waves of swoonlike tension coursing through my body may be impeding that effort. I mean, it's him. It's really him. The sinewy body, the postmodern Bumble and Bumble tousled hair, the deliciously quirky demeanor. It is actually him.

"Uh, are you Ryan?" he asks.

I tell my head to move in an up-and-down motion, but I can't be sure it's complying.

"Jimmy," he says, offering me his hand.

I flimsily shake his hand.

I'm completely unclear as to how this whole thing is to proceed. This is, after all, my first random celebrity makeout session. Am I to make the first move? Should I just hit and run, so to speak, or should there be a little get-to-know-you conversation?

Luckily, he speaks before I get the chance to screw it up, "Uh, I've never done this before." Animated correction on that point. "Not the kissing—that I *have* done. But, uh . . . I'm just going to uh . . . dive in. Does that sound all right?"

"Yeah, absolutely," I say cheerily, trying to contain the hysterical jitters now doing a mambo somewhere between my lungs and my legs.

He places his hands gently, timidly, on either side of my face. I smile in an attempt to ease his understandable shyness in this situation. And as he smiles back, I feel his hands relax, and the apprehension and discomfort between us melt into the ebony-colored walls of the hallway.

His lips are tender and sweet, yielding and responsive. His touch, gentle, delicate, sensitive—so easy, it almost borders on suave. His hair smells crisp, like lemongrass and peppermint. For one or two brief moments I slip away, out of my head and out of myself, to a euphoric metaphysical enclave where all silly, romantic, and unrealistic fantasies come true.

I mumble, "Thank you."

He replies with a wry, "No. Thank *you*."

I slowly back out of the hallway, powerless to suppress my instinctive female urges. Thus, sadly, I commence with the furious batting of eyelashes, smoothing of hair, and fits of coy giggles.

Cross off Number 16.

I practically bounce into Charlie's vicinity, throwing my exhilaration at him like so much confetti. "Oh. My. God!"

He quickly leads me by the hand out of the restaurant and onto the sidewalk, no doubt because I have suddenly become an auditory health hazard.

"Thank you. Thank you. *Thank you!*" I scream, frantically tugging on his jacket sleeve. "That was amazing!"

"I'm glad you—"

"I don't think you understand. It was, quite possibly, the most awesome thing that has ever happened to me. I've never been pimped out before, but I gotta say, I don't know what all the fuss is about. It rocks!"

"I take it, then, he's a good kisser?" Charlie asks.

"You have *no* idea!" I cheer. "I can't tell you how— Wait a second—yes I can." I take a deep breath to keep myself from hyperventilating. "Okay, so he puts his hands on my cheeks. How dreamy is that? And I won't get too graphic here but *wow*—I mean, *WOW*. Such an incredible kisser, so sweet and tender and—"

"Really?" Charlie cuts me off. He starts off down the street, moving in serpentine fashion up the sidewalk.

I race to catch up. "But that's not it. Charlie, I mean . . . it was really him and—"

"Where the hell is Tom?" he mutters.

I take him by the arms and force him to stand still, face me. "Let me finish," I implore.

"No," he mumbles.

"Charlie?"

"I don't want to hear it," he says sharply.

"What is your problem?" I bite back.

"I just don't want to hear about it." He walks away from me, looks up and down the street. "Where the hell is the car?"

I race around and get eye to eye with him again, but he looks straight over me. "Charlie," I try again. "Charlie!" He finally looks at me, though more at my nose than my eyes. "What is wrong with you?"

"Why do you have to make this a thing?" he snaps. "I just don't want to hear how *dreamy* and *amazing* it was to kiss this other guy. Is that too hard for you?"

"'Other guy'?" Is he saying what I think he's saying? I stutter out, "You mean as in . . . some other guy than . . . you?"

His face contorts a bit; his eyes squish together, making a little *V* between his eyebrows. He huffs and grumbles, then stomps away from me again.

"Answer me, damnit!" What a relief to get that one out. He continues his futile search for Tom on the horizon. I repeat at a slightly higher decibel level, "Answer me!"

He stops his pacing and throws his hands up in the air. "Yes, all right? Happy now? Yes!"

All the urge to scream and shout is sucked out of me, though more than a little joy creeps into my voice. "You're jealous?"

On his mouth, words form, then swiftly dissolve. In the end, only a sigh makes it past his lips. I think I'm going to take that as a yes.

I know I should stop, should accept what he's given, and not push it. But the tantalizing proximity of real answers is too much to bear. I approach him slowly, graze my hand against his shoulder. "Are you . . . do you love Marisa?"

"Ryan." It comes out like a plea. His eyes implore. *Don't make me say it.*

I stand my ground and demand again, "Are you in love with her?"

He shrugs my hand off his shoulder. His face goes rigid, except for his eyes. Methodical control, betrayed by two honey-brown windows. He locks onto my gaze, willing me to believe. He says, "I am."

It's a lie. It is a total lie, and this isn't my own wild jealousy talking, either. Though I can taste a hint of its bitterness on my tongue. No, he's really lying. He registers the traces of pity and sorrow on my face, and looks away. I see through him, and he knows it. A great woeful tide crashes into my chest. This incredible man has sunk to such a lonely, sad place. I know that place.

Tom pulls up in front of us. The promise of reprieve from my impromptu inquisition shows clearly in Charlie's demeanor. He opens the rear car door and points for me to get in.

A gruff "Huh" spews out from deep inside me. I grasp his forearms and whisper, "Who are you? Did I do this to you?"

He stares across the street, refusing to look me in the eye, offering no response. I reluctantly let go of him and climb into the car.

Charlie slams the door and pounds on the roof for Tom to go.

CHAPTER Thirty-two

What a grotesque encounter with irony. I thought irony was reserved exclusively for the complex and interesting. I mean, doesn't it usually involve intricate plots and schemes, startling acts of karmic retribution, and several thousand hours of therapy? Well, I guess that's what I get for switching from Lifetime to the Independent Film Channel—I was lulled into believing such a thing could never happen to me. Yet, here I am sans Charlie, even though it's painfully clear he has feelings for me, and that his relationship with Marisa is a sham.

"You're pretty much in love with him again, aren't you?" asks Audrey.

"He hooked me up with Jimmy Fallon, for God's sake. It's only natural," I reply.

"I don't think you are," declares Veronica. "I think you're in love with the *idea* of him. What you used to have, and who he used to be."

Audrey and I stare bewildered at Veronica's sudden transformation into her own worst nightmare—a touchy-feely type. I say, "You've really got to cut back on the *Oprah.*"

"I know," she replies, shaking her head. Then adds, "But I'm right."

"But he's lying, Veronica."

"Is he?" she replies skeptically.

I can only groan in frustration. I want to grab Charlie and shake him. I want to wake him up and make him mine. I want to go back to that stupid day at the stupid Mozart statue and scream "Yes!" at the top of my lungs. It's hopeless. . . .

I light a cigarette, rest my head against The Gaf's plate-glass window. Fat drops of rain slide into one another, pooling and cascading down, forming their own bloated rivers. "I can't have him. That's all. If he's bound and determined to marry Marisa, so be it. I won't even pine," I say finally.

"Now you're talking," says Veronica.

Yeah, I hope it's not just talk. I need to break this thing, nip it in the bud—again. I've got to concentrate on something that may actually benefit my future. "You know what?" I say. "I'm going to take the website live tonight."

Audrey rouses from her hunched-over drinking position. "Really?"

"Why not?" I proclaim.

"And you'll still go to the show?" Audrey asks.

The show? Shit. Delicate Blunder at someplace called Puget.

"Oh. Forgot about that." I don't mind butting heads with Charlie and Marisa, so long as it's only virtually.

"Oh, no you don't," presses Veronica. "There's no backing out now."

"Of which," I ask, "the site or the show?"

Veronica stares me down and grins. "Both."

Damn. I hate it when she's right.

I click the button on the mouse. My computer whirs, its low-voltage hum like a chorus of tiny wishes aching to be fulfilled. As much as I enjoy the feeling of accomplishment, the satisfaction of setting and meeting this goal—the beginning, middle, and end of it mine and mine alone—it will mean nothing if Delicate Blunder doesn't like it.

I pick up my cell phone and dial Will's number.

"Will?" I ask.

A swell of "Hey" and "Hi, Ryan!" ripples through the grainy crackle of his speakerphone.

"We're all here, Ry," Will says, "ready and waiting."

Oh, God, they're all together. My voice cracks: "It should be up and running."

They cheer and clap.

"We'll call you in a little bit," cries Audrey.

"Okay!" I reply.

They click off, and I sit paralyzed. What if they don't like it? What if I'm wrong and it totally sucks? What do I do then? I probably should have thought this through. I have no backup plan ready, no excuses for failure prepared. What was I thinking? Oh, that's right—failure is not an option.

• • •

I go through my going-out-on-the-town ritual to take my mind off the waiting. The getting-dressed part is easy, but my hands are shaking with such violence that I've already stabbed myself in the eye with a kohl pencil twice, and my lipstick looks like it was applied by a rabid monkey.

The phone rings and I jump straight out of my skin. Luckily, the toilet breaks my fall. Thank God, the lid was down.

I hop up and race to the phone.

"Hello?" I say tentatively.

"Ryan, it's Will," he moans gravely. Oh, shit. They hate it. I suck at web design. I was afraid of that. Deep down I knew . . . "We love it!" he says, lightening his tone.

"Seriously? You're not just saying that?" I exclaim.

"No. It's incredible. Really great. The Flash stuff is so professional."

"Thanks," I say, barely able to speak through my enormous grin.

There's an odd crackling pause then. "Hey, it's Dane. Excellent work. Really slick."

Before I can get a word out, Ben's voice rings through, notched up about an octave, "You go, girl." What a goofball.

Audrey gets on the line, "Hey, honey! I know this may sound a little silly coming from me, but I'm proud of you."

"I love you, Audrey," I reply.

"I love you, too, Ry. Now get dressed, 'cause we're going to celebrate."

• • •

I amble through the streets of Manhattan a new person, and carry out Vera's standing orders—head up, shoulders back—so easily, it's scary. The city is somehow open to me now. I don't feel so much the outsider, don't feel like I'm the only one in this city who doesn't know where they're going. It's like I've recovered some of the excitement, the promise of opportunity and success, that I felt when I first got here.

I step into the bar called Puget, and though it is new and unfamiliar, I am ready for anything. The crowd is thick; the smell of countless warm bodies and their myriad perfumes, colognes, and heavily scented hair products saturate the air. But the place has already been loosened by countless shots and pints, making the mass of people twist and swell with the jazz drifting from the speakers.

Man, so many good-looking guys here tonight. I have *got* to figure out a way to mention that I designed the website without sounding conceited. Maybe "Hey there, sexy. I'm with the band. Ever been to delicateblunder.com?" Well, maybe not.

Audrey and Veronica wave to me from the backstage entrance. As soon as I'm within arm's reach, they envelop me in a great big group hug.

"Thanks, you guys. You realize, it's only a website."

"It is not," says Veronica. "It's a *kick-ass* website."

They usher me through the door and down a greasy narrow hallway to the dressing rooms. Audrey almost opens the door, then stops herself.

"One thing, Ryan. You can't get upset, though."

"Why?"

"Just promise," Audrey says ominously.

I don't like the sound of this but "Okay, I promise."

She whispers, "Will sent the link to Charlie and Marisa."

"What?" I scream.

She points at me emphatically. "You promised!"

"I lied!" I knew it would happen eventually, but tonight? As Audrey's hand turns the knob on what will almost certainly be an evening of awkward silences and thinly veiled insults, my shoulders, amazingly, do not revert instinctively back to their default position—the unattractive slump. Instead, I raise my head higher and fortify my sensitive bits against the coming assault.

We enter the dressing room, if you can call it that, and I am instantly assailed by a barrage of backslaps and hugs from Delicate Blunder and a few additional waves from the ever-increasing entourage. There's Molly, of course, but Ben and Sammy have apparently become very popular with the wannabe groupie crowd. There are no less than five fairly pretty rock-and-roll–girlfriend types displaying themselves on countertops and chairs. They all have long floppy limbs and that perpetually bored/jaded facial expression most commonly found in Prada ads. I guess the rumors are true: a record deal = ass.

Lounging ever so comfortably on a grungy sofa is Marisa. She leans back like a centerfold, crossed arms plumping up her breasts. One leg hangs over the other, showing off her willowy thighs in jeans that cost more than my weekly salary. I wonder how long it took her to master that routine?

Fortunately, she doesn't acknowledge my presence. But

there's no way she doesn't know I'm here. Charlie, who sits beside her like a lump of useless man-clay, glances at me for three and a half nanoseconds, then looks away. I suddenly find it very hard to feel sorry for him.

The door behind me swings wildly on its hinges and smacks me hard on my massive rear. The head of Jerry Garcia, or a reasonably close facsimile, peeks into the dressing room. He calls out, "Marisa Campanella!"

Marisa unknots her willowy limbs and saunters across the room. I do my best to scoot out of her way but unfortunately can't avoid scampering through her line of sight. She sweeps by me with a flick of her hair and stabs me in the eye with one of her split-less ends.

The very second Marisa is out of the room, Charlie leaps to his feet.

He tiptoes toward me.

"The site is good," he says in an almost believable tone.

"Oh, yeah?" I bite.

"Really good."

An uncomfortable silence ensues in which Charlie strains to think of something to say, and I won't let him off the hook by either talking first or walking away. I stand stoically, poised and calm. I can do this all night if you make me, Charlie.

Charlie finally opens his mouth. "I wanted to say—"

Marisa blows in through the door like she's been waiting for her cue to bust something up. She says, "Ryan, what a pleasant surprise." Wow, good thing she didn't go into acting.

"Good to see you, Marisa," I say coolly.

"We saw the website."

"Yes, Charlie was just telling me." Charlie shoves his hands deep in his pockets and looks only at Marisa. You are in control of this now, Ryan. Hit her. "What do you think?"

Marisa smiles in that way that all predatory carnivores do—teeth exposed and clenched—showing me her superiority by displaying her expensive cosmetic dentistry. "It's nice." "Nice" comes out like a hiss.

Do not feed the animals, Ryan. "Thank you," I reply warmly.

She flicks her hair again, chuckles nefariously. "And it saves us from having to pay someone to do it. Isn't that right, Charlie?" She paws at his neck.

Charlie's only reply is an apathetic tilt of the head.

Delicate Blunder takes the stage to a standing O from the crowd. Well, most of the people don't have chairs, but even those who do are standing up.

Will graciously accepts the applause, then quiets everyone with a wave of his hand. He takes the mike and shouts, "Big news. Tonight we launched delicateblunder-dot-com." The hardcore fans scream back and clap like crazy. Will catches my eye and points. A million (or so) hungry eyes scan our table. He continues, "And it's all thanks to our good friend Ryan Hadley."

Veronica and Audrey each grab one of my arms and raise them triumphantly in the air. A wave of admiration strikes me head-on. A couple hundred strangers who, it must be said, haven't had time to even see the site pour out their happiness—at me. Because of me. I did this.

As casually as I can, I give a beauty queen–ish wave back to them and sit down. Still eyes fixed on me, still with the staring—and I like it. Especially since some of those eyes are lodged in handsome faces. Unfortunately, Charlie's is not one of them.

"Who does your hair?" asks one of the pouty hangers-on.

There is brief moment of flattered shock before I realize she's talking to Marisa.

"I haven't been able to find anyone here. I think I'm going to have to get back to L.A. for a trim," she says coolly, as though this is something reasonable and expected.

Veronica rolls her eyes for the thirteenth time in the last five minutes.

The whole situation at our table is about as bizarre as it gets. I am sitting here across from Charlie, who hasn't taken his eyes off the stage for even a second. Meanwhile, Marisa and the floppy-limbettes have perfected an air of casual disinterest at their surroundings. They join in the applause at the end of each song but aren't actually paying attention to the performance.

We should be dancing, damnit. We should be hanging off the edge of the stage like the girls-with-the-band we are. Instead, Audrey and Molly have lapsed into love-induced trances, unable to do anything but make goo-goo eyes at Will and Dane. Veronica is enthralled with eavesdropping on, and rolling her eyes at, Marisa. And I, sad and petty as it may be, am having way too much fun making Charlie uncomfortable. He slouches, he squirms, and still I stare and wonder. I stare and silently ridicule. I stare and wish that I could hit him with something.

Must probe his frozen innards. "Ben's doing better with the bridge."

"What?" Charlie asks.

"Ben. He's handling the bridge better than he used to. He had trouble with the tempo change." I really hope I'm getting all the lingo right. Will yammered on to me about Ben and the stupid bridge to this song, like, four months ago.

"Oh. Yeah." He turns back to the stage.

Marisa leans over to Charlie, pokes him in the arm. "Honey, guess what? Kimber knows the guy who does special-event booking at Blue Fin."

"Good," he replies halfheartedly.

Marisa pokes again. "You know what this means? We might be able to get it for the rehearsal dinner."

"Good," he repeats. His attention wanders back to the stage.

Marisa shakes her head at him, for the benefit of her newfound minions—oops, I mean confidantes. "He's been so touchy since we heard that my dad is coming to town. I think he's nervous."

The hanger-on—the one who apparently calls herself Kimber—coos, "Awwww, that is soooo sweeeet."

I think Veronica's eyes may spin right out of her skull.

Marisa melodramatically smiles at Kimber and lovingly caresses her engagement ring. "That's Charlie."

A great rush of bile and beer threatens to make its way up my esophagus.

Another girl asks, "This'll be, like, the first time they meet?"

"Oh, God, no," Marisa says with flourish. "My dad gave Charlie his first job in the business. That's how we met."

Veronica suddenly perks up, elbows Audrey, and gives me a look that says *Are you hearing this?*

Kimber resumes the hollow cutesy routine. "Awww, did your dad, like, bring him to dinner and then you fell madly in love?"

"It was courtside at a Lakers game," Marisa claims proudly. She leans over to Charlie and kisses him dramatically on the cheek. She glances at me, then takes Charlie's hand in hers—yanking him out of his Delicate stupor.

Veronica switches over to viper mode and crashes the conversation. "So, Marisa, that would make your father . . . what, exactly?"

"Now he's the CEO." Holy shit.

Veronica pushes gently, as if she were leading a scared lamb to the slaughter. "Of the record company?"

Charlie swallows hard and squeezes Marisa's hand—so hard that her fingernails look like they're about to pop off. Marisa squints at Charlie, then says, "Yes."

Oh. My. God.

"So technically that makes him your boss?" continues Veronica.

This is all beginning to make sense. Glaring at Charlie, I add, "And Charlie's."

Marisa notices that Audrey, Veronica, and I are slowly turning red and are shooting a torrent of tiny invisible daggers straight between Charlie's eyes. She raises an eyebrow and answers, "Yes."

So that's it. That's why he's lying. It all makes perfect sense. The bastard! I can't believe it! His plan—his very future—depends on Marisa. I am merely an obstacle in his plan for success. I am the one who gets crushed in his rise up the corporate ladder.

An indignant huff escapes my lips. Charlie opens his mouth

to say something to me, but my hand flies up to silence him.

Veronica grabs my arm and pulls me out of my seat. "Why don't we dance, Ryan? Isn't this your favorite song? Audrey? You coming?"

Audrey takes my other arm and they force me away from the table. But my eyes are fixed on Charlie's, hopefully communicating my contempt and disappointment.

Like two well-heeled linebackers, Audrey and Veronica plow through the throng of DB fans and push me out of sight.

"That hypocritical bastard," I scream. "All this time, the one thing keeping us apart is nepotism? Nepotism! Veronica, you were so right about me liking the old him. I don't even know who he is now. I have no idea who he is."

Audrey strokes my back. "Don't worry about him, Ryan. Let it go. He'll get his punishment being married to Marisa."

"I don't want to punish him. I want to slap him."

Veronica takes my hand in hers. "He's not your responsibility anymore."

I spot Charlie heading to the restrooms. I bellow, "You think?"

CHAPTER Thirty-three

Audrey and Veronica call after me as I race toward the restrooms, trying to warn me off and calm me down from a distance. Luckily for my wavering nerves, their cautionary screams are muffled by Delicate Blunder pandemonium.

The hall to the restrooms is eerily empty, no crush of perfumed women impatiently waiting their turn. I'll just stand here and wait till he comes out, collect my thoughts, and . . . What the hell am I talking about?

I pound my fists on the door and march in. Immediately, three heads whip around at me. I set my hands on my hips, make myself an immovable object. Two of the men swiftly shift their focus back to the urinals, finishing their business as fast as they can. Charlie's jaw drops to the sticky brown floor.

"Jesus, Ryan!" he yelps before turning back around.

"Oh, please. Don't you dare 'Jesus, Ryan' me."

The other guys scurry out, clearly not wanting to get caught in the crossfire.

Charlie faces me. "I wanted to tell you. I thought about it hundreds of times. I couldn't think of—"

"Zip it," I command.

He closes his mouth tight and rolls his eyes at me indignantly, like a teenager steeling himself for word of how many months he's to be grounded.

"I actually meant your pants, but the shutting-up thing is good too."

Charlie scowls at me while he zips his pants. His tone softens. "I know your feelings are hurt, and I'm sorry, but—"

"*My* feelings? Fuck *my* feelings. I'm here about you. Granted, I feel a bit cheated—and angry. But that's beside the point, Charlie." I take a deep breath. "What are you doing? Do you *know* what you're doing?"

"I—"

"Wait. First I'd like to ask you something. Was dating Marisa your *way* to the top, or was it sort of a thank-you gift to her father? Like, 'Oh, Mr. Campanella, to show my gratitude for your helping me be a success, what do you say I marry your daughter?' "

"Ryan, you have no right to—"

"Really? How about this one, Charlie: you told me I should live my life, my way. Was that some kind of Do-as-I-say, not-as-I-do advice? I mean, is *this* really your way, Charlie? Is this . . . *relationship* with Marisa, if you can call it that, how you saw yourself getting what you wanted in life?"

Charlie crosses the small room, shies away from looking in

the dirty mirror. He folds his arms tight over his chest and leans a shoulder against a paper escort-service flyer taped to the wall. "You don't know what it's like out there, Ryan. The competition, how many people fail because they don't know the right people . . . I have nothing to be ashamed of."

Who *is* this person? "You don't think I know where you are, Charlie? I know what it's like to take the easy way. True, yours has considerably more perks than mine did, but I guarantee you'll regret it just the same. Don't you already? Even a little?"

He rolls his eyes at me.

I respond, "Being at Marisa's beck and call, doing everything in your power not to ruffle her pristine feathers. You've got your lips so firmly planted on her ass, I'm amazed you can even talk."

"Cute, Ryan. Very cute," he says acerbically.

"Can you really see yourself doing that till death do you part? Or are you planning to divorce her once you make it to the top? Don't you think you're losing a bit of yourself in all this?"

"Give me a break. That's a bunch of glossy fashion magazine psychobabble." Oh, boy.

"You know what's sadder than your lying to me? Lying to yourself." I stomp over to him, force myself into his personal space. "Life is fucking scary, okay? But you know what I finally figured out? You've got to take a chance. When you play it safe and easy, the victories are hollow and meaningless. Then you wake up one day and realize you've been sleepwalking and wasted all this time on crap that doesn't make you happy."

He turns away. Oh, no—you can't avoid me, Charlie. I go

nose-to-nose and toe-to-toe. "You think failure freaks you out? Wait till you find out that you're fine and nothing more. Wait till you realize that you've spent your life avoiding the scary stuff, at the expense of really living your life. Let me tell you, that'll *really* freak you the fuck out."

His expression is suddenly so empty, so sallow—the violent jolt of truth smashing into rationalizations. All the anger, the bluster of my argument, drifts away, and I just want to console him, repair the damage I've done.

The desire to touch him is too great to resist. I gently place my hand on his face, stroke his strong, smooth jaw line—and he doesn't turn away. He trains his honeyed eyes on mine. At this distance, the smell of his skin hits me like a hammer, its soft manly purity made even more striking against the stench of industrial cleaner permeating the place.

I take a deep whiff of him and whisper, "*You* are special, Charlie." With my heart in my throat, I press my lips firmly on his. Tears trickle down my face and land on his cheek. "Don't waste it."

His face is a mottled mix of grief and rage. He is still, but I know how his insides are churning. I remember the feeling, the swells of panic and disappointment.

I have changed the trajectory of my life. I see that now—through Charlie's eyes. The simple act of putting it all on paper, and then putting one foot in front of the other—it changed things. It changed *me*. I know how Charlie's feeling, I was there once.

But I'm not there anymore.

I back away and step proudly toward the bathroom door, as

slowly as I possibly can. Plenty of time for him to grab me from behind and profess his undying love.

He doesn't budge.

Veronica and Audrey tackle me as I step out of the men's room.

"What did you say?"

"Are you all right?"

"Oh, God. You're crying."

"I'm okay," I say, recovering. We walk back out into the loud and chaotic revelry of the bar.

Audrey grabs a wad of tissues from her purse and thrusts them in my hand. "Come on, we'll go somewhere and get your mind off everything."

"No. You guys stay. Congratulate the band for me. I'm just going to go home, curl up with Darcy, and wallow."

"You sure?" asks Audrey.

I nod and attempt a smile. "Please. Stay and have fun."

They eye me, trying to work out for themselves my true mental state.

I repeat, "Seriously, you guys. I just need to be alone. Stay. For me?"

Veronica says, "Do you have cigarettes and tissues?"

"Yes," I reply.

"Ice cream and/or Oreos?"

"Yes."

Veronica takes my hand. "Okay. Then let's get you a cab."

In an attempt to lift my spirits, I add delicateblunder.com to my résumé. It takes roughly five minutes of editing and rereading and seven minutes of *Mansfield Park* before I stumble back into a wispy blue funk.

Fictional movie heroes no longer interest me. They can't give me what I want. The usual all-over-tingle is now more like an itch. It's an itch I can't scratch because the only thing that will sooth it is Charlie—*my* Charlie, not that guy I saw tonight in the club. I yearn for the guy I remember, the one who was unguarded and honest with himself, and . . . *fearless*. He was so fearless.

I walk out of my bathroom and imagine the old Charlie lying on the couch waiting for me, arms outstretched. I remember him standing in my kitchenette, laughing, and strain my ears to hear it. I close my eyes and try to recapture the feeling of his lips on mine. All I'm left with is fantasy—again.

As much as I've gained in the last couple of months—as hard as I've worked to make something of myself and transform—there are some things I cannot change no matter how many times I write them down on paper. I could make Charlie numbers 52 through 90, but it wouldn't change a thing. The real Charlie is gone, eaten alive by a desire to reach the top by the quickest and least demanding means. And I want no part of this new guy. This new guy is stuck, and I've moved on from there. I can't go back.

Sadly, no matter how many times I tell myself this, the old Charlie still lingers. Now that so many things in my life are looking up, I can't help but obsess on the one part that isn't. Is this how it always works? The one thing in your life that isn't quite right gets hold of your brainpower? It begs the question: What the hell does Julia Roberts think about all day?

CHAPTER Thirty-four

Vera's Park Slope Academy of Dance is in a state of utter chaos. The makeshift backstage-slash-hallway is a hurricane of pink tulle and sparkly Bonne Bell cosmetics. I splurged on my own modest tutu. Well, it's a little fluttery wrap skirt, but I bought it at Capezio, so technically it qualifies for tutu status.

This will be the final test, proof once and for all that I have vanquished the old me. I have signed on to make an ass out of myself in front of roughly forty strangers and all of my friends. This is, after all, a recital. And we all know they're not really about showing off new skills and improved technique. Recitals are little Darwinian experiments, the embarrassing results of which are to be dragged out at family gatherings or, in my case, over beers at The Gaf. This particular experiment will be a success if I can make it through my number without crumbling into a million tiny pieces or wetting my pants. I might not be alone in this measure of success. Then again, I think I'm the only one in the troupe who isn't wearing protective plastic undies. Sadly, they don't make them in my size.

As I stretch out my tense limbs, Audrey and Veronica traipse through the obstacle course of doting mothers and fidgeting minidancers.

"You ready?" asks Veronica.

"As I'll ever be, I suppose," I say with a sigh.

"You're going to do great," says Audrey.

"Well, I'm going to do it. Then, good or bad, we'll go out and get hammered. Deal?"

"Will we have time for that?"

"Audrey, all my classmates have to be in bed by nine."

"Right."

The tinny piano starts up and I count down the beats in my head. Onetwothreefour, fivesixseveneight . . . My partners in this number, the sweet ballerino and two of the *y*'s, tap out the chords with their new ballet slippers.

One by one we make our way out of the hall and in front of the crowd. At seeing the fifty or so eager faces, my heart jumps way before I do. By my calculation, only six people aren't focused on my excessively large limbs—and they have to be the parents of my three partners. Will and the rest of Delicate Blunder stand along the back wall, looking fairly uncomfortable and very out of place. But when they see me, they smile. This makes all the difference—for me, at least. I see Audrey and Veronica ever so slightly wringing their hands. Man, I have amazing friends. Absolutely amazing.

I try and focus on Vera, who stands in the corner, waving her finger with the music and giving us subtle cues.

I do my steps as precisely as I can. I try to appear breezy and fluid, keeping my head up and shoulders back. I smile at the crowd, but not too big. I plié and point, I stretch and bounce, with the three little ones in tow. Vera's grand plan for my group? A goofy take on *Swan Lake* whereby I am the swan and the kids are ducklings. It seems to be working. We get laughs and motherly "Awww"-ing at the appropriate moments. And before I know it, just when I'm getting to like it, I hit my last pose. The music comes to a triumphant stop.

A torrent of cheers ensues. The unbelievably loud whistling and yelling of Delicate Blunder echoes through the small room. Audrey and Veronica clap with their hands over their heads.

I take a bow and let the joy wash over me.

I am not, at this moment, a graceful and worldly sophisticate. I am neither terribly poised nor a very good horsewoman. My credit gets worse by the minute and, in my haste to get here on time, I completely forgot to floss. I am no goddess of city living, and a man has yet to be so completely bewitched by me that he throws himself at my mercy—and maybe he never will. But you know what? I am so much closer to superb than I was a couple of months ago, it's staggering. I'm not a different person, I'm just not so afraid of *me* anymore. I stand a little straighter than I used to, look ahead instead of at my feet. And though my rise may not be meteoric, I know I'm moving up. I am comfortable with slow and steady. It's the momentum that counts, anyway.

• • •

"A toast to my best friends, who fake genuine interest in beginner's ballet with style and class," I shout over The Gaf's jukebox.

Will gasps in mock shock. "Me, fake it? I am a connoisseur of the amateur arts."

We laugh and dance several hours away under the haze of cheap beer and overpriced cigarettes. I don't think there's anyplace I'd rather be.

I sit with Veronica at our usual booth, watching Audrey and Will fondle each other to the Allman Brothers.

"I think *I* should have Ben and *you* should have Sammy," Veronica declares.

"Oh, but, Veronica, think how proud your mother would be if you came home with a bassist."

"He told me tonight he's giving serious thought to getting a mullet."

"Oooh."

"Yeah . . ." Veronica's eyes wander over my head and widen to saucer size; her face goes slack.

"What?" I turn around, expecting to see a three-headed monster, or something equally as frightening. Yikes, worse—it's Charlie.

He gives me a weak smile and makes a beeline for Will and the guys. Delicate Blunder crowds around him, suddenly grave and out of sorts. Veronica and I quickly, and not so subtly, squeeze in behind them, plopping down on a tabletop.

Charlie pulls out a stack of papers from inside his leather jacket. "I have some bad news and some good news. Which do you want first?"

Ben and Dane say, "Good."

Will and Sammy say, "Bad."

Will rolls his eyes and repeats, "Bad."

Charlie inhales slowly, exhales with the force of a gale, and bellows, "Cranky Tank has vacated your contract."

A storm of nervous hair pulling and foot shuffling ensues. Will screams, *"What the hell happened?"*

Charlie barks back with "Hold on! Do you want the good news?"

"Please!" replies Will angrily.

"I have with me . . . a contract offer with Insurrection Records."

Sammy and Ben look at each other quizzically, scratching their respective heads.

Will shakes his head. "Charlie, man," he pleads, "I've never even heard of it. Who the hell—"

Charlie gives Will a wry smile. He looks to me, locks onto me with those honey-brown eyes. "It's mine. I run it."

Like I've been hit by an unexpected tackle, my lungs deflate and my chest goes heavy. I slap my hand over my mouth to quiet the wave of elation that's about to make itself audible.

Veronica pokes me in the arm and says, "Breathe."

Will practically explodes with laughter.

Dane says, "Show me where to sign."

Charlie shoves the stack of papers in Dane's hands.

He walks toward me.

Is this really happening? To *me?*

Charlie wraps his arms tight around my waist, buries his face in my hair. He whispers, "Thank you."

Yep. It's really happening.

I wipe the smile off my face long enough to kiss him—hard. All the years of daydreams, the months of uncertainty, were all worth it. In one kiss—a simple thing that happens millions of times a day the world over—all the hurt and doubt are wiped clean, surrendered to a pure moment of happiness.

Charlie beams at me. "How soon can you put in your notice?"

"What?" I yelp.

"I'm gonna need a partner."

I sputter, "Are you serious?"

In classic Charlie deadpan, he says, "Babe, I have got a shit-load of data."

Epilogue

The look on The Dirk's face was priceless. He *really* thought I would be his protégé. However, I think his consternation had more to do with the inconvenience of finding someone new rather than any real distress. Honestly, Mrs. Wheatley took it harder than The Dirk. But then, she wasted two months of bohemian dreamboat time—Veronica had a date with a lute player not three days later.

Betsy, on the other hand, was genuinely thrilled for me. On my last day she gave me a potted violet and a replica of her coveted kitty-shaped pencil holder. For a very brief moment, as I made my final trek past her desk, I felt a pang of sadness at leaving Geiger Data Systems. But the second I saw Charlie standing on the sidewalk waiting for me, it all slipped away and Geiger was pushed firmly into the murky puddles of my past.

My life now is a blur of busy, blissfully exhausting days. I wake up one day and find that it's tomorrow before I lay my head down. And I love it.

I now hold two sets of official-sounding titles:

Set 1. Webmaster for Delicate Blunder and Insurrection Records.

Set 2. CEO, CFO, head designer, secretary, and unpaid intern for Plan B Designs (my own web-design firm—if you can call one girl and a laptop a firm).

Sadly, I took a pay cut to gain these lofty titles, but it's totally worth it and, I'm confident, only temporary. I've already had interest from a few other New York bands about using me to expand into the web, and I have a feeling that Insurrection Records will probably kick a few clients my way. Besides, my rent is now only $450 a month. I suggested we get a one-bedroom somewhere, but Charlie wants to wait on "the door." So, what precious few items Marisa didn't smash, Charlie has brought to the apartment, adding yet another multipurpose to our teeny-tiny abode. It is a home for two, and the international headquarters for Insurrection Records and Plan B Designs. We even have a fax machine/photocopier/laser printer. It's just one of the many things paid for by the liquidation of two pricey assets: one-half of a swank West Village apartment, and one massive diamond ring.

Charlie and I stumble through the door at about three A.M. and drop our coats and bags onto the floor like deadweight.

"Are you tired?" I ask him.

"No."

"Me either." I guess your first CD release party will do that to you. "What do you want to do?" I ask coyly.

"I have an idea."

I raise an eyebrow. "Do you, now?"

He bends down and riffles through his jacket, finally coming up with a CD. He pops it in the stereo/alarm clock and kicks away the coffee table and area rug.

Charlie takes my hand and pulls me close as the opening notes of "Fresh" gurgle from Delicate Blunder. Oh, cross off Number 11.

He gently sweeps a lock of hair from my face and tucks it gingerly behind my ear. I clutch the back of his shirt to steady myself, press my knuckles firmly against his shoulder blade—a desperate attempt to keep my feet on the ground.

Charlie leans in close, so close I can feel his heartbeat, almost in time with the music. He whispers the first few words of the song—my song: *"Sweet, Ryan. Where you're going . . . can I come?"*

Now *this* is a wonderful day.

The Authors Get Up Close and Personal With Each Other

SARAH: How long have you known me?

EMILY: Do you mean known in the sense that I was aware of your existence, or known *you* in the metaphysical sense? Because we met in 1981. But I don't think I saw the *real* you until we were singing Madonna songs into a hairbrush some ten years later.

Sarah laughs uproariously.

SARAH: Um, Emily, I don't think I "laughed uproariously." I think "chuckles weakly" would be more accurate.

EMILY: It's called poetic license, Sarah.

SARAH: It's called journalism, Emily. We are supposed to be reporting, not wildly exaggerating.

EMILY: Fine. You win.

Sarah laughs maniacally.

SARAH: To continue: A little birdie tells me that our pseudonym has some secret meaning. Is that true?

EMILY: I think you were in on that meeting. Remember, it was you and me on the phone?

Sarah rolls her eyes.

SARAH: I am trying to take this seriously. Tell the people what it means.

Sarah's eyes shoot daggers at poor, innocent Emily.

SARAH: Really, "poor, innocent Emily"? A little over-the-top, don't you think?

EMILY: So you admit, then, that you were "shooting daggers."

SARAH: I neither confirm nor deny the daggers. But wouldn't you say "poor, innocent Emily" makes you sound a little meek and defenseless?

EMILY: Okay. I agree.

Emily's eyes shoot daggers at poor, innocent Sarah.

SARAH: Funny.

EMILY: Thanks.

SARAH: Now answer the question.

EMILY: What was the question?

SARAH: What is the significance of the pseudonym Libby Street?

EMILY: When you and I met, at the tender age of five and four, we lived on Liberty Drive in Dover, Delaware—

SARAH: And afterward, in high school too, when you came back from . . . Where was it that time?

EMILY: Alabama. Yeah, my family lived in three houses on Liberty Drive over the years. So, after we wrote the book, we turned Liberty to Libby and Drive to Street, and there you have it: our pseudonym, Libby Street.

SARAH: That was a great place to grow up. Don't you think?

EMILY: I do.

SARAH: Now, how did we decide to write this book?

EMILY: Well, you and I had been reading a lot of books about young single girls in the city and were really entertained by them.

SARAH: We had been reading a lot of those books.

EMILY: That's what I said, a lot.

SARAH: No, a lot.

EMILY: We had been reading a lot of them, but sometimes couldn't really identify with the main characters.

SARAH: We wanted to read about a woman who reflected who we were, with problems more like those that we were facing.

EMILY: A woman going through a quarter-life crisis, of sorts, and wondering if she'd made the right choices so far.

SARAH: Exactly.

SARAH: We wanted Ryan to be a girl like us, with friends like ours.

EMILY: Smart, sassy, and fun.

SARAH: Did you just say "sassy"?

Sarah laughs uproariously.

EMILY: That was just uncalled-for.

SARAH: Continue.

EMILY: I think that about sums it up.

SARAH: *Sassy* sums it up?

EMILY: Hey, why don't I ask you some questions. For instance . . . how long have you known *me*?

Sarah lets out an exasperated sigh.

EMILY: Okay, seriously. Here we go. So, does that mean Ryan's story is autobiographical?

SARAH: I wish.

EMILY: Yeah, me too.

SARAH: Aw, thanks.

EMILY: I meant for me, silly. You're married. I am single, single, single.

SARAH: Oh, my God. That was a total advertisement.

Emily smiles wryly.

EMILY: Moving on . . . Do you have a list of things you want to do with your life?

SARAH: I didn't have one before we started writing. As we were making Ryan's list, I decided it was a good idea. My list is shorter—and I'm not relying on it to change my life—but yes, I do have a list.

EMILY: Name one that you haven't done yet, and one that you have.

SARAH: Done: Moved to New York and made it my home. Not done: After five years in NYC, I'm *still* not on "Top. Of. The. Heap." Your turn.

EMILY: Done: Have a book published. Not done: Become the queen of a small island nation.

SARAH: Still with that island business.

EMILY: If I've learned one thing from Ryan, it's to never give up.

SARAH: It's time.

Emily glares at Sarah while imagining herself in a tiara.

Sarah imagines herself stealing Emily's tiara.

EMILY: How dare you!

Sarah bats her eyelashes in mock innocence.

EMILY: That brings me to my next question: How have we managed to stay friends for so long?

SARAH: I think we owe a lot of that to our parents and the United States Air Force. Your family moved all over the place while mine stayed still in Delaware. Since our parents were also friends, there was no problem shipping me off to Alabama or Hawaii to see you, or taking the whole family on a trip to Ohio. The USAF thankfully shipped you guys back to Delaware in time for high school, but I think it was really in college—you in Ohio, me in Pittsburgh—when we really became . . . whatever it is we are.

EMILY: We were always friends, but thankfully you, me, and Jen — the third part of *our* triple threat, who also happened to live on Liberty Drive—drifted in and out of other groups too.

SARAH: It's made us more well rounded.

EMILY: I think you mean less pathetic.

SARAH: That too. Hey, do you think people think we're weird? Because we're so close?

EMILY: And eerily, freakishly alike in a million different ways?

SARAH: Yeah.

EMILY: Sarah . . .

SARAH: Yeah?

EMILY: We *are* weird.

SARAH: And really lucky.

EMILY: And *really* lucky.

SARAH: I just said that.

EMILY: I was agreeing with you.

SARAH: I have one more question: You want to go out for a beer?

EMILY: Mmmm. Let me think about it. . . . Yes.

NATIONWIDE AUTHOR SEARCH!

Be the Next Downtown Girl!

Are you a downtown girl at heart and an aspiring writer with a story?

Ever dreamed of having that story published?

Downtown Press is looking for an author with a fresh, new voice whose story will be published in one of our future Downtown Press anthologies. The first prize winner will also receive $500 (for that new pair of stilettos!).

Before you start writing, visit **www.simonsaysthespot.com** to register your name for the contest. If you choose, we'll provide you with writing tips from our authors, hints from our senior editors, info on online chats, and a newsletter with the latest from Downtown Press.

The rest is up to you! Good Luck!

Stories must be received by July 31, 2005.

www.downtownpress.com • www.simonsaysthespot.com

116

Be the Next Downtown Girl

Contest Rules

NO PURCHASE NECESSARY TO ENTER.

) ENTRY REQUIREMENTS:

egister to enter the contest on ww.simonsaysthespot.com. Enter by ubmitting your story as specified elow.

) CONTEST ELIGIBILITY:

his contest is open to nonprofessional riters who are legal residents of the nited States and Canada (excluding uebec) over the age of 18 as of ecember 7, 2004. Entrant must not ave published any more than two hort stories on a professional basis or n paid professional venues. Employees r relatives of employees living in the ame household) of Simon & Schuster, IACOM, or any of their affiliates are ot eligible. This contest is void in uerto Rico, Quebec, and wherever rohibited or restricted by law.

) FORMAT:

ntries must not be more than 7,500 ords long and must not have been reviously published. Entries must be yped or printed by word processor, ouble spaced, on one side of noncor-asable paper. Do not justify right-side margins. Along with a cover letter, the uthor's name, address, email address, nd phone number must appear on the irst page of the entry. The author's ame, the story title, and the page umber should appear on every page. lectronic submissions will be accepted and must be sent to owntowngirl@simonandschuster.com. All electronic submissions must be sent as an attachment in a Microsoft Word document. All entries must be original and the sole work of the Entrant and the sole property of the Entrant.

All submissions must be in English. Entries are void if they are in whole or n part illegible, incomplete, or dam-aged or if they do not conform to any of the requirements specified herein. Sponsor reserves the right, in its absolute and sole discretion, to reject any entries for any reason, including but not limited to based on sexual content, vulgarity, and/or promotion of violence.

4) ADDRESS:

Entries submitted by mail must be postmarked by July 31, 2005 and sent to:

Be The Next Downtown Girl
Author Search

Downtown Press Editorial Department
Pocket Books
1230 Sixth Avenue, 13th floor
New York, NY 10020

Or Emailed By July 31, 2005
at 11:59 PM EST as a
Microsoft Word document to:

downtowngirl@simonandschuster.com

Each entry may be submitted only once. Please retain a copy of your submission. You may submit more than one story, but each submission must be mailed or emailed, as applicable, separately. Entries must be received by July 31, 2005. Not responsible for lost, late, stolen, illegible, mutilated, postage due, garbled, or misdirected mail/entries.

5) PRIZES:

One Grand Prize winner will receive:

Simon & Schuster's Downtown Press Publishing Contract for Publication of Winning Entry in a future Downtown Press Anthology, Five Hundred U.S. Dollars ($500.00), and

Downtown Press Library
(20 books valued at $260.00)

Grand Prize winner must sign the Publishing contract which contains additional terms and conditions in order to be published in the anthology.

Ten Second Prize winners will receive:

A Downtown Press Collection
(10 books valued at $130.00)

No contestant can win more than one prize.

6) STORY THEME

We are not restricting stories to any specific topic, however they should embody what all of our Downtown Press authors encompass—they should be smart, savvy, sexy stories that any Downtown Girl can relate to. We all know what uptown girls are like, but girls of the new millennium prefer the Downtown Scene. That's where it happens. The music, the shopping, the sex, the dating, the heartbreak, the family squabbles, the marriage, and the divorce. You name it. Downtown Girls have done it. Twice. We encourage you to register for the contest at www.simonsaysthespot.com in order to receive our monthly emails and updates from our authors and read about our titles on www.downtownpress.com to give you a better idea of what types of books we publish.

7) JUDGING:

Submissions will be judged on the equally weighted criteria of (a) basis of writing ability and (b) the originality of the story (which can be set in any time frame or location). Judging will take place on or about October 1, 2005. The judges will include a freelance editor, the editor of the future Anthology, and 5 employees of Sponsor. The decisions of the judges shall be final.

8) NOTIFICATION:

The winners will be notified by mail or phone on or about October 1, 2005. The Grand Prize Winner must sign the publishing contract in order to be awarded the prize. All federal, local, and state taxes are the responsibility of the winner. A list of the winners will be available after October 20, 2005 on:

http://www.downtownpress.com

http://www.simonsaysthespot.com

The winners' list can also be obtained by sending a stamped self-addressed envelope to:

Be The Next Downtown Girl
Author Search
Downtown Press Editorial Department
Pocket Books
1230 Sixth Avenue, 13th floor
New York, NY 10020

9) PUBLICITY:

Each Winner grants to Sponsor the right to use his or her name, likeness, and entry for any advertising, promotion, and publicity purposes without further compensation to or permission from such winner, except where prohibited by law.

10) INTERNET:

If for any reason this Contest is not capable of running as planned due to an infection by a computer virus, bugs, tampering, unauthorized intervention, fraud, technical failures, or any other causes beyond the control of the Sponsor which corrupt or affect the administration, security, fairness, integrity, or proper conduct of this Contest, the Sponsor reserves the right in its sole discretion, to disqualify any individual who tampers with the entry process, and to cancel, terminate, modify, or suspend the Contest. The Sponsor assumes no responsibility for any error, omission, interruption, deletion, defect, delay in operation or transmission, communications line failure, theft or destruction or unauthorized access to, or alteration of, entries. The Sponsor is not responsible for any problems or technical malfunctions of any telephone network or telephone lines, computer on-line systems, servers, or providers, computer equipment, software, failure of any email or entry to be received by the Sponsor due to technical problems, human error or traffic congestion on the Internet or at any website, or any combination thereof, including any injury or damage to participant's or any other person's computer relating to or resulting from participating in this Contest or downloading any materials in this Contest. CAUTION: ANY ATTEMPT TO DELIBERATELY DAMAGE ANY WEBSITE OR UNDERMINE THE LEGITIMATE OPERATION OF THE CONTEST IS A VIOLATION OF CRIMINAL AND CIVIL LAWS AND SHOULD SUCH AN ATTEMPT BE MADE, THE SPONSOR RESERVES THE RIGHT TO SEEK DAMAGES OR OTHER REMEDIES FROM ANY SUCH PERSON(S) RESPONSIBLE FOR THE ATTEMPT TO THE FULLEST EXTENT PERMITTED BY LAW. In the event of a dispute as to the identity or eligibility of a winner based on an email address, the winning entry will be declared made by the "Authorized Account Holder" of the email address submitted at time of entry. "Authorized Account Holder" is defined as the natural person 18 years of age or older who is assigned to an email address by an Internet access provider, online service provider, or other organization (e.g., business, education institution, etc.) that is responsible for assigning email addresses for the domain associated with the submitted email address. Use of automated devices are not valid for entry.

11) LEGAL Information:

All submissions become sole property of Sponsor and will not be acknowledged or returned. By submitting an entry, all entrants grant Sponsor the absolute and unconditional right and authority to copy, edit, publish, promote, broadcast, or otherwise use, in whole or in part, their entries, in perpetuity, in any manner without further permission, notice or compensation. Entries that contain copyrighted material must include a release from the copyright holder. Prizes are nontransferable. No substitutions or cash redemptions, except by Sponsor in the event of prize unavailability. Sponsor reserves the right at its sole discretion to not publish the winning entry for any reason whatsoever.

In the event that there is an insufficient number of entries received that meet the minimum standards determined by the judges, all prizes will not be awarded. Void in Quebec, Puerto Rico, and wherever prohibited or restricted by law. Winners will be required to complete and return an affidavit of eligibility and a liability/publicity release, within 15 days of winning notification, or an alternate winner will be selected. In the event any winner is considered a minor in his/her state of residence, such winner's parent/legal guardian will be required to sign and return all necessary paperwork.

By entering, entrants release the judges and Sponsor, and its parent company, subsidiaries, affiliates, divisions, advertising, production, and promotion agencies from any and all liability for any loss, harm, damages, costs, or expenses, including without limitation property damages, personal injury, and/or death arising out of participation in this contest, the acceptance, possession, use or misuse of any prize, claims based on publicity rights, defamation or invasion of privacy, merchandise delivery, or the violation of any intellectual property rights, including but not limited to copyright infringement and/or trademark infringement.

Sponsor:
Pocket Books,
an imprint of Simon & Schuster, Inc.
1230 Avenue of the Americas,
New York, NY 10020

TM, ®, and © 2004 Pocket Books.
All Rights Reserved

Good books are like shoes...
You can never have too many.

Best of Friends
Cathy Kelly

Yes, you can have it all! Just be sure to share...

I'm With Cupid
Diane Stingley

What happens when Cupid wastes your arrow on a guy who isn't worthy of true like—let alone love?

Irish Girls Are Back in Town
Cecelia Ahern, Patricia Scanlan, Gemma O'Connor, and many more of your favorite Irish writers!

Painting the town green was just the beginning...

The Diva's Guide to Selling Your Soul
Kathleen O'Reilly

Sign on the dotted line—and get everything you *ever* wanted.

Exes and Ohs
Beth Kendrick

When new loves meet old flames, stand back and watch the fireworks.

Dixieland Sushi
Cara Lockwood

Love is always a culture shock.

Balancing in High Heels
Eileen Rendahl

It's called *falling* in love for a reason... and she's working without a net.

Cold Feet
Elise Juska, Tara McCarthy, Pamela Ribon, Heather Swain, and Lisa Ticker

Something old, something new, something borrowed—and a fast pair of running shoes.

Around the World in 80 Dates
Jennifer Cox

What if your heart's desire isn't in your own backyard? You go out and find him.

Great storytelling just got a new address.

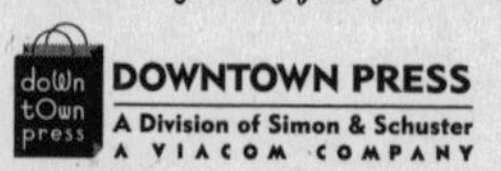

Look for them wherever books are sold or visit us online at www.downtownpress.com.

Published by Pocket Books

11910-1